THE MINECRAFT-INSPIRED MISADVENTURES OF

FRIGIEL AND FLUFFY

VOL 4

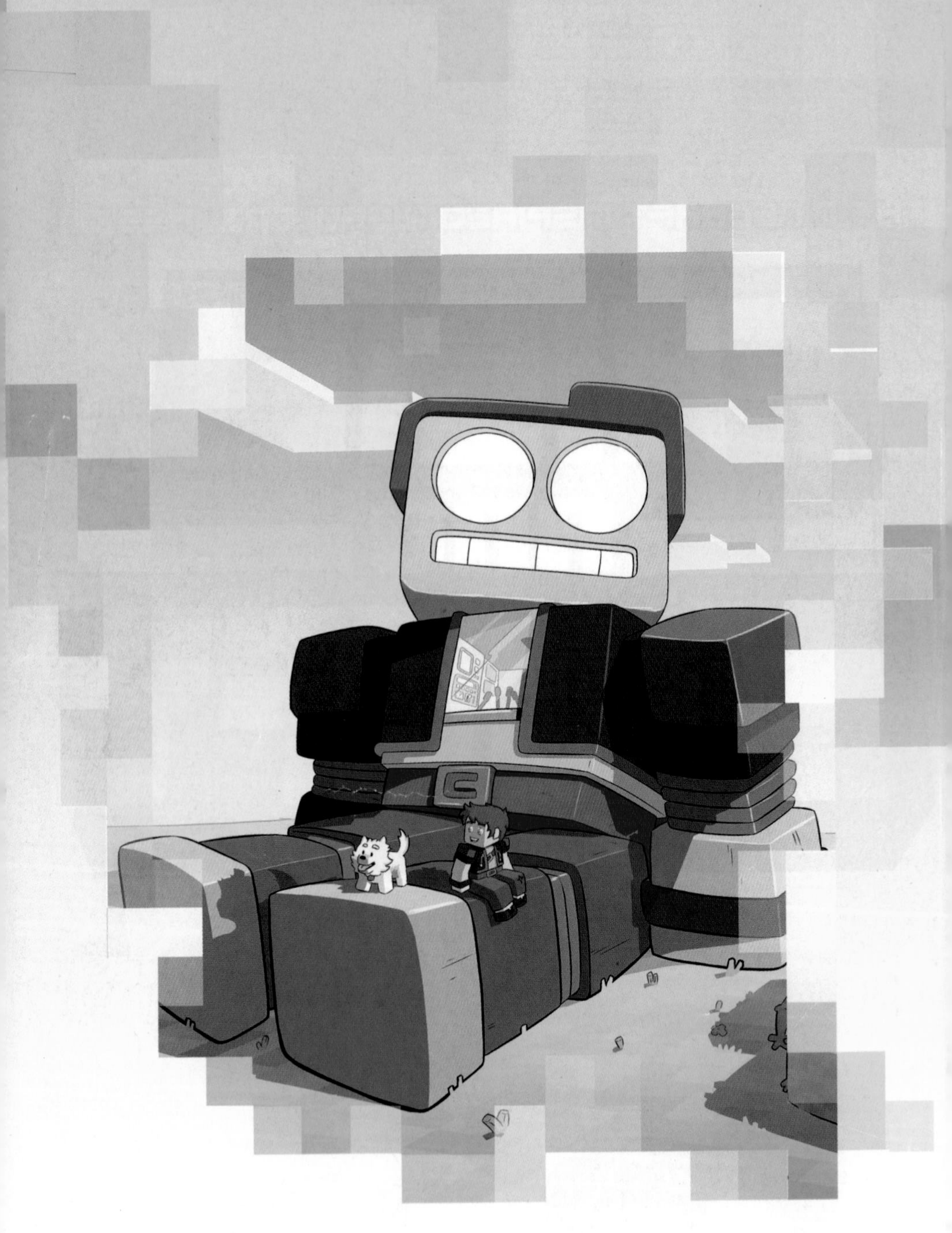

THE MINECRAFT-INSPIRED MISADVENTURES OF

FRIGIEL AND FLUFFY

VOL 4

WRITERS:
JEAN-CHRISTOPHE DERRIEN, FRIGIEL

ARTISTS:
STUDIO MINTE

TRANSLATION
FABRICE SAPOLSKY

LETTERS
MARIANO BENITEZ CHAPO

FOR ABLAZE

MANAGING EDITOR
RICH YOUNG

EDITOR
KEVIN KETNER

DESIGNER
CINTHIA TAKEDA CAETANO
RODOLFO MURAGUCHI

Publisher's Cataloging-in-Publication Data

Names: Derrien, Jean-Christophe, author. I Frigiel, author. I Minte, illustrator.
Title: The Minecraft-inspired misadventures of Frigiel and Fluffy , vol. 4 /
[written by] Jean-Christophe Derrien and Frigiel; [illustrated by] Minte.
Description: Portland, OR: Ablaze Publishing, 2022.
Identifiers: ISBN 978-1-68497-091-9
Subjects: LCSH Minecraft (Game)—Comic books, strips, etc. I Video game characters—
Comic books, strips, etc. I Video games—Comic books, strips, etc. I Graphic
novels. I BISAC JUVENILE FICTION / Comics & Graphic Novels / Media Tie-In
Classification: LCC PZ7.7 .D502 Mi 2022 I DDC 741.5—dc23

THE MINECRAFT-INSPIRED MISADVENTURES OF FRIGIEL & FLUFFY VOL 4. First printing. Published by Ablaze Publishing, 11222 SE Main St. #2290
Portland, OR 97269. Frigiel et Fluffy, volume 7, by Jean-Christophe Derrien, Frigiel and Minte © Editions Soleil – 2019, adapted from the novel "Frigiel e
Fluffy – La Bataille de Meraîm" by Frigiel and Nicolas Digard © SLALOM, a department of Place des Editeurs, 2018; Frigiel et Fluffy, volume 8, by Jean
Christophe Derrien, Frigiel and Minte © Editions Soleil – 2020, adapted from the novel "Frigiel et Fluffy – Le Retour de l'Ender Dragon" by Frigiel and
Nicolas Digard © SLALOM, a department of d'Edi8, 2016. Ablaze TM & © 2022 ABLAZE, LLC. All rights reserved. For the English edition: © 2022 ABLAZE
LLC. All Rights Reserved. Ablaze and its logo TM & © 2022 Ablaze, LLC. All Rights Reserved. All names, characters, events, and locales in this publicatio
are entirely fictional. Any resemblance to actual persons (living or dead), events or places, without satiric intent is coincidental. No portion of this boo
may be reproduced by any means (digital or print) without the written permission of Ablaze Publishing except for review purposes. Printed in China.

For advertising and licensing email: info@ablazepublishing.com

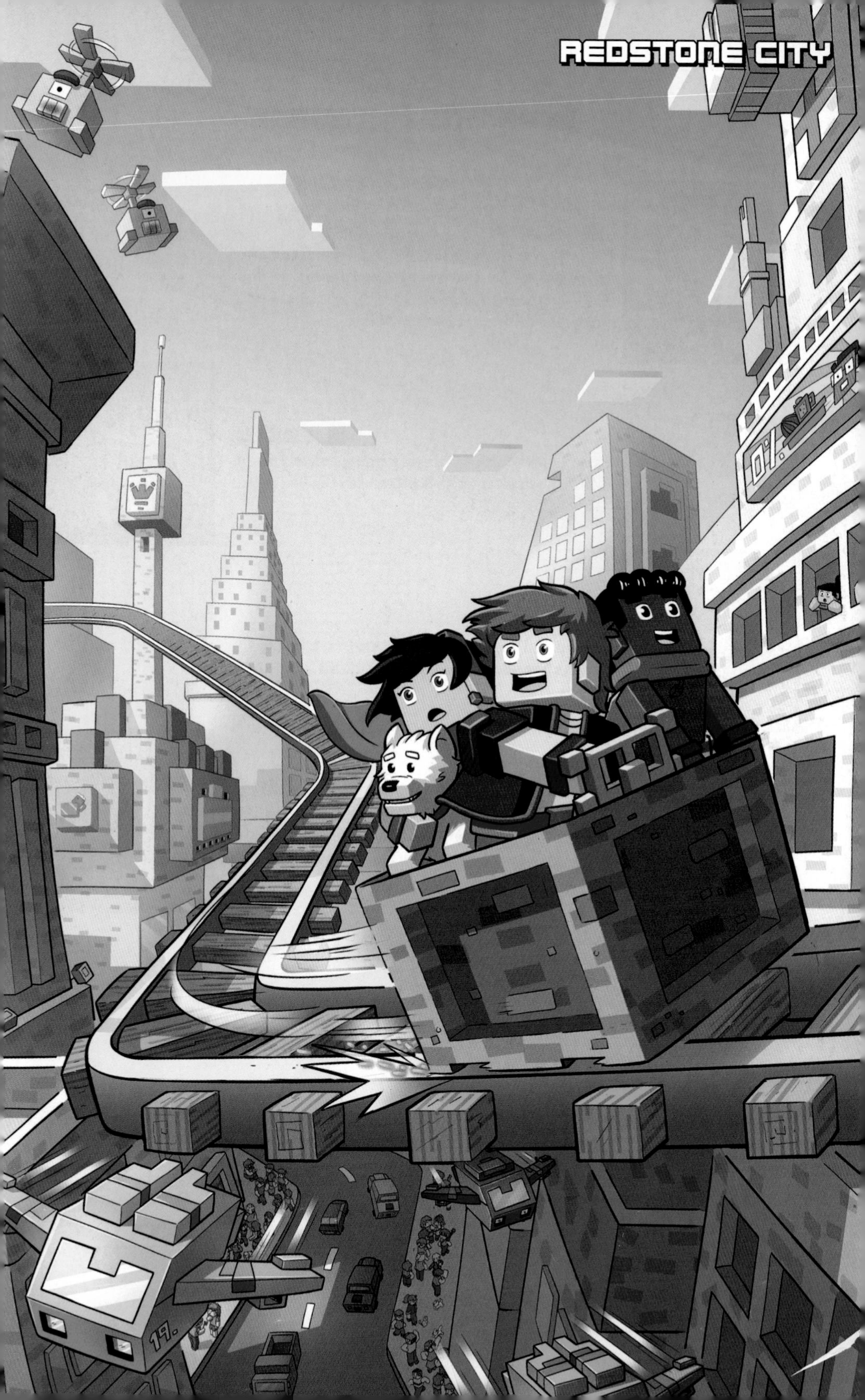
REDSTONE CITY

Dramatis Personae

■ Frigiel

A brave sorcerer's apprentice ever-ready to give his all for his friends. He dreams of one day becoming a true adventurer. His chance to discover the world begins today...

■ Fluffy

Frigiel's faithful canine companion, as cuddly with his master as he is bitey with the bad guys.

■ Alice

Proud and passionate, this thief-in-training keeps her secrets close to her heart...

■ Abel

A clever builder, and a somewhat mocking friend, he doesn't always see the irony of the situation.

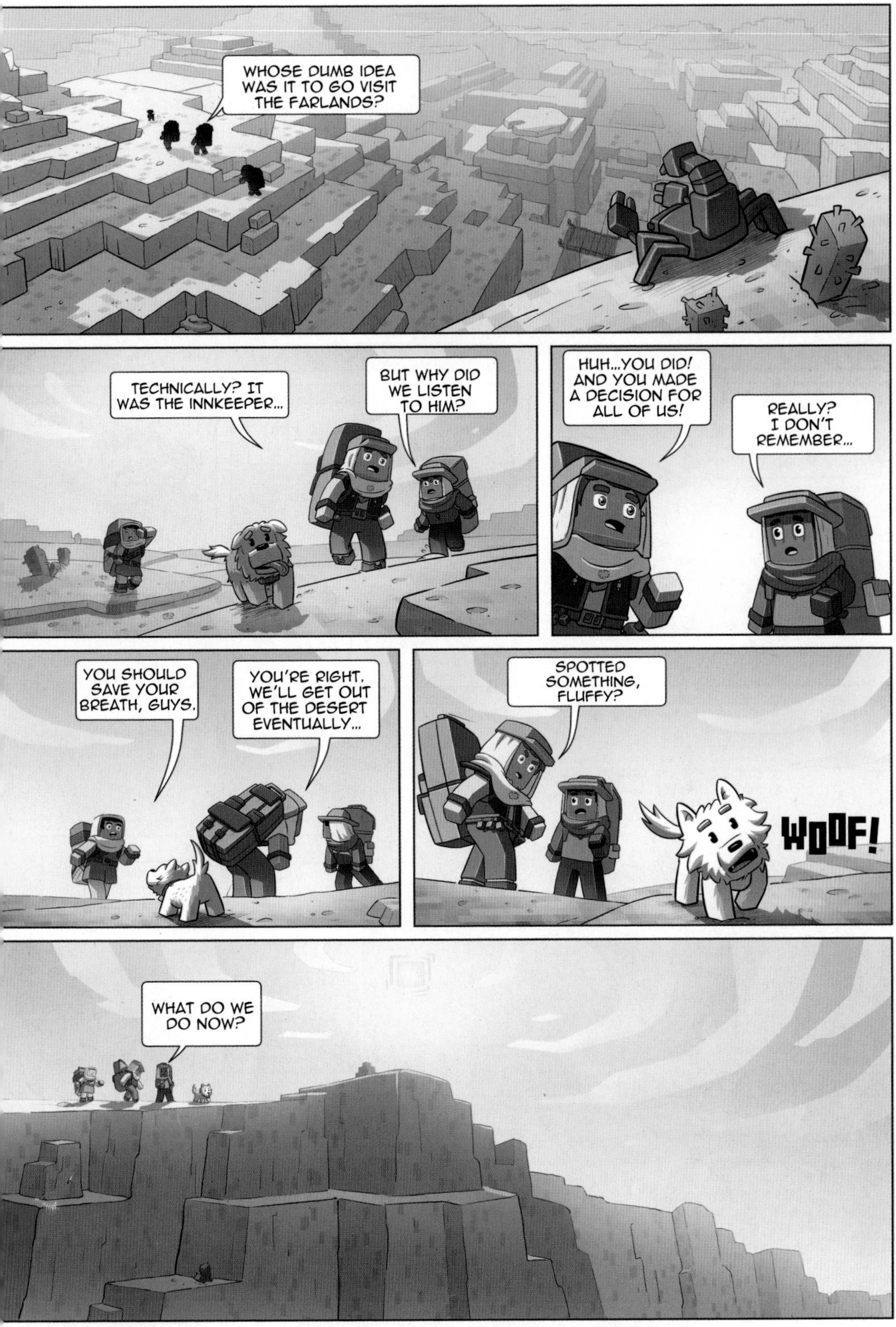
WHOSE DUMB IDEA WAS IT TO GO VISIT THE FARLANDS?
TECHNICALLY? IT WAS THE INNKEEPER...
BUT WHY DID WE LISTEN TO HIM?
HUH...YOU DID! AND YOU MADE A DECISION FOR ALL OF US!
REALLY? I DON'T REMEMBER...
YOU SHOULD SAVE YOUR BREATH, GUYS.
YOU'RE RIGHT. WE'LL GET OUT OF THE DESERT EVENTUALLY...
SPOTTED SOMETHING, FLUFFY?
WOOF!
WHAT DO WE DO NOW?

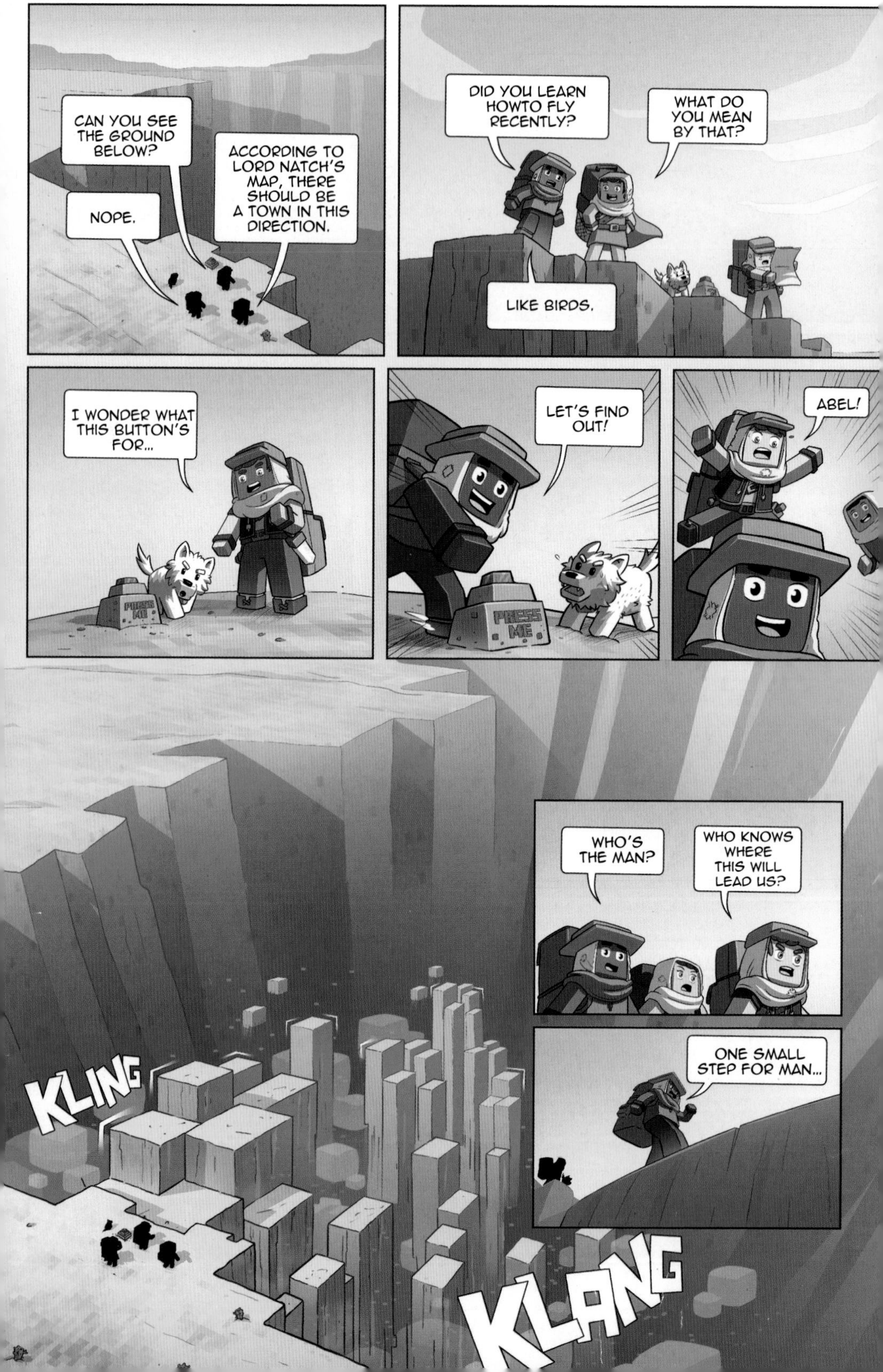
CAN YOU SEE THE GROUND BELOW?
NOPE.
ACCORDING TO LORD NATCH'S MAP, THERE SHOULD BE A TOWN IN THIS DIRECTION.
DID YOU LEARN HOWTO FLY RECENTLY?
WHAT DO YOU MEAN BY THAT?
LIKE BIRDS.
I WONDER WHAT THIS BUTTON'S FOR...
PRESS ME
LET'S FIND OUT!
PRESS ME
ABEL!
WHO'S THE MAN?
WHO KNOWS WHERE THIS WILL LEAD US?
ONE SMALL STEP FOR MAN...
KLING
KLANG

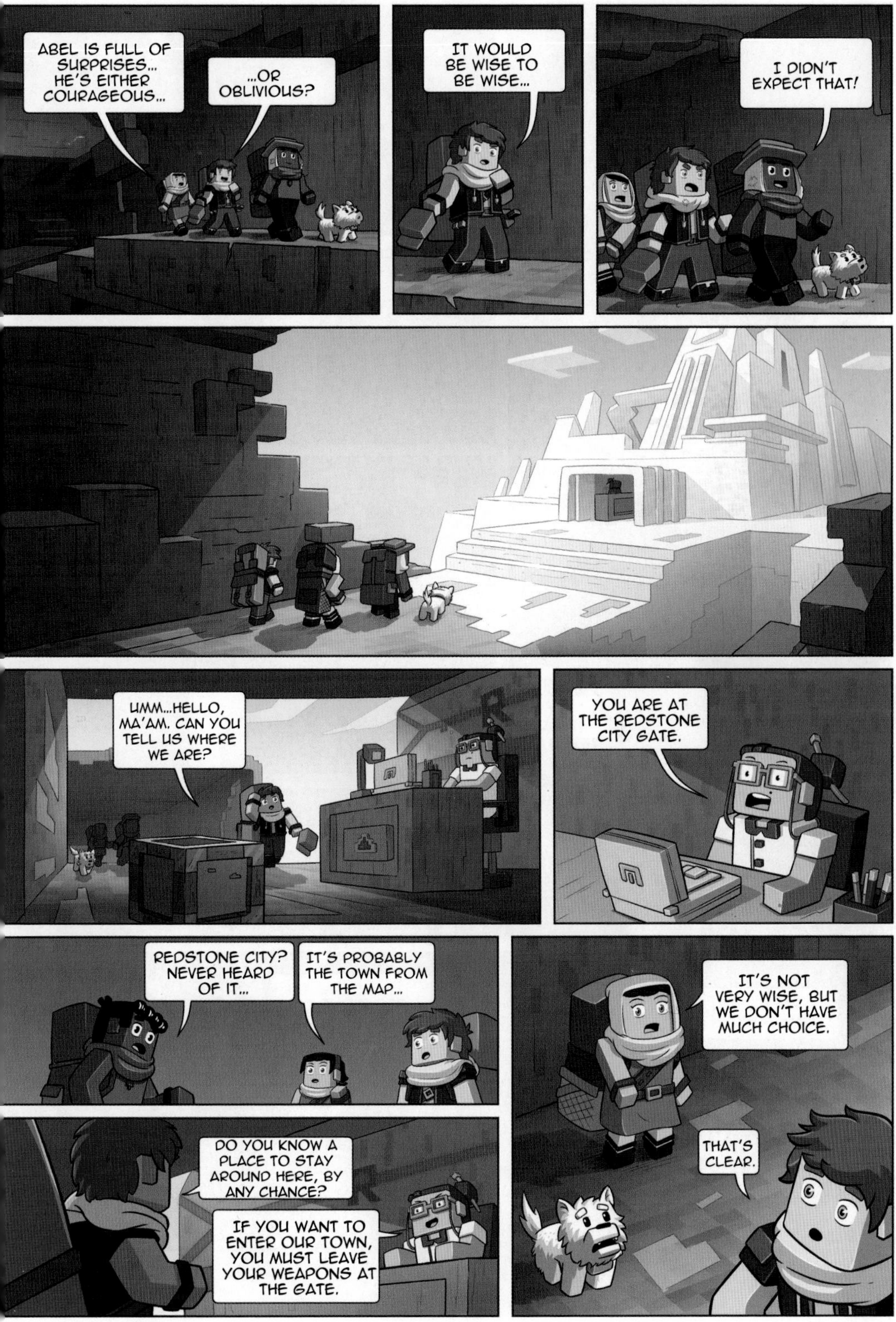
ABEL IS FULL OF SURPRISES... HE'S EITHER COURAGEOUS...
...OR OBLIVIOUS?
IT WOULD BE WISE TO BE WISE...
I DIDN'T EXPECT THAT!
UMM...HELLO, MA'AM. CAN YOU TELL US WHERE WE ARE?
YOU ARE AT THE REDSTONE CITY GATE.
REDSTONE CITY? NEVER HEARD OF IT...
IT'S PROBABLY THE TOWN FROM THE MAP...
DO YOU KNOW A PLACE TO STAY AROUND HERE, BY ANY CHANCE?
IF YOU WANT TO ENTER OUR TOWN, YOU MUST LEAVE YOUR WEAPONS AT THE GATE.
IT'S NOT VERY WISE, BUT WE DON'T HAVE MUCH CHOICE.
THAT'S CLEAR.

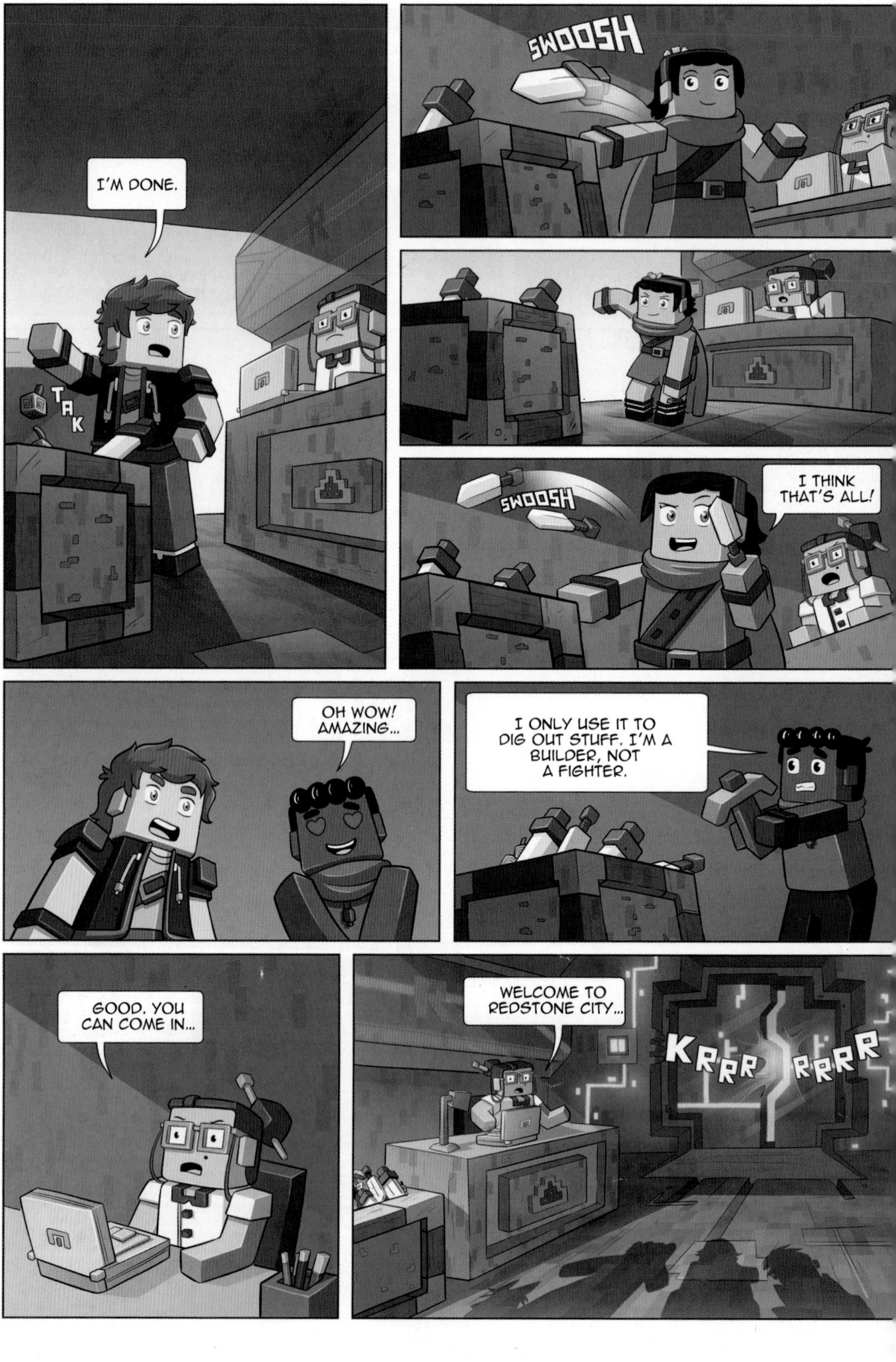
I'M DONE.
TAK
SWOOSH
SWOOSH
I THINK THAT'S ALL!
OH WOW! AMAZING...
I ONLY USE IT TO DIG OUT STUFF. I'M A BUILDER, NOT A FIGHTER.
GOOD. YOU CAN COME IN...
WELCOME TO REDSTONE CITY...
KRRR RRRR

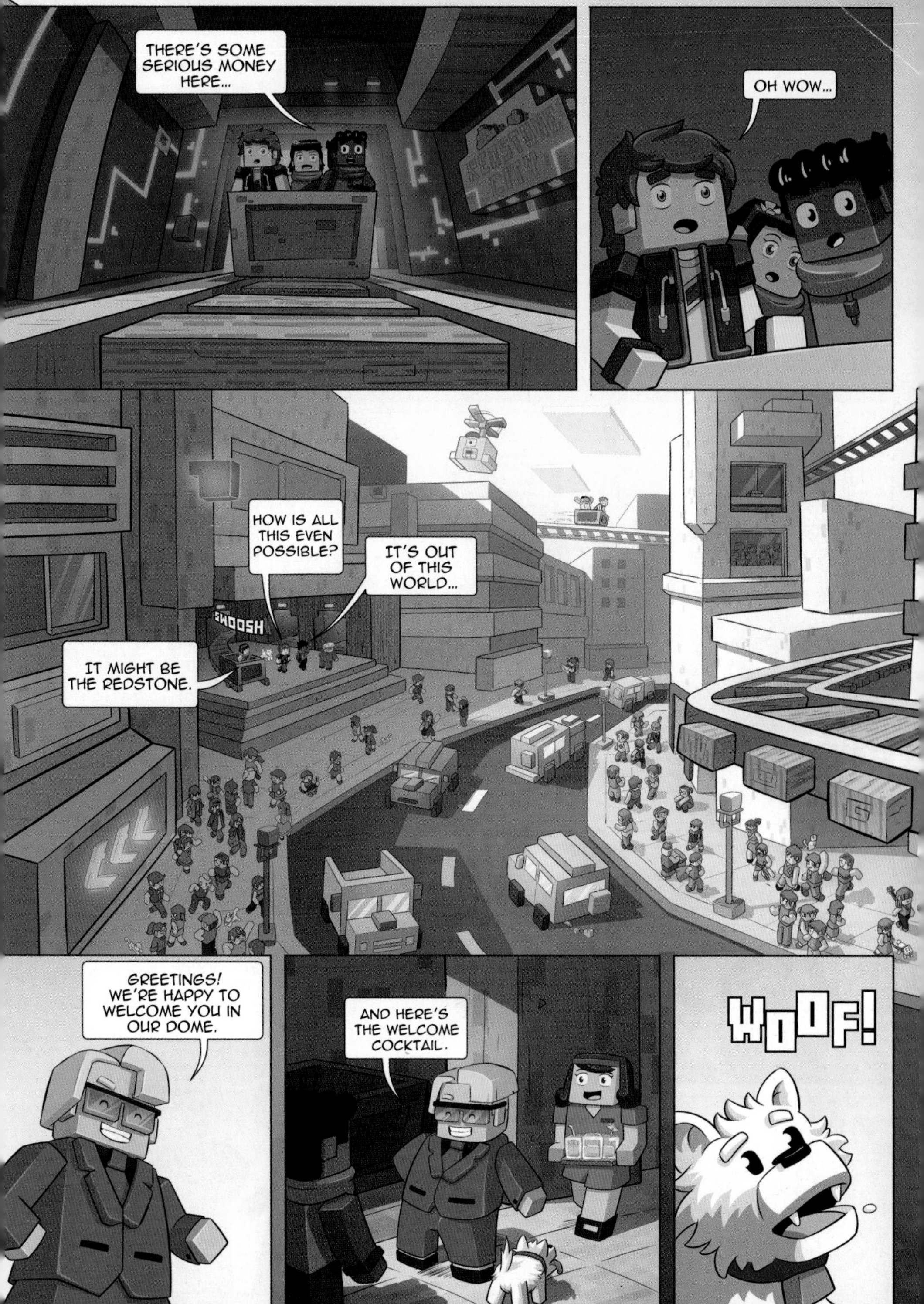
THERE'S SOME SERIOUS MONEY HERE...
OH WOW...
HOW IS ALL THIS EVEN POSSIBLE?
IT'S OUT OF THIS WORLD...
SHOOSH
IT MIGHT BE THE REDSTONE.
GREETINGS! WE'RE HAPPY TO WELCOME YOU IN OUR DOME.
AND HERE'S THE WELCOME COCKTAIL.
WOOF!

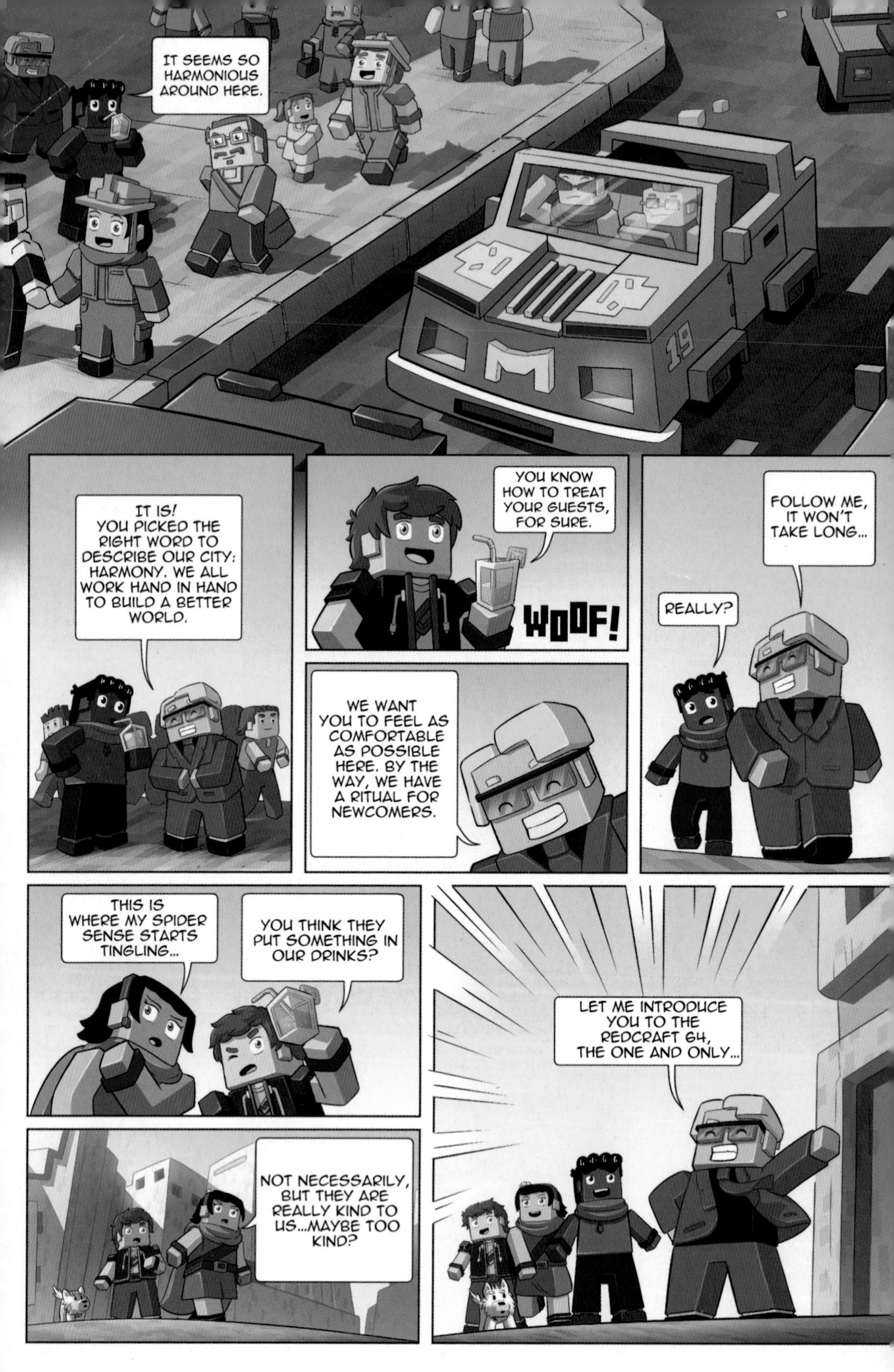
IT SEEMS SO HARMONIOUS AROUND HERE.
IT IS! YOU PICKED THE RIGHT WORD TO DESCRIBE OUR CITY: HARMONY. WE ALL WORK HAND IN HAND TO BUILD A BETTER WORLD.
YOU KNOW HOW TO TREAT YOUR GUESTS, FOR SURE.
WOOF!
WE WANT YOU TO FEEL AS COMFORTABLE AS POSSIBLE HERE. BY THE WAY, WE HAVE A RITUAL FOR NEWCOMERS.
FOLLOW ME, IT WON'T TAKE LONG...
REALLY?
THIS IS WHERE MY SPIDER SENSE STARTS TINGLING...
YOU THINK THEY PUT SOMETHING IN OUR DRINKS?
NOT NECESSARILY, BUT THEY ARE REALLY KIND TO US...MAYBE TOO KIND?
LET ME INTRODUCE YOU TO THE REDCRAFT 64, THE ONE AND ONLY...

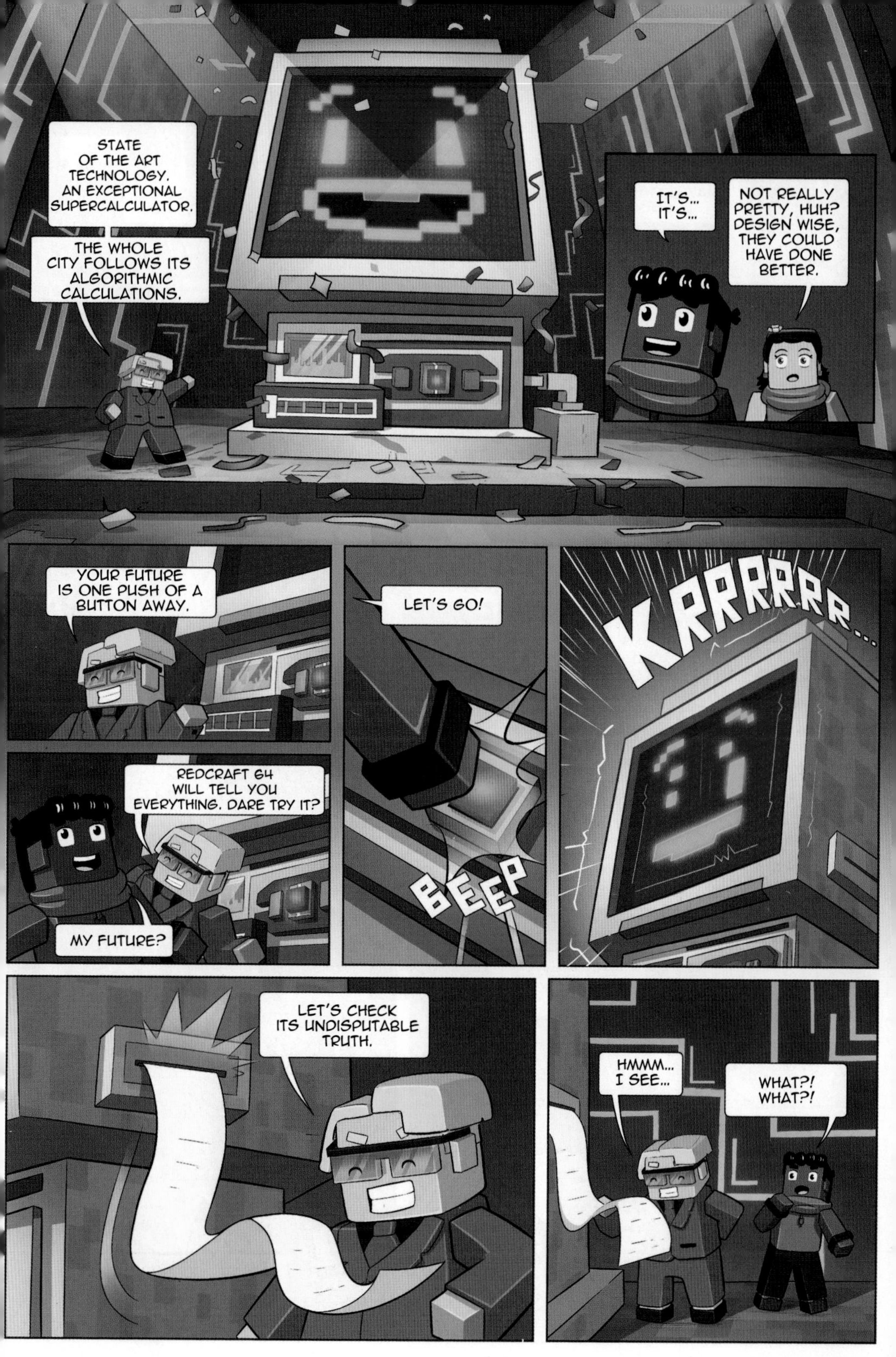
STATE OF THE ART TECHNOLOGY. AN EXCEPTIONAL SUPERCALCULATOR.
THE WHOLE CITY FOLLOWS ITS ALGORITHMIC CALCULATIONS.
IT'S... IT'S...
NOT REALLY PRETTY, HUH? DESIGN WISE, THEY COULD HAVE DONE BETTER.
YOUR FUTURE IS ONE PUSH OF A BUTTON AWAY.
REDCRAFT 64 WILL TELL YOU EVERYTHING. DARE TRY IT?
MY FUTURE?
LET'S GO!
BEEP
KRRRRRR...
LET'S CHECK ITS UNDISPUTABLE TRUTH.
HMMM... I SEE...
WHAT?! WHAT?!

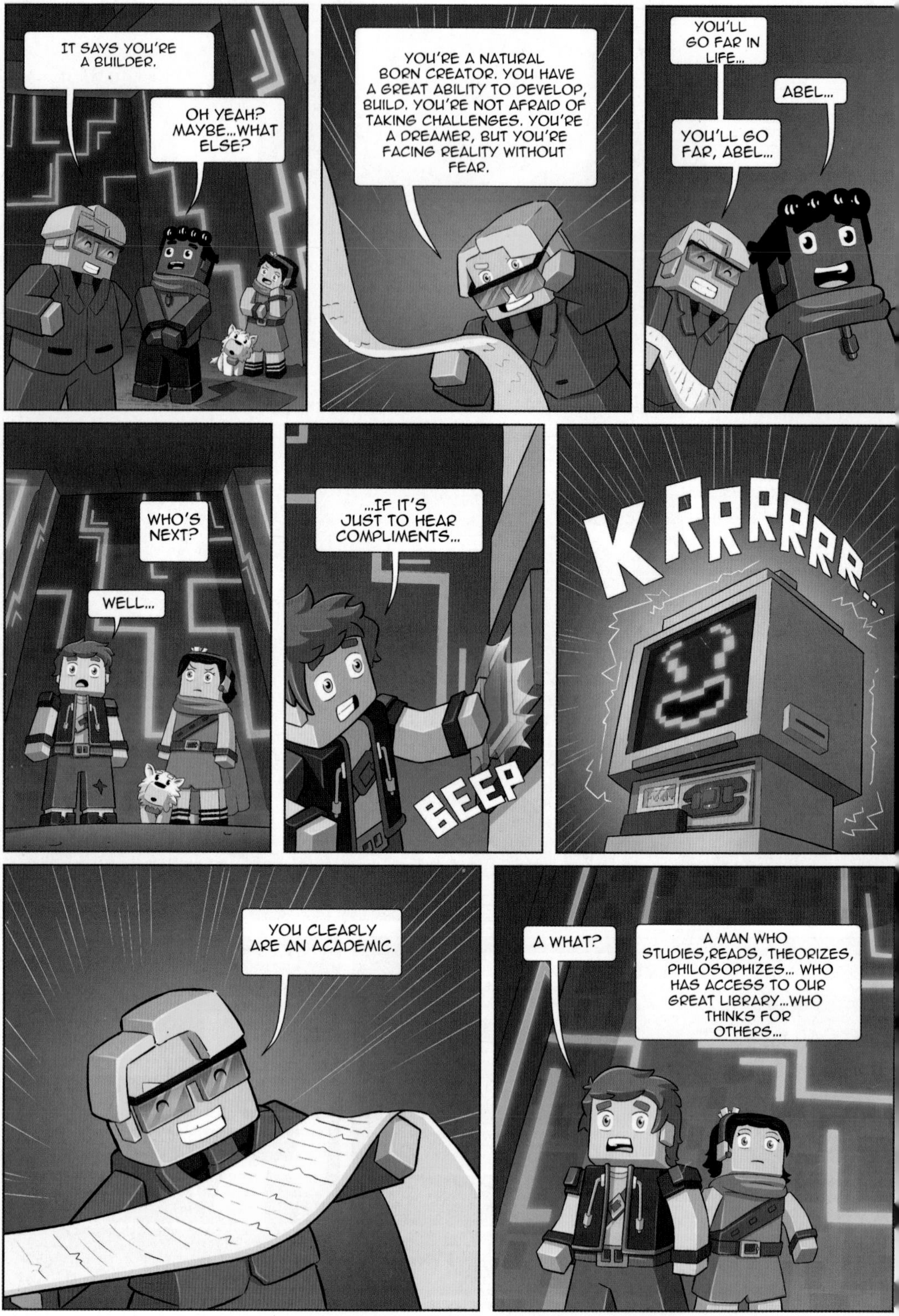
IT SAYS YOU'RE A BUILDER.
OH YEAH? MAYBE...WHAT ELSE?
YOU'RE A NATURAL BORN CREATOR. YOU HAVE A GREAT ABILITY TO DEVELOP, BUILD. YOU'RE NOT AFRAID OF TAKING CHALLENGES. YOU'RE A DREAMER, BUT YOU'RE FACING REALITY WITHOUT FEAR.
YOU'LL GO FAR IN LIFE...
YOU'LL GO FAR, ABEL...
ABEL...
WHO'S NEXT?
WELL...
...IF IT'S JUST TO HEAR COMPLIMENTS...
BEEP
KRRRRRR...
YOU CLEARLY ARE AN ACADEMIC.
A WHAT?
A MAN WHO STUDIES,READS, THEORIZES, PHILOSOPHIZES... WHO HAS ACCESS TO OUR GREAT LIBRARY...WHO THINKS FOR OTHERS...

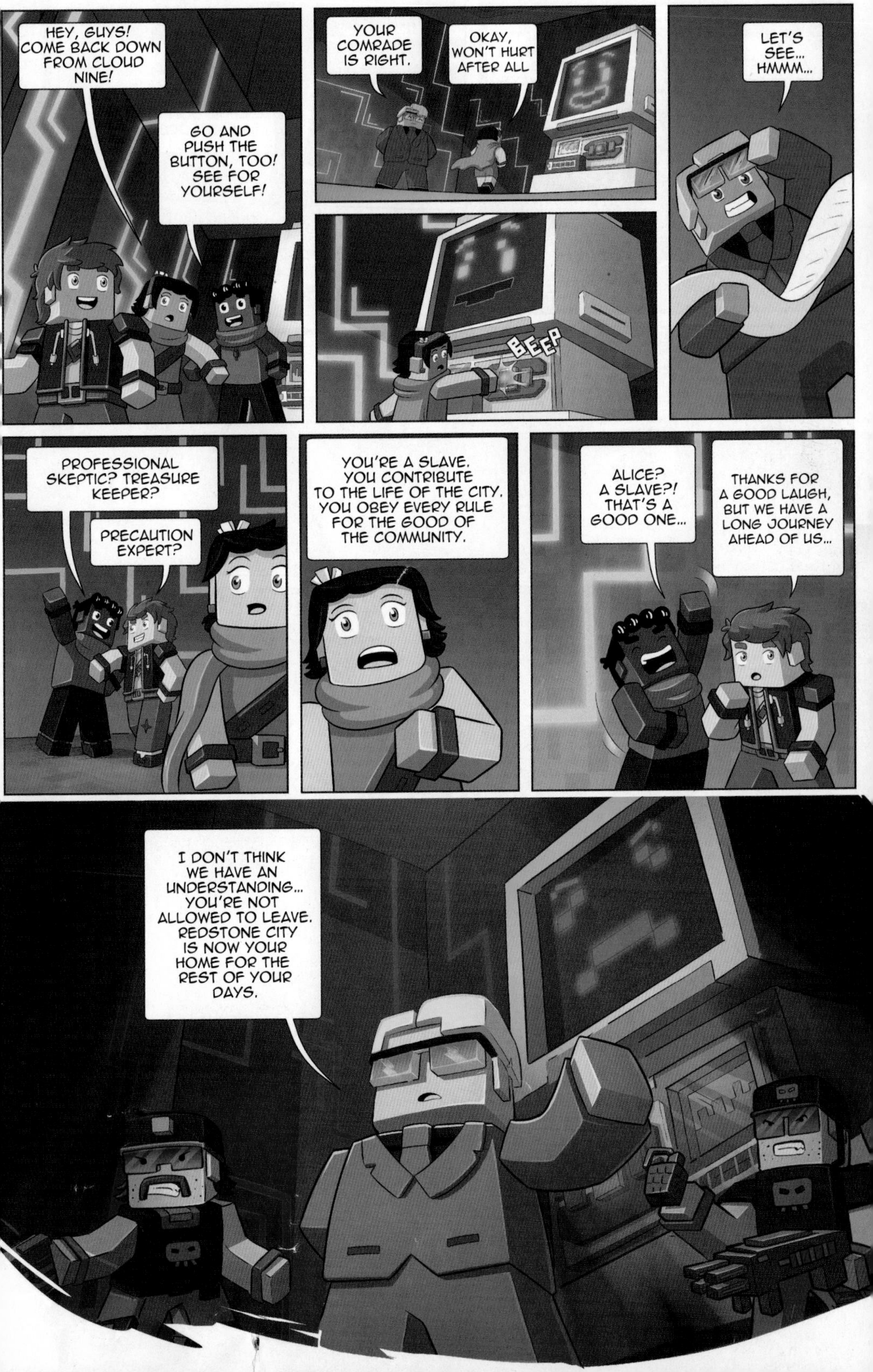
HEY, GUYS! COME BACK DOWN FROM CLOUD NINE!
GO AND PUSH THE BUTTON, TOO! SEE FOR YOURSELF!
YOUR COMRADE IS RIGHT.
OKAY, WON'T HURT AFTER ALL
BEEP
LET'S SEE... HMMM...
PROFESSIONAL SKEPTIC? TREASURE KEEPER?
PRECAUTION EXPERT?
YOU'RE A SLAVE. YOU CONTRIBUTE TO THE LIFE OF THE CITY. YOU OBEY EVERY RULE FOR THE GOOD OF THE COMMUNITY.
ALICE? A SLAVE?! THAT'S A GOOD ONE...
THANKS FOR A GOOD LAUGH, BUT WE HAVE A LONG JOURNEY AHEAD OF US...
I DON'T THINK WE HAVE AN UNDERSTANDING... YOU'RE NOT ALLOWED TO LEAVE. REDSTONE CITY IS NOW YOUR HOME FOR THE REST OF YOUR DAYS.

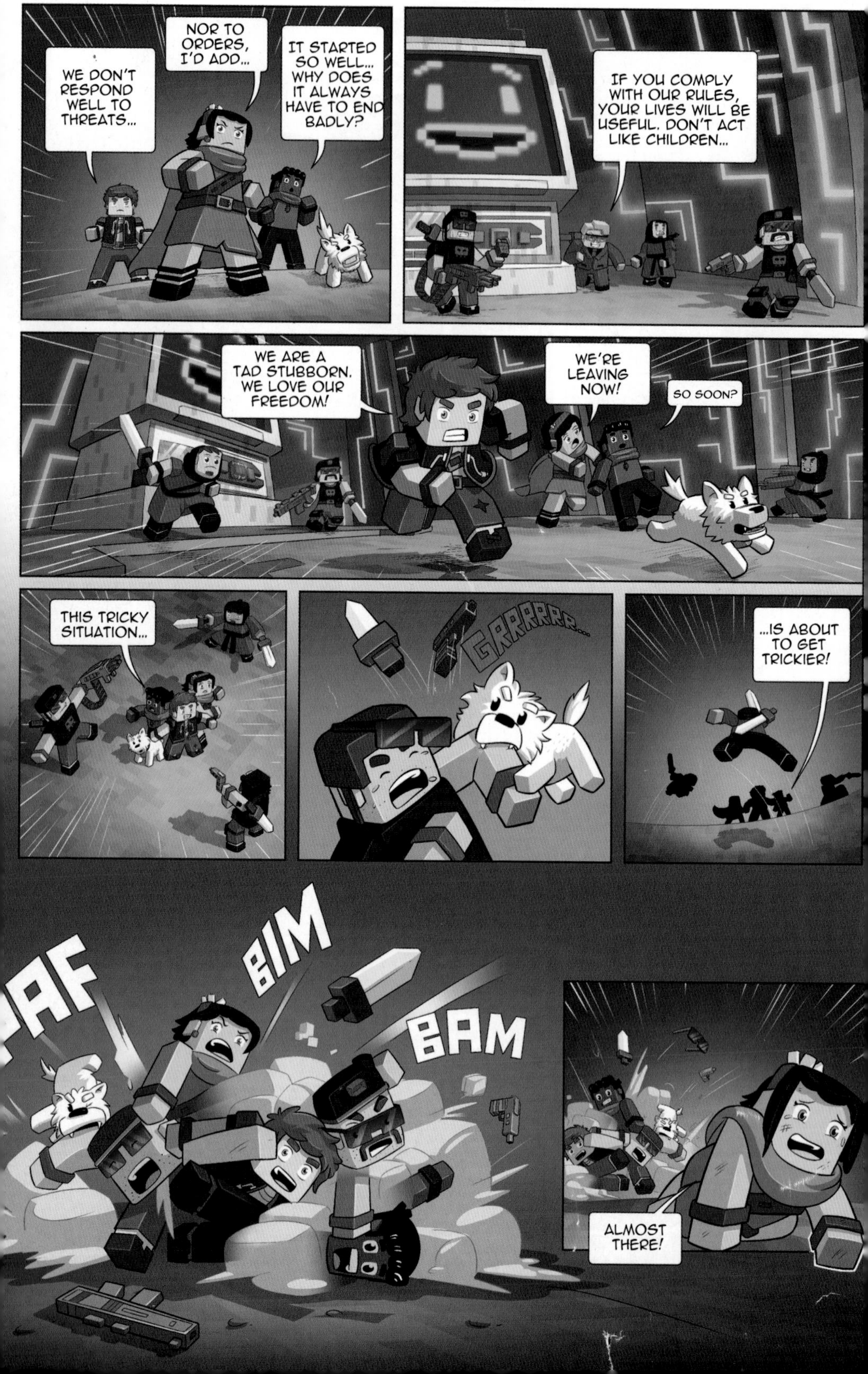
NOR TO ORDERS, I'D ADD...
WE DON'T RESPOND WELL TO THREATS...
IT STARTED SO WELL... WHY DOES IT ALWAYS HAVE TO END BADLY?
IF YOU COMPLY WITH OUR RULES, YOUR LIVES WILL BE USEFUL. DON'T ACT LIKE CHILDREN...
WE ARE A TAD STUBBORN. WE LOVE OUR FREEDOM!
WE'RE LEAVING NOW!
SO SOON?
THIS TRICKY SITUATION...
GRRRRRR...
...IS ABOUT TO GET TRICKIER!
PAF
BIM
BAM
ALMOST THERE!

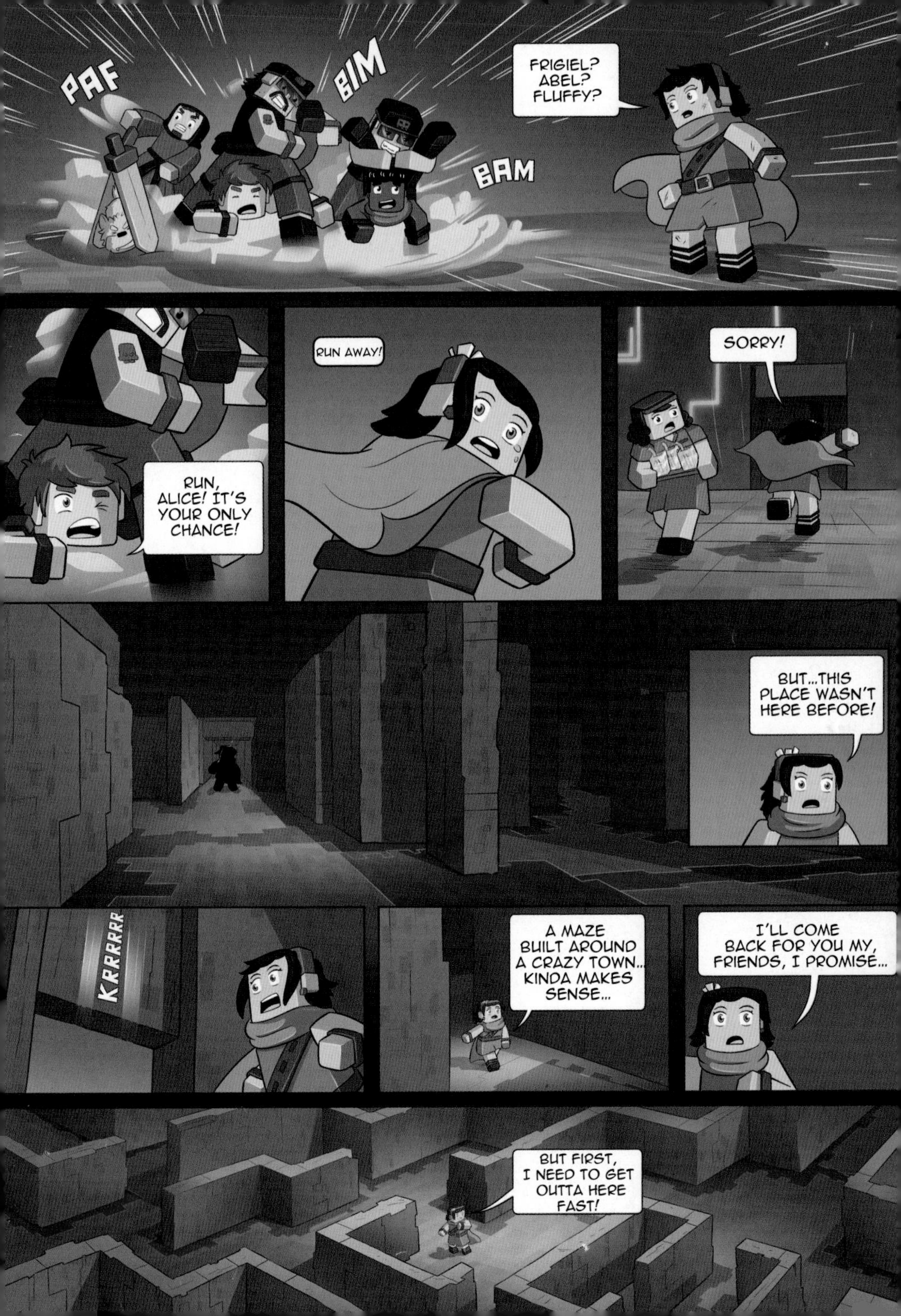
PAF
BIM
BAM
FRIGIEL? ABEL? FLUFFY?
RUN, ALICE! IT'S YOUR ONLY CHANCE!
RUN AWAY!
SORRY!
BUT...THIS PLACE WASN'T HERE BEFORE!
KRRRRRR
A MAZE BUILT AROUND A CRAZY TOWN... KINDA MAKES SENSE...
I'LL COME BACK FOR YOU MY, FRIENDS, I PROMISE...
BUT FIRST, I NEED TO GET OUTTA HERE FAST!

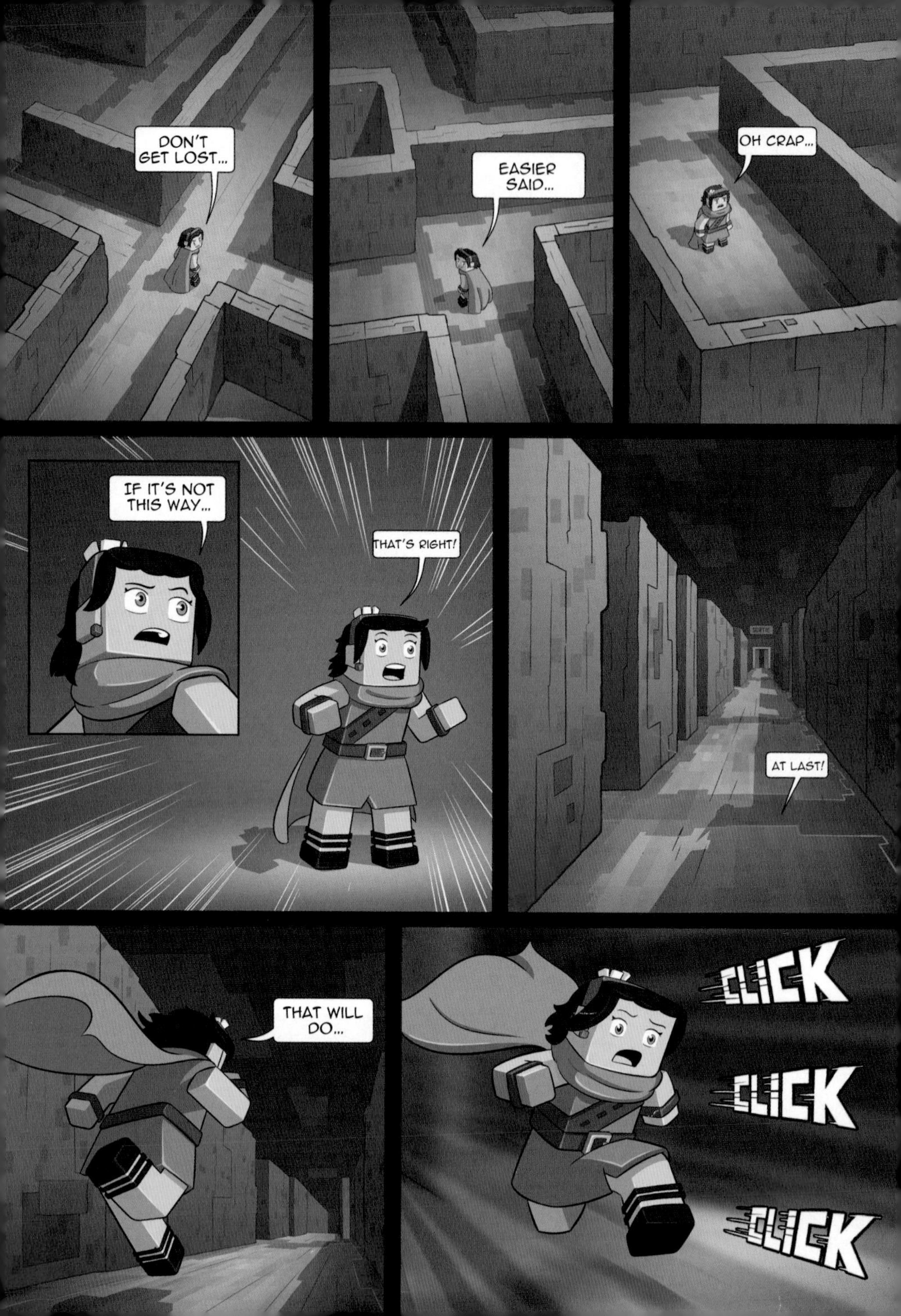
DON'T GET LOST...
EASIER SAID...
OH CRAP...
IF IT'S NOT THIS WAY...
THAT'S RIGHT!
AT LAST!
THAT WILL DO...
CLICK
CLICK
CLICK

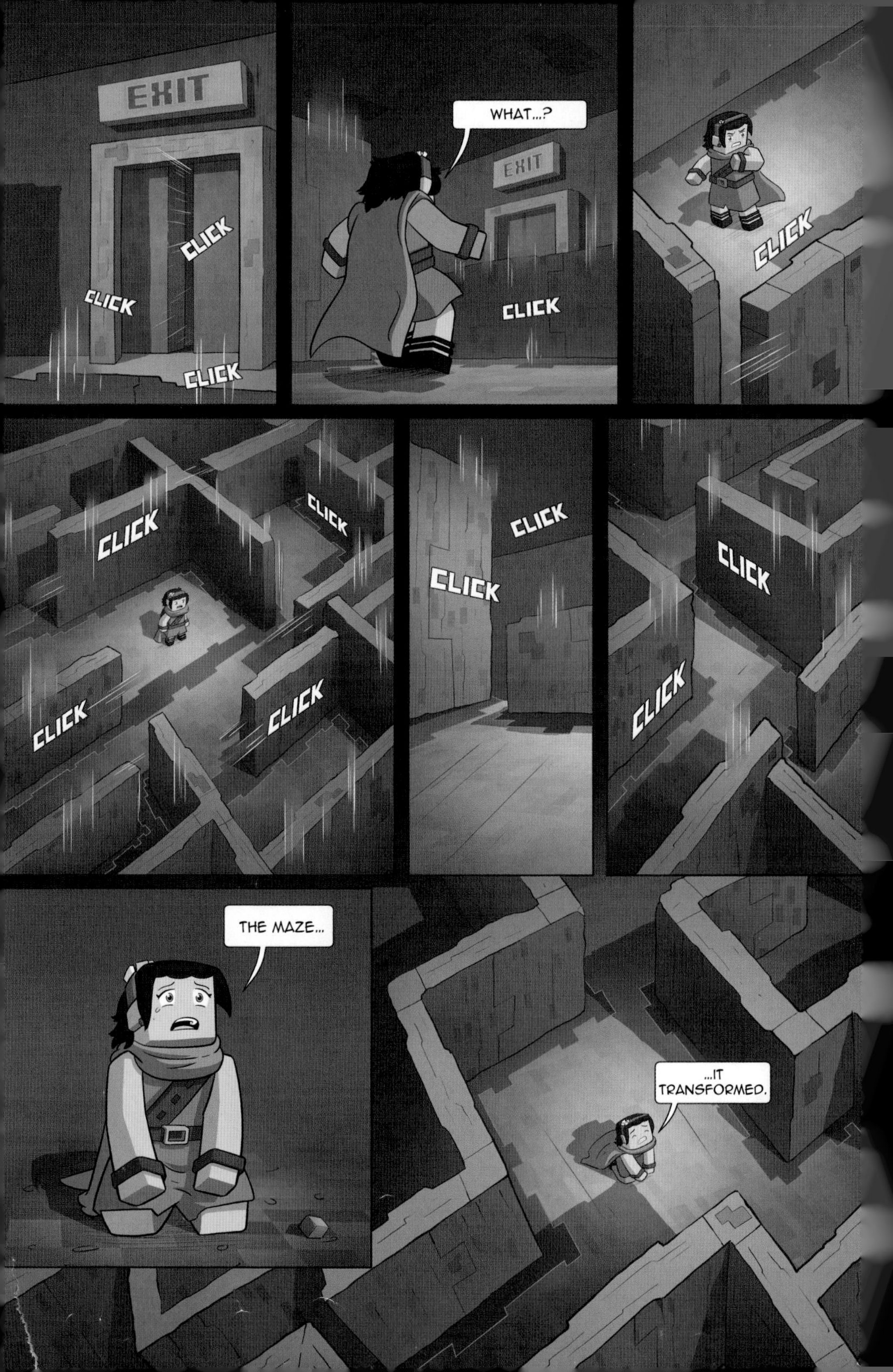
EXIT
CLICK
CLICK
CLICK
WHAT...?
EXIT
CLICK
CLICK
CLICK
CLICK
CLICK
CLICK
CLICK
CLICK
CLICK
CLICK
CLICK
THE MAZE...
...IT TRANSFORMED.

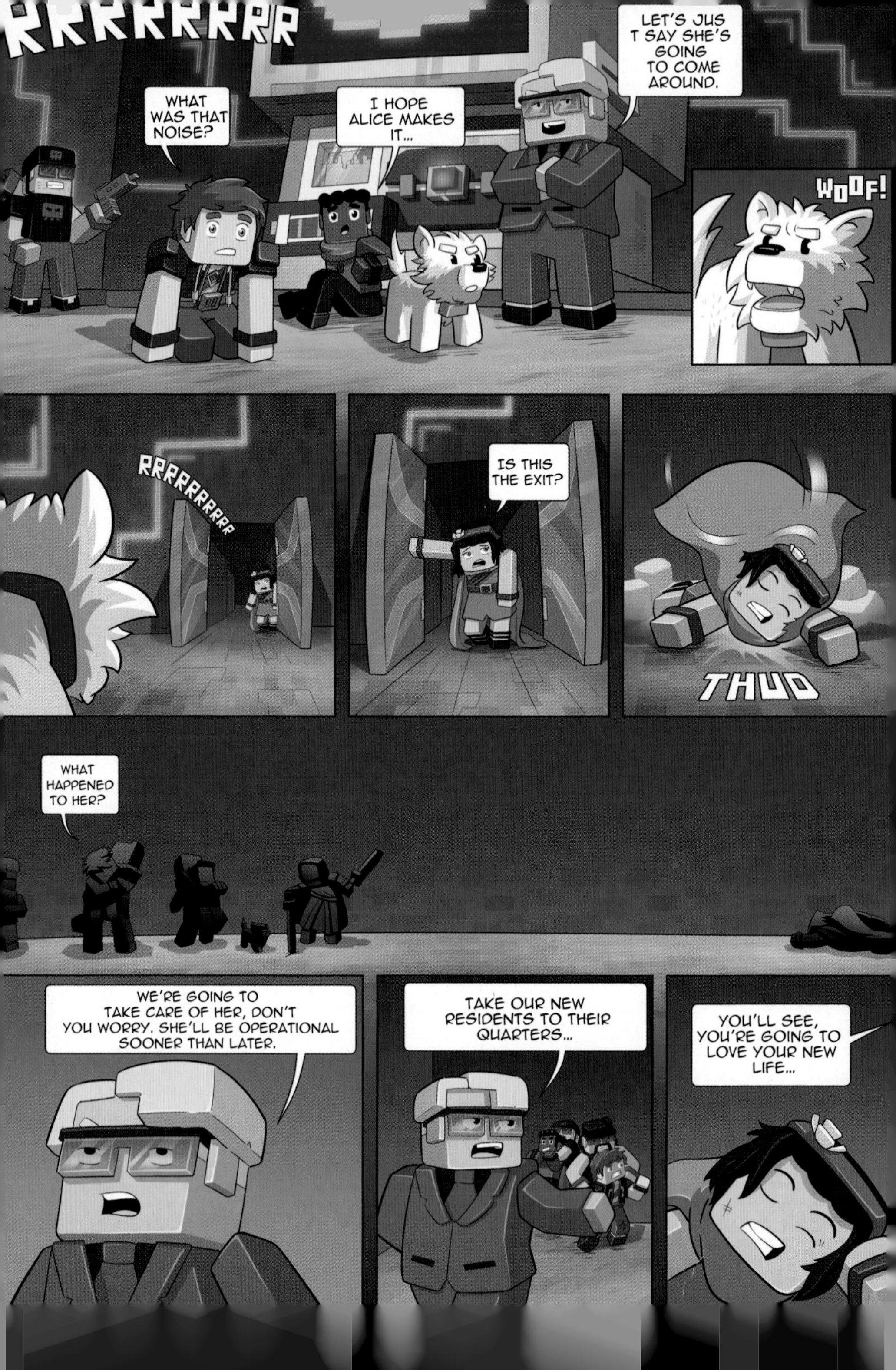
RRRRRRRRR
WHAT WAS THAT NOISE?
I HOPE ALICE MAKES IT...
LET'S JUS T SAY SHE'S GOING TO COME AROUND.
WOOF!
RRRRRRRRRR
IS THIS THE EXIT?
THUD
WHAT HAPPENED TO HER?
WE'RE GOING TO TAKE CARE OF HER, DON'T YOU WORRY. SHE'LL BE OPERATIONAL SOONER THAN LATER.
TAKE OUR NEW RESIDENTS TO THEIR QUARTERS...
YOU'LL SEE, YOU'RE GOING TO LOVE YOUR NEW LIFE...

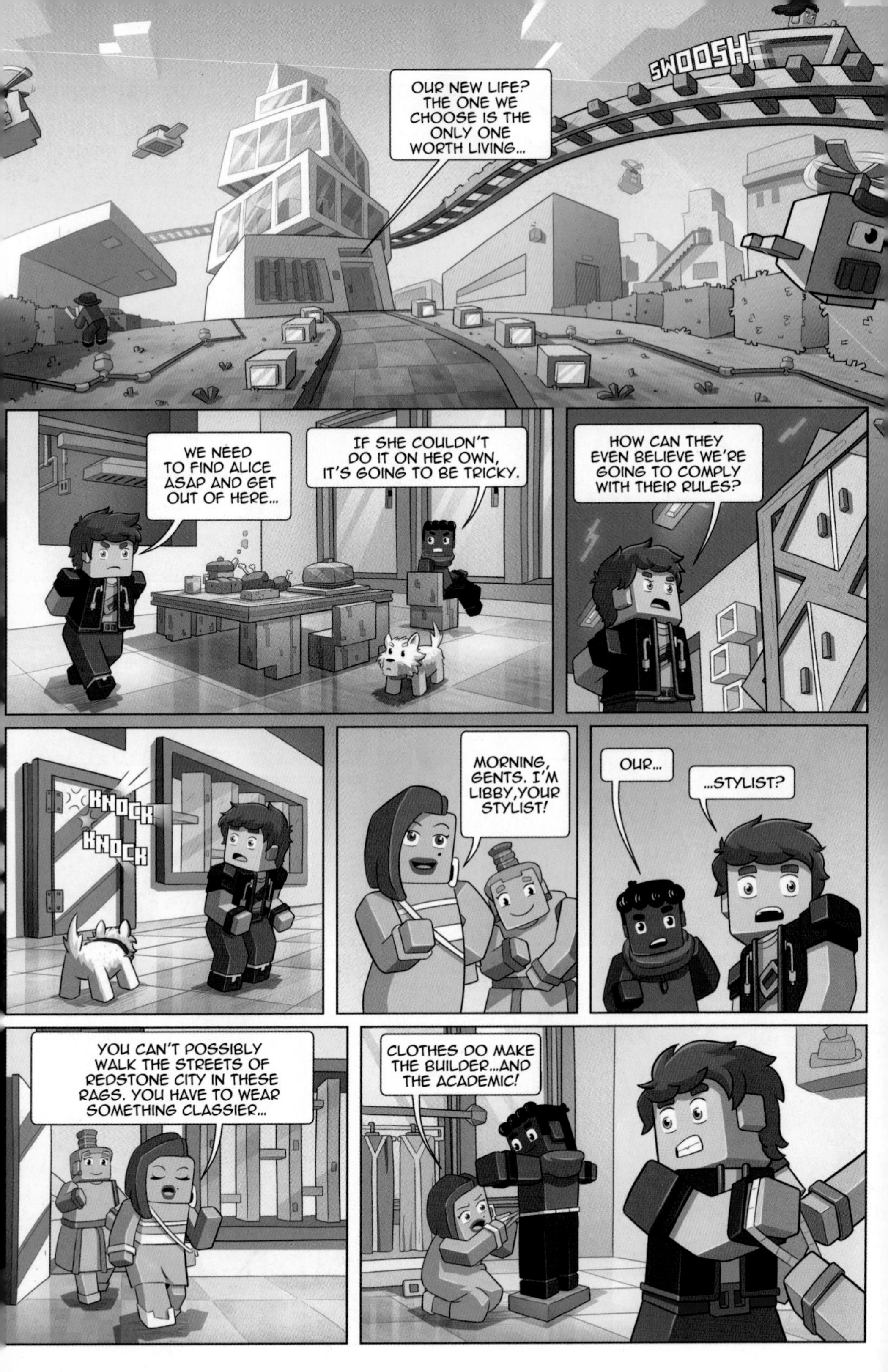
SWOOSH
OUR NEW LIFE? THE ONE WE CHOOSE IS THE ONLY ONE WORTH LIVING...
WE NEED TO FIND ALICE ASAP AND GET OUT OF HERE...
IF SHE COULDN'T DO IT ON HER OWN, IT'S GOING TO BE TRICKY.
HOW CAN THEY EVEN BELIEVE WE'RE GOING TO COMPLY WITH THEIR RULES?
KNOCK
KNOCK
MORNING, GENTS. I'M LIBBY,YOUR STYLIST!
OUR...
...STYLIST?
YOU CAN'T POSSIBLY WALK THE STREETS OF REDSTONE CITY IN THESE RAGS. YOU HAVE TO WEAR SOMETHING CLASSIER...
CLOTHES DO MAKE THE BUILDER...AND THE ACADEMIC!

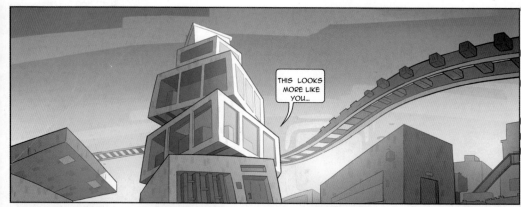

THIS LOOKS MORE LIKE YOU...

I'M NOT SURE...

YES, COME ON. YOU'LL GET USED TO IT...

WELL, THANKS...

LIBBY.

THANK YOU, LIBBY. HOW LONG HAVE YOU LIVED HERE?

I CAN'T REMEMBER EVER LEAVING TOWN, ACTUALLY.

YOU'VE ALWAYS BEEN A FASHION DESIGNER?

AT FIRST, I DIDN'T KNOW WHAT TO DO...THEN THE COMPUTER DECIDED FOR ME AND...I THINK IT WAS RIGHT.

WHAT IF IT WAS WRONG?

THAT'S IMPOSSIBLE. THE COMPUTER IS NEVER WRONG!

A BUILDER BUILDS, AN ACADEMIC LEARNS!

WHAT ARE WE DOING NOW?

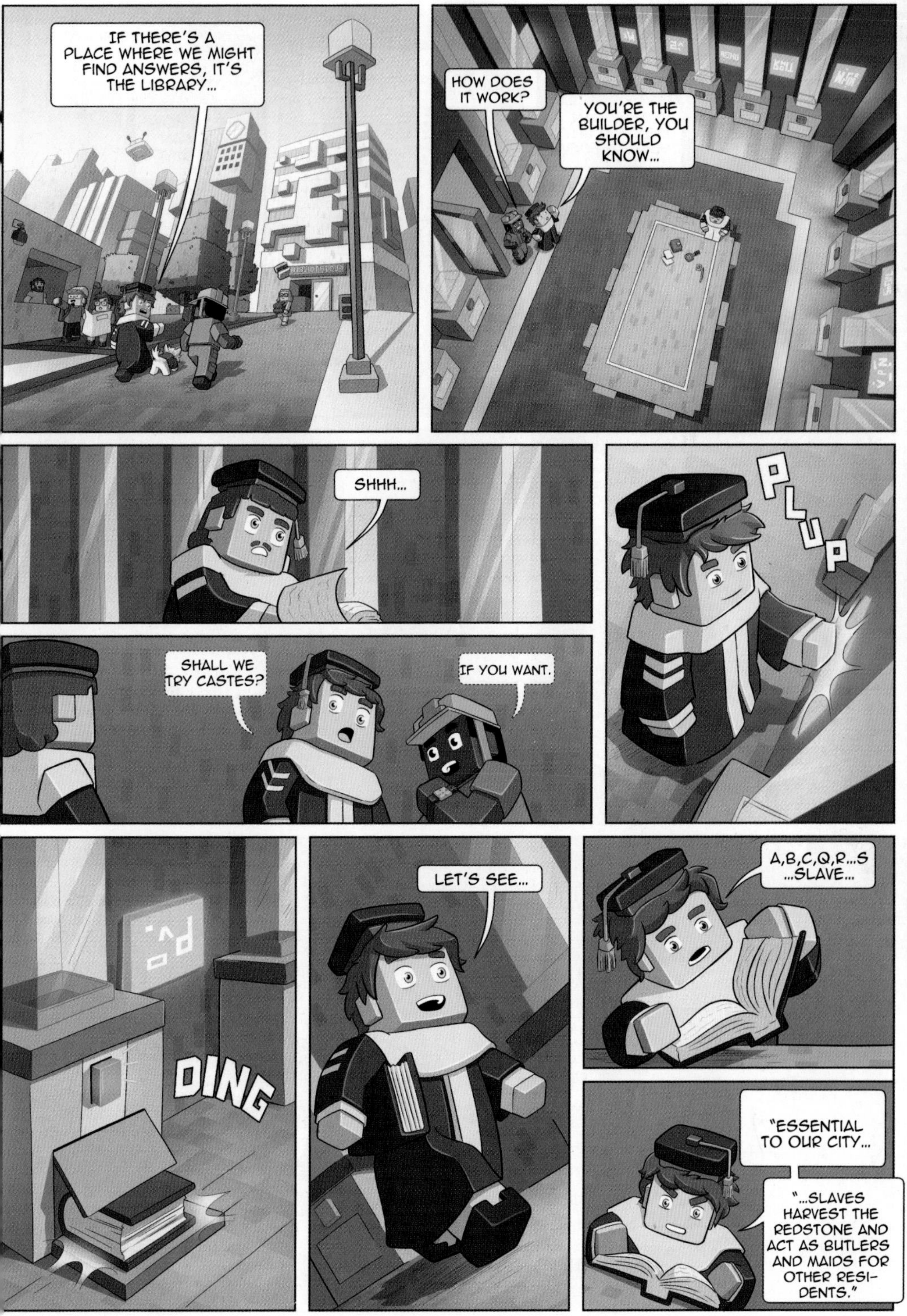

IF THERE'S A PLACE WHERE WE MIGHT FIND ANSWERS, IT'S THE LIBRARY...
HOW DOES IT WORK?
YOU'RE THE BUILDER, YOU SHOULD KNOW...
SHHH...
PLUP
SHALL WE TRY CASTES?
IF YOU WANT.
DING
LET'S SEE...
A,B,C,Q,R...S ...SLAVE...
"ESSENTIAL TO OUR CITY...
"...SLAVES HARVEST THE REDSTONE AND ACT AS BUTLERS AND MAIDS FOR OTHER RESI-DENTS."

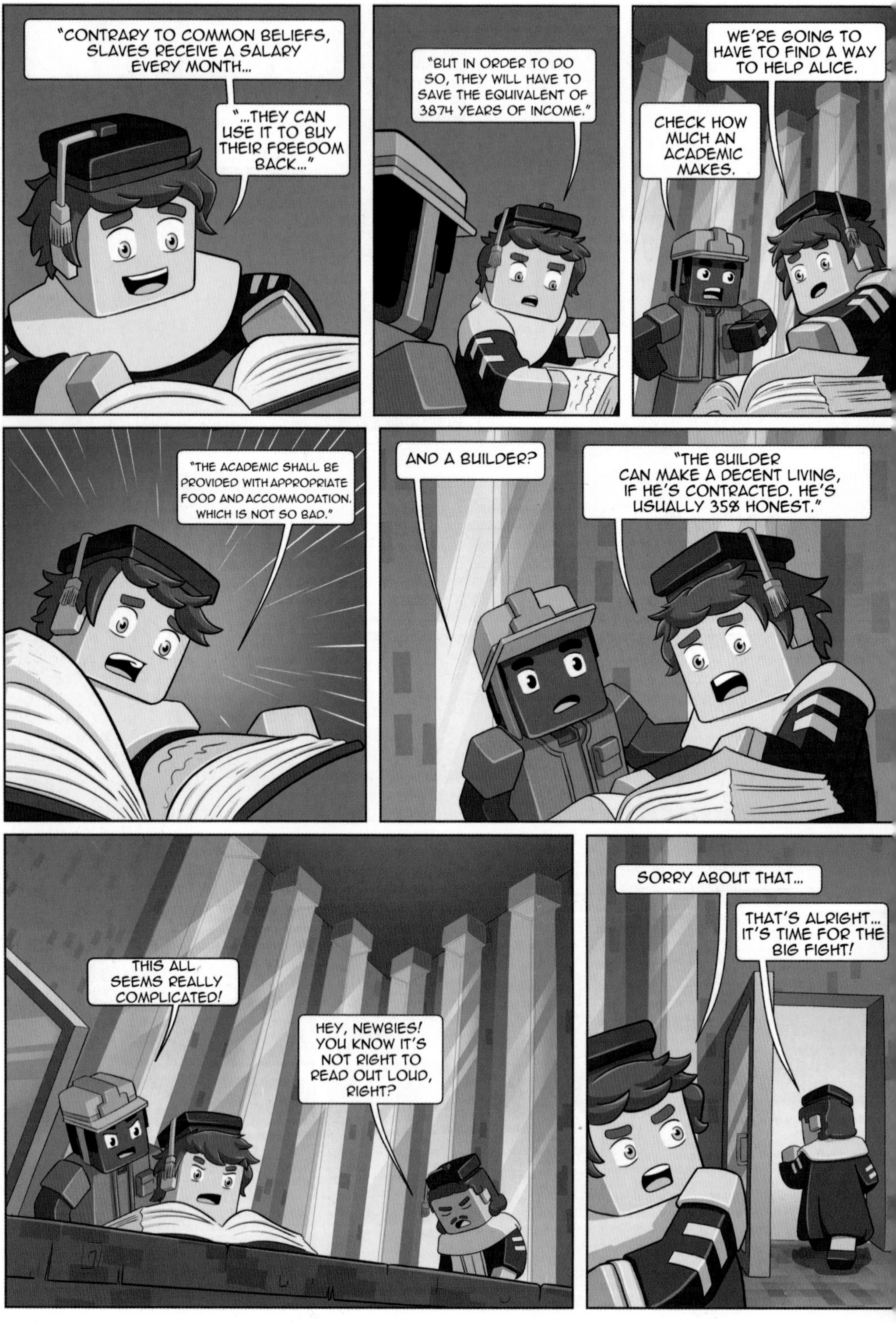
"CONTRARY TO COMMON BELIEFS, SLAVES RECEIVE A SALARY EVERY MONTH...
"...THEY CAN USE IT TO BUY THEIR FREEDOM BACK..."
"BUT IN ORDER TO DO SO, THEY WILL HAVE TO SAVE THE EQUIVALENT OF 3874 YEARS OF INCOME."
WE'RE GOING TO HAVE TO FIND A WAY TO HELP ALICE.
CHECK HOW MUCH AN ACADEMIC MAKES.
"THE ACADEMIC SHALL BE PROVIDED WITH APPROPRIATE FOOD AND ACCOMMODATION. WHICH IS NOT SO BAD."
AND A BUILDER?
"THE BUILDER CAN MAKE A DECENT LIVING, IF HE'S CONTRACTED. HE'S USUALLY 35% HONEST."
THIS ALL SEEMS REALLY COMPLICATED!
HEY, NEWBIES! YOU KNOW IT'S NOT RIGHT TO READ OUT LOUD, RIGHT?
SORRY ABOUT THAT...
THAT'S ALRIGHT... IT'S TIME FOR THE BIG FIGHT!

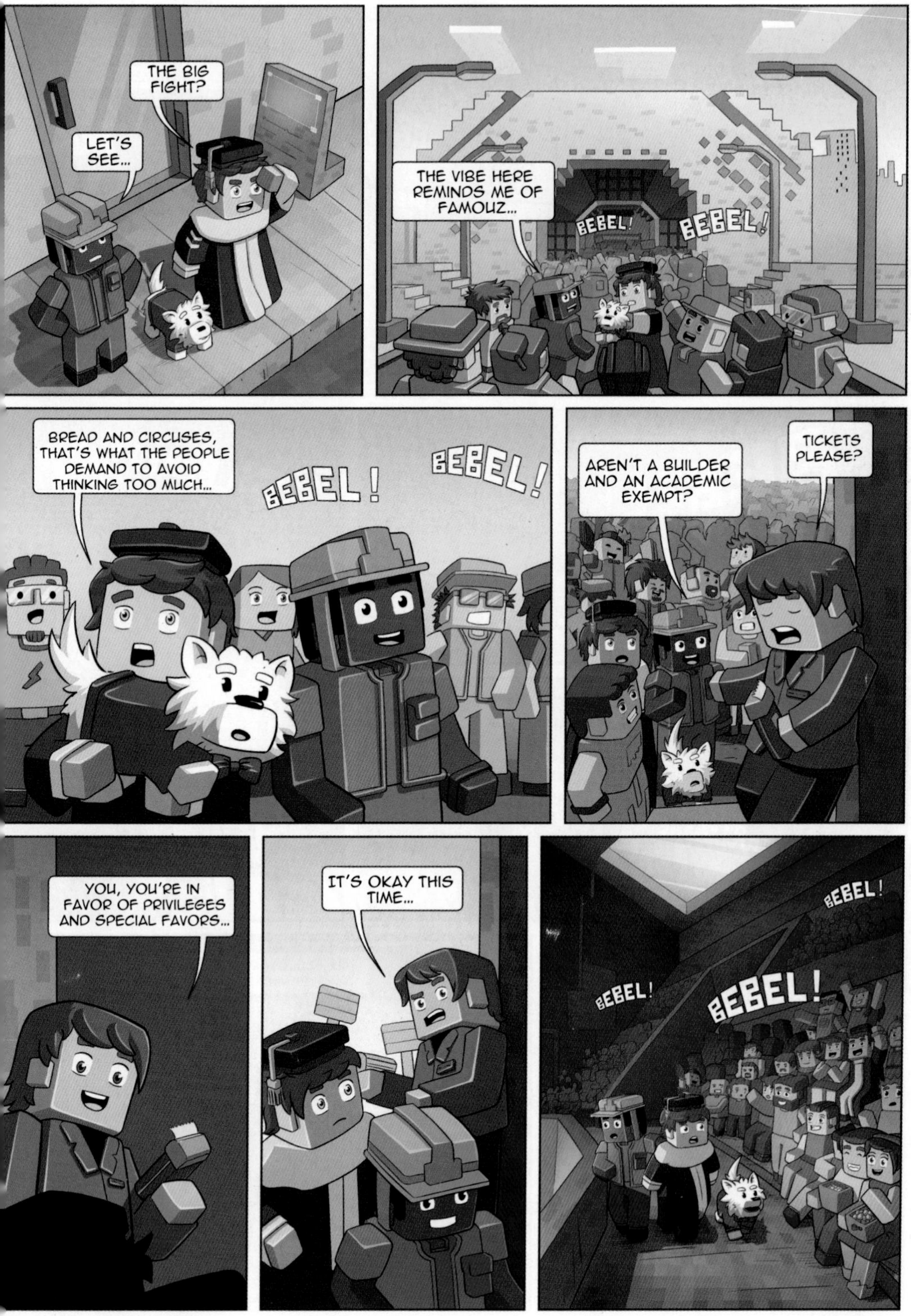
THE BIG FIGHT?
LET'S SEE...
THE VIBE HERE REMINDS ME OF FAMOUZ...
BEBEL!
BEBEL!
BREAD AND CIRCUSES, THAT'S WHAT THE PEOPLE DEMAND TO AVOID THINKING TOO MUCH...
BEBEL!
BEBEL!
TICKETS PLEASE?
AREN'T A BUILDER AND AN ACADEMIC EXEMPT?
YOU, YOU'RE IN FAVOR OF PRIVILEGES AND SPECIAL FAVORS...
IT'S OKAY THIS TIME...
BEBEL!
BEBEL!
BEBEL!

BEBEL!

BEBEL!

BEBEL!

I THINK THE PILOT OF THE ROBOT'S NAME IS BEBEL...

WHAT MAKES YOU SAY THAT?

BEBEL!

BEBEL!

GILBERTO!

GILBERTO!

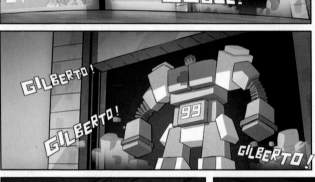

GILBERTO!

GILBERTO!

GILBERTO!

SO, TWO GIANT ROBOTS ARE GOING TO FIGHT TO PLEASE THE CROWD...

IT'S GREAT THAT THEY SPORT DIFFERENT COLORS...OR IT'D BE DIFFICULT TO DIFFERENTIATE THEM...

MY FELLOW REDSTONIANS, WELCOME TO THE WEEKLY CLASH OF THE TITANS.

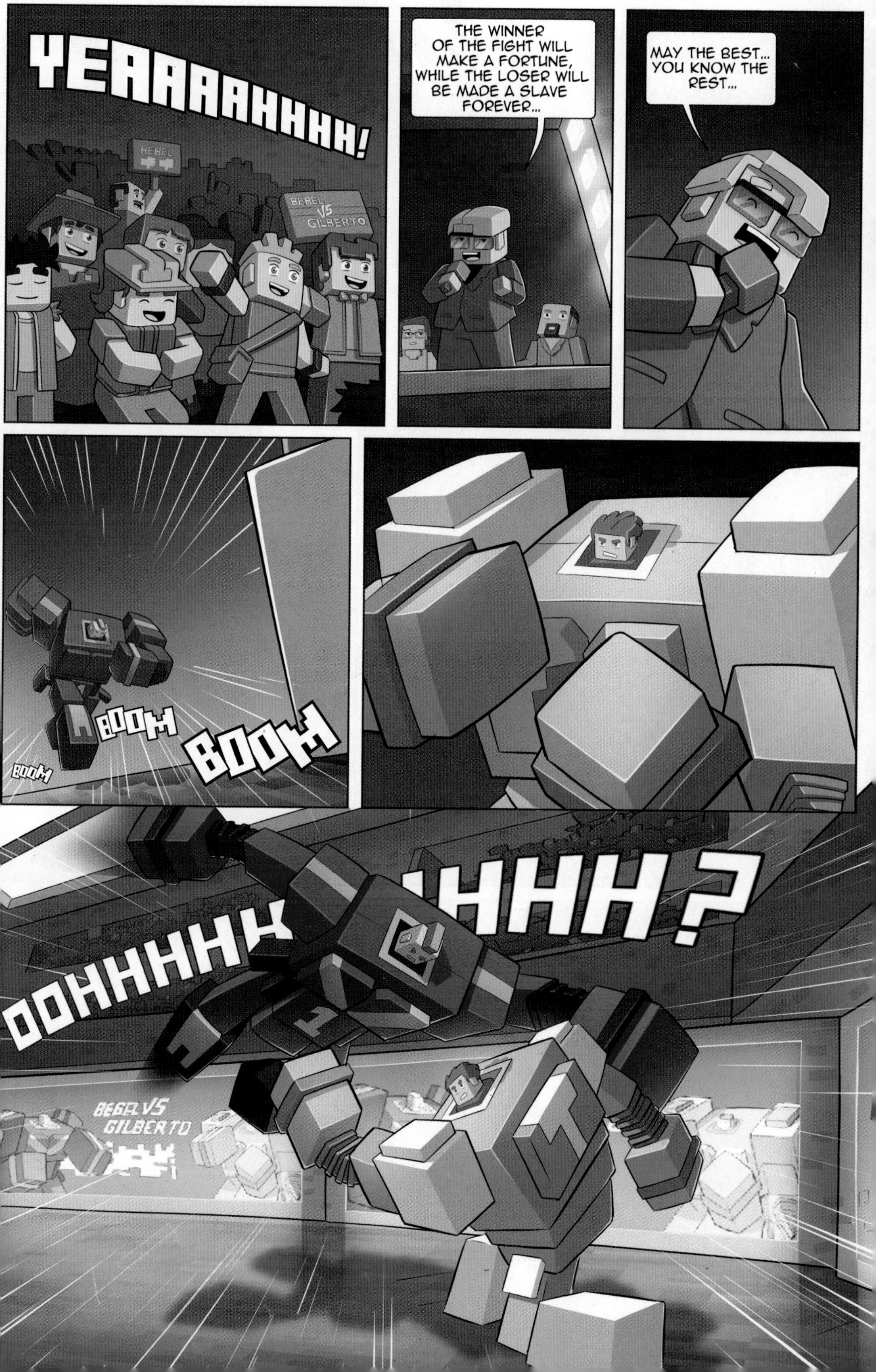
YEAAAAHHHH!
BEBEL
BEBEL VS GILBERTO
THE WINNER OF THE FIGHT WILL MAKE A FORTUNE, WHILE THE LOSER WILL BE MADE A SLAVE FOREVER...
MAY THE BEST... YOU KNOW THE REST...
BOOM
BOOM
BOOM
OOHHHHHHHHH?
BEBEL VS GILBERTO

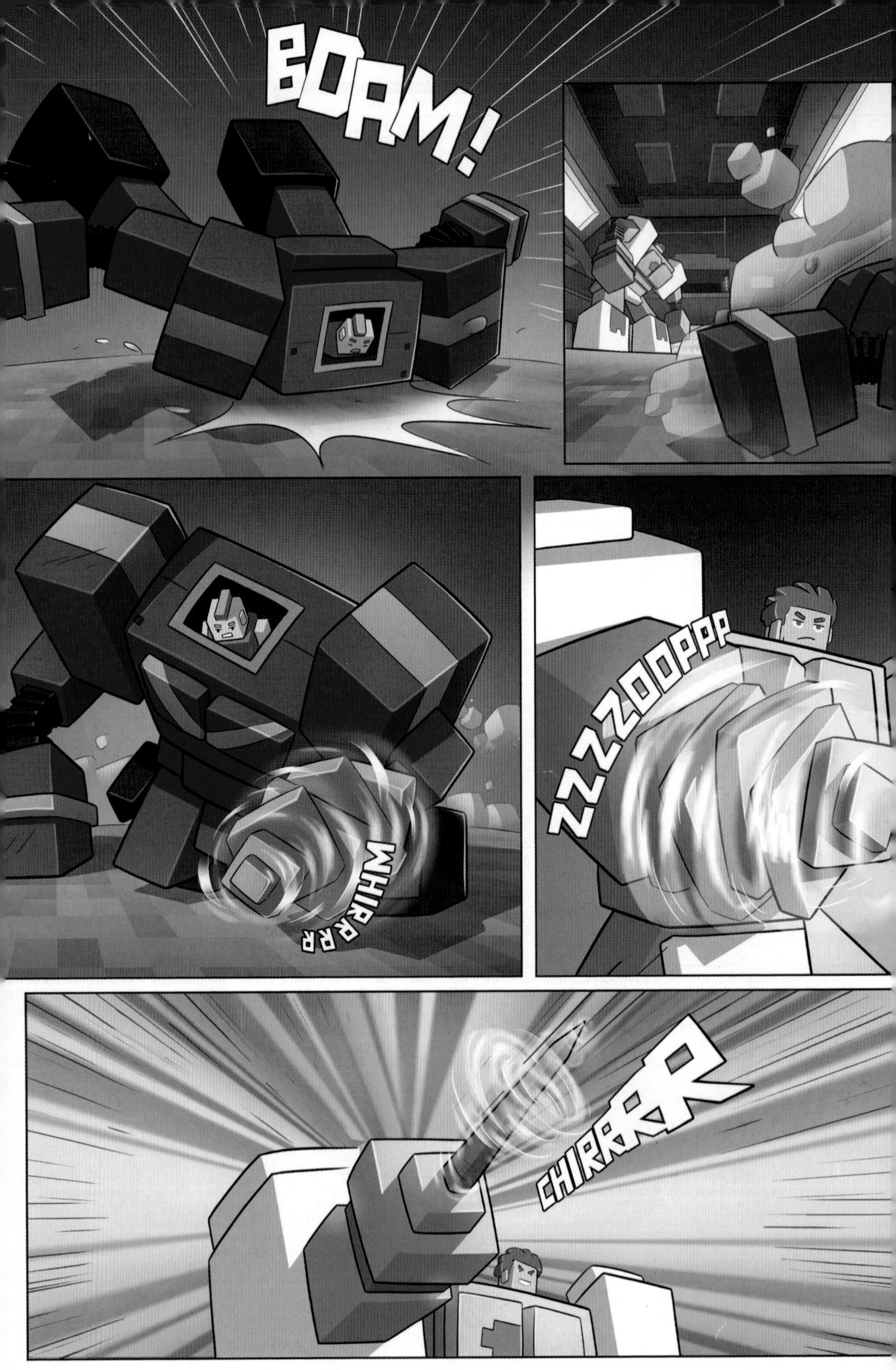
BOOM!
WHIRRRR
ZZZZOOPPP
CHIRRRRR

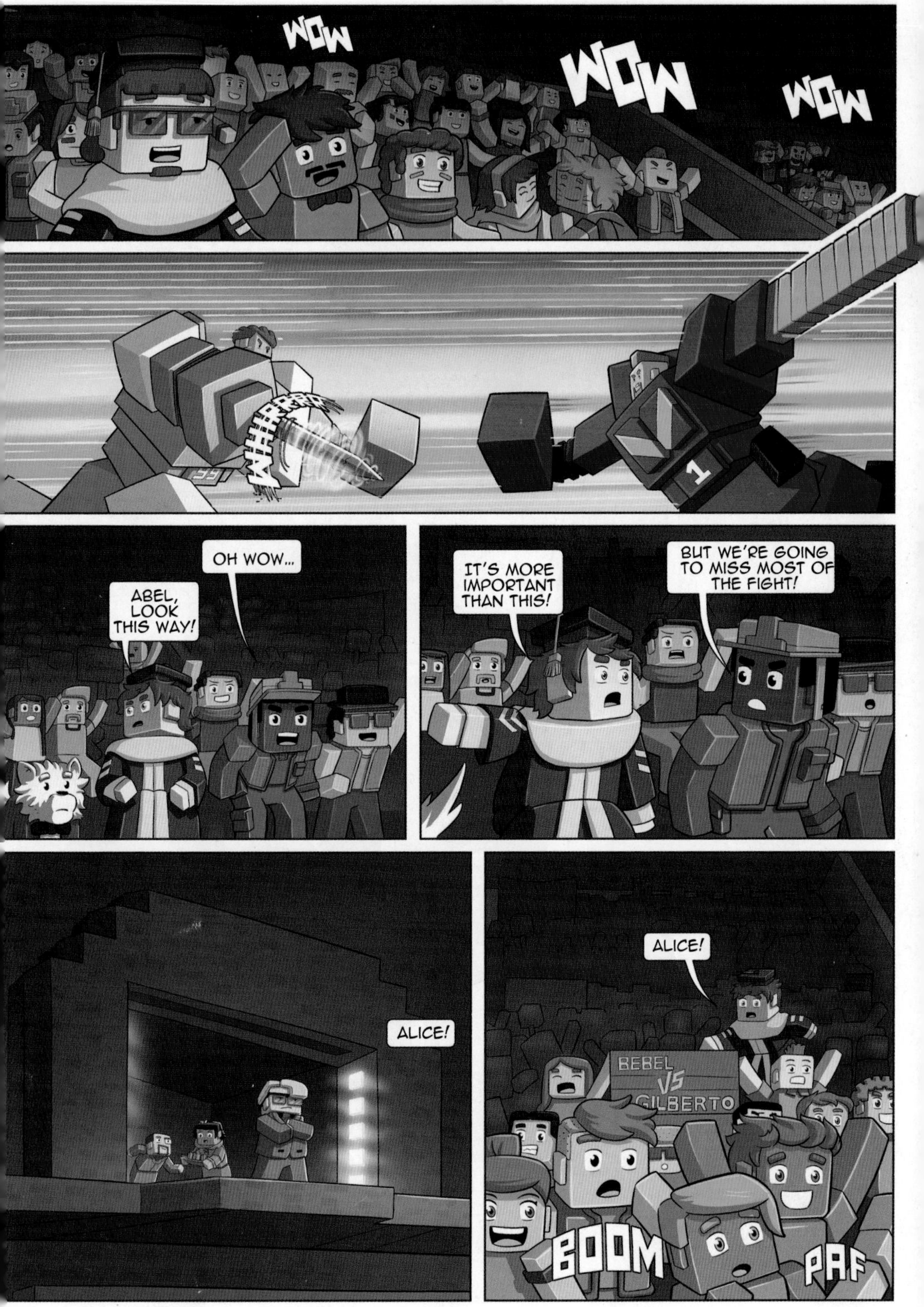
WOW
WOW
WOW
OH WOW...
ABEL, LOOK THIS WAY!
IT'S MORE IMPORTANT THAN THIS!
BUT WE'RE GOING TO MISS MOST OF THE FIGHT!
ALICE!
ALICE!
BEBEL VS GILBERTO
BOOM
PAF

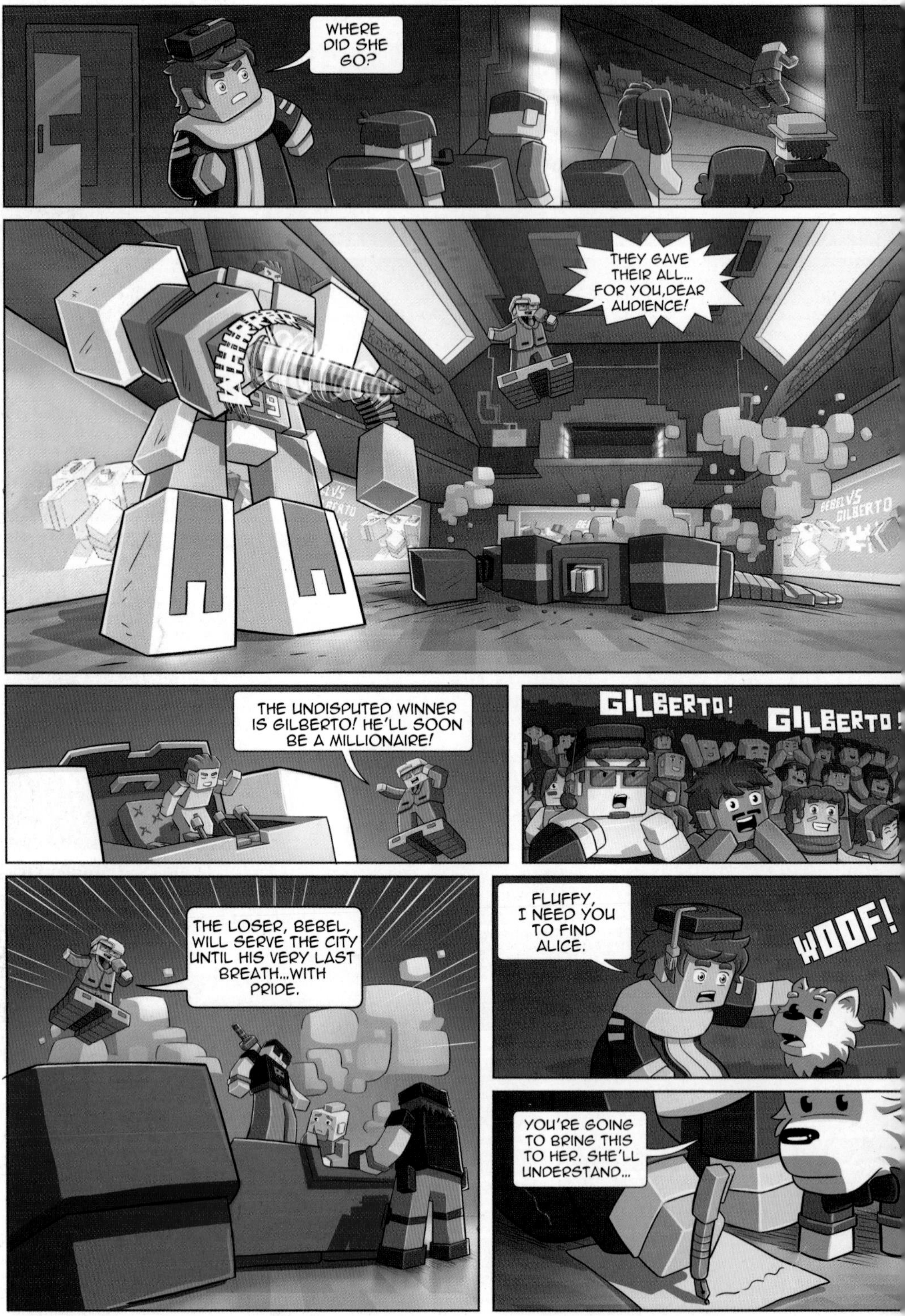
WHERE DID SHE GO?
WHIRRR
THEY GAVE THEIR ALL... FOR YOU,DEAR AUDIENCE!
BEBEL VS GILBERTO
THE UNDISPUTED WINNER IS GILBERTO! HE'LL SOON BE A MILLIONAIRE!
GILBERTO!
GILBERTO!
THE LOSER, BEBEL, WILL SERVE THE CITY UNTIL HIS VERY LAST BREATH...WITH PRIDE.
FLUFFY, I NEED YOU TO FIND ALICE.
WOOF!
YOU'RE GOING TO BRING THIS TO HER. SHE'LL UNDERSTAND...

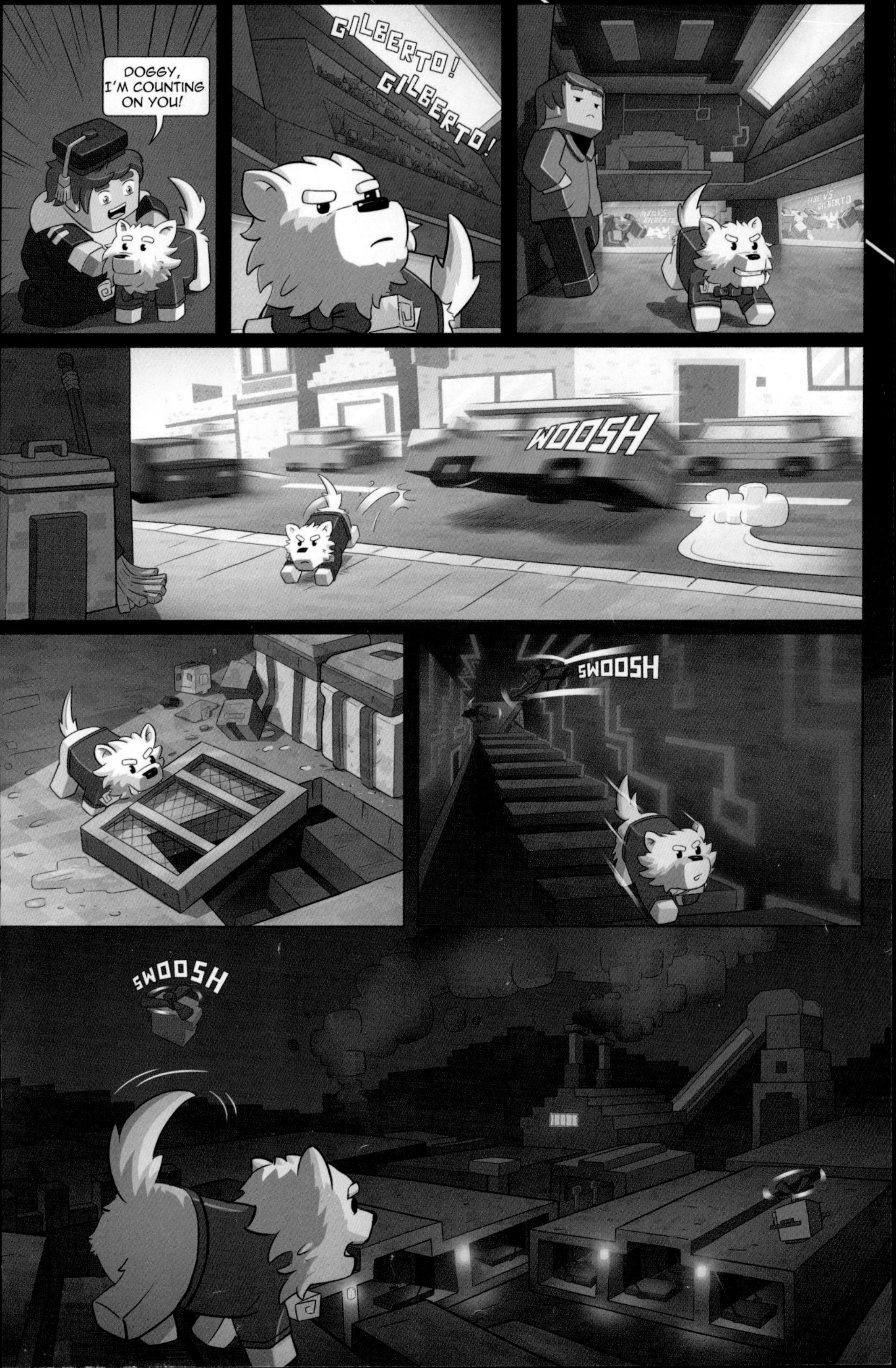
DOGGY, I'M COUNTING ON YOU!
GILBERTO! GILBERTO!
WOOSH
SWOOSH
SWOOSH

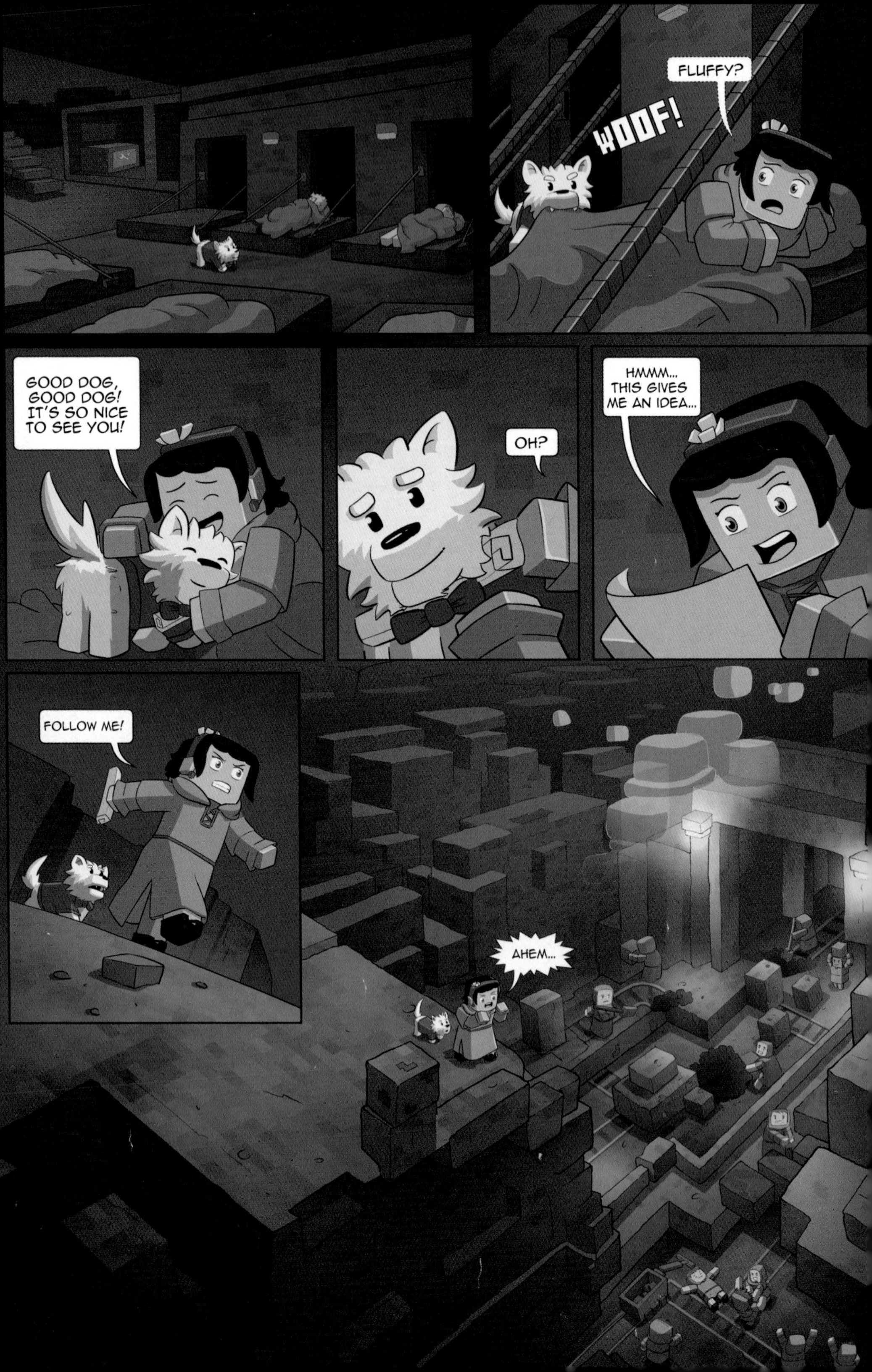

FLUFFY?
WOOF!
GOOD DOG, GOOD DOG! IT'S SO NICE TO SEE YOU!
OH?
HMMM... THIS GIVES ME AN IDEA...
FOLLOW ME!
AHEM...

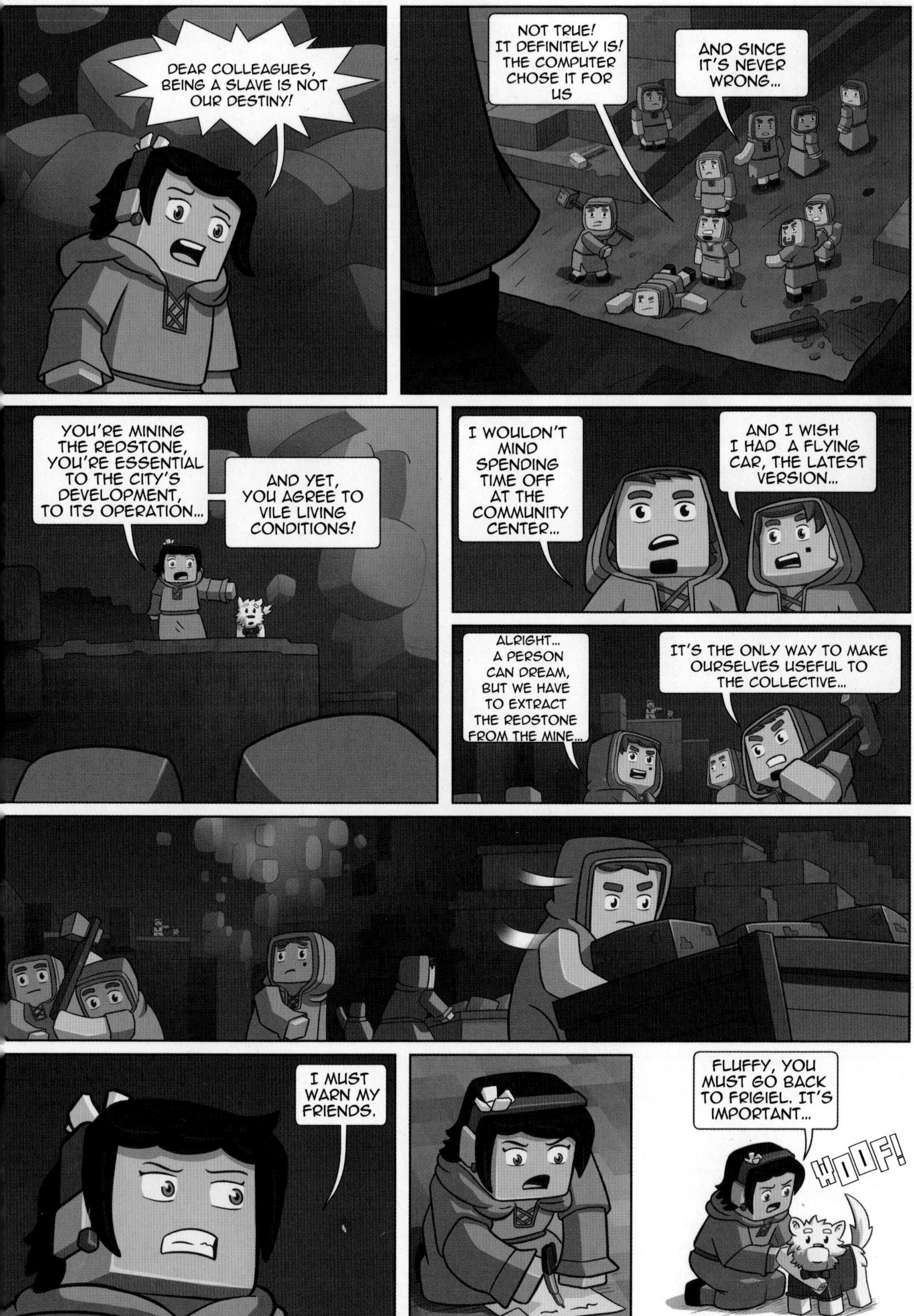
DEAR COLLEAGUES, BEING A SLAVE IS NOT OUR DESTINY!
NOT TRUE! IT DEFINITELY IS! THE COMPUTER CHOSE IT FOR US
AND SINCE IT'S NEVER WRONG...
YOU'RE MINING THE REDSTONE, YOU'RE ESSENTIAL TO THE CITY'S DEVELOPMENT, TO ITS OPERATION...
AND YET, YOU AGREE TO VILE LIVING CONDITIONS!
I WOULDN'T MIND SPENDING TIME OFF AT THE COMMUNITY CENTER...
AND I WISH I HAD A FLYING CAR, THE LATEST VERSION...
ALRIGHT... A PERSON CAN DREAM, BUT WE HAVE TO EXTRACT THE REDSTONE FROM THE MINE...
IT'S THE ONLY WAY TO MAKE OURSELVES USEFUL TO THE COLLECTIVE...
I MUST WARN MY FRIENDS.
FLUFFY, YOU MUST GO BACK TO FRIGIEL. IT'S IMPORTANT...
WOOF!

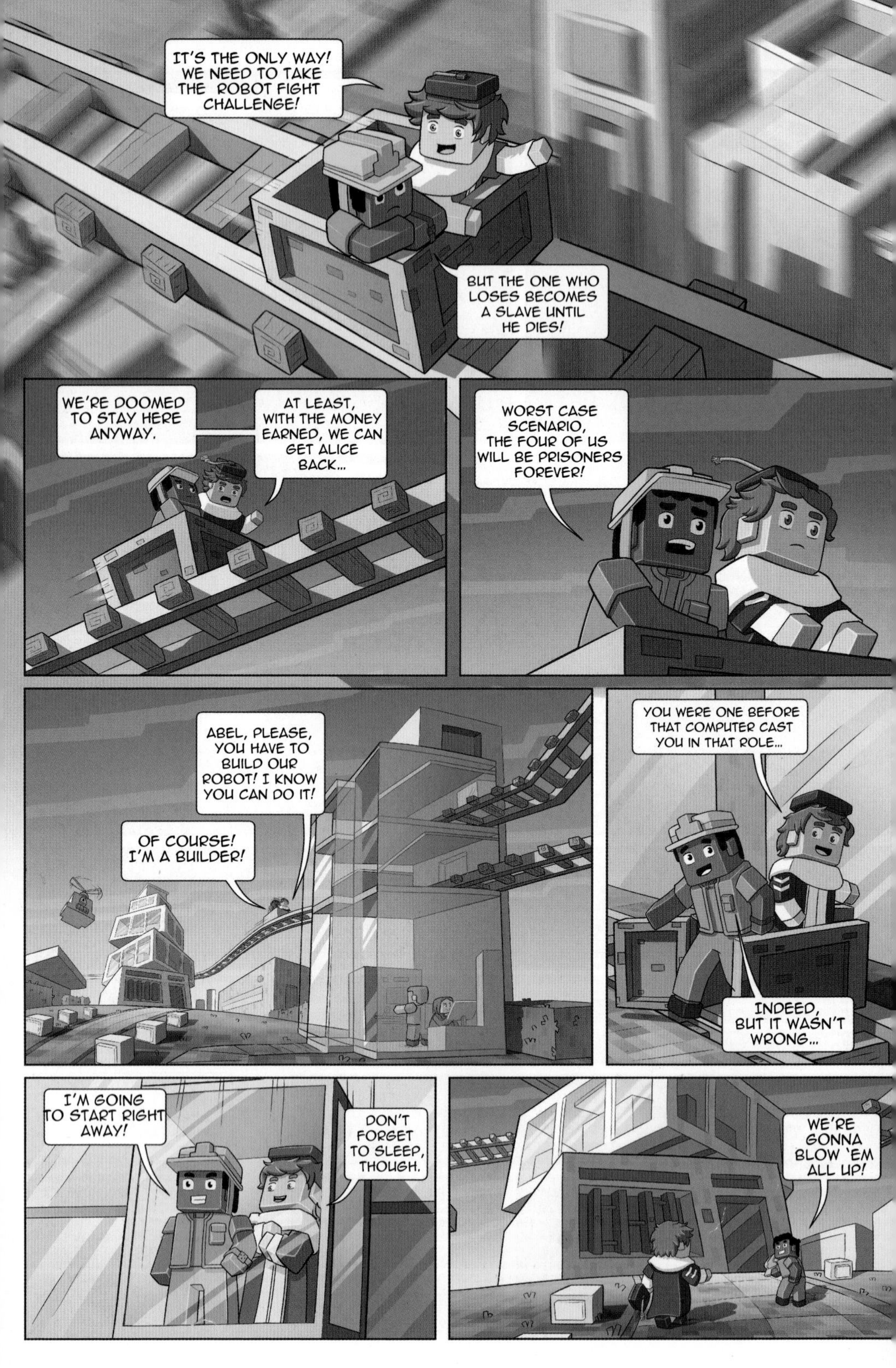
IT'S THE ONLY WAY! WE NEED TO TAKE THE ROBOT FIGHT CHALLENGE!
BUT THE ONE WHO LOSES BECOMES A SLAVE UNTIL HE DIES!
WE'RE DOOMED TO STAY HERE ANYWAY.
AT LEAST, WITH THE MONEY EARNED, WE CAN GET ALICE BACK...
WORST CASE SCENARIO, THE FOUR OF US WILL BE PRISONERS FOREVER!
ABEL, PLEASE, YOU HAVE TO BUILD OUR ROBOT! I KNOW YOU CAN DO IT!
OF COURSE! I'M A BUILDER!
YOU WERE ONE BEFORE THAT COMPUTER CAST YOU IN THAT ROLE...
INDEED, BUT IT WASN'T WRONG...
I'M GOING TO START RIGHT AWAY!
DON'T FORGET TO SLEEP, THOUGH.
WE'RE GONNA BLOW 'EM ALL UP!

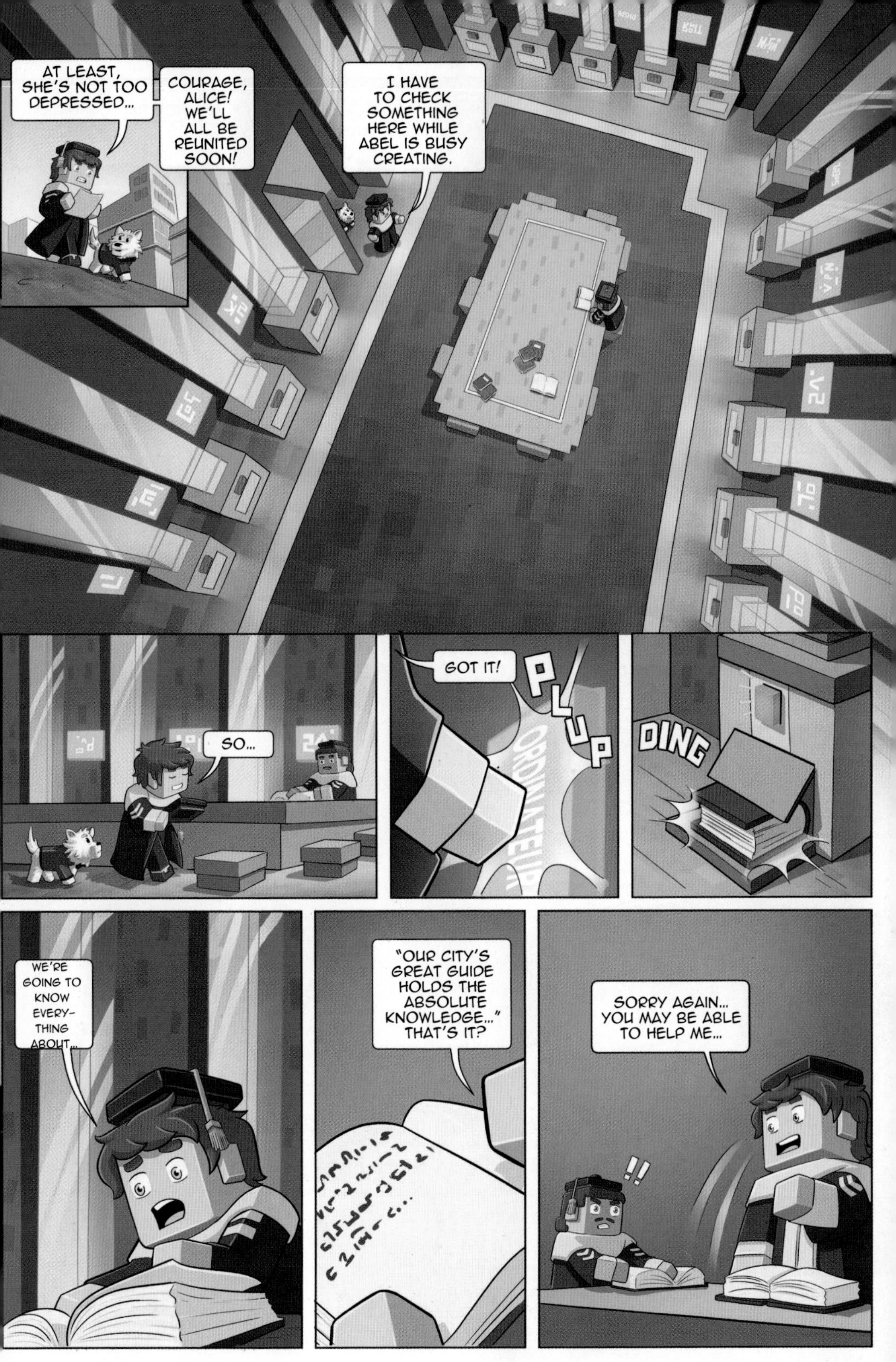
AT LEAST, SHE'S NOT TOO DEPRESSED...
COURAGE, ALICE! WE'LL ALL BE REUNITED SOON!
I HAVE TO CHECK SOMETHING HERE WHILE ABEL IS BUSY CREATING.
SO...
GOT IT!
PLUP
ORDINATEUR
DING
WE'RE GOING TO KNOW EVERY-THING ABOUT...
"OUR CITY'S GREAT GUIDE HOLDS THE ABSOLUTE KNOWLEDGE..." THAT'S IT?
!!
SORRY AGAIN... YOU MAY BE ABLE TO HELP ME...

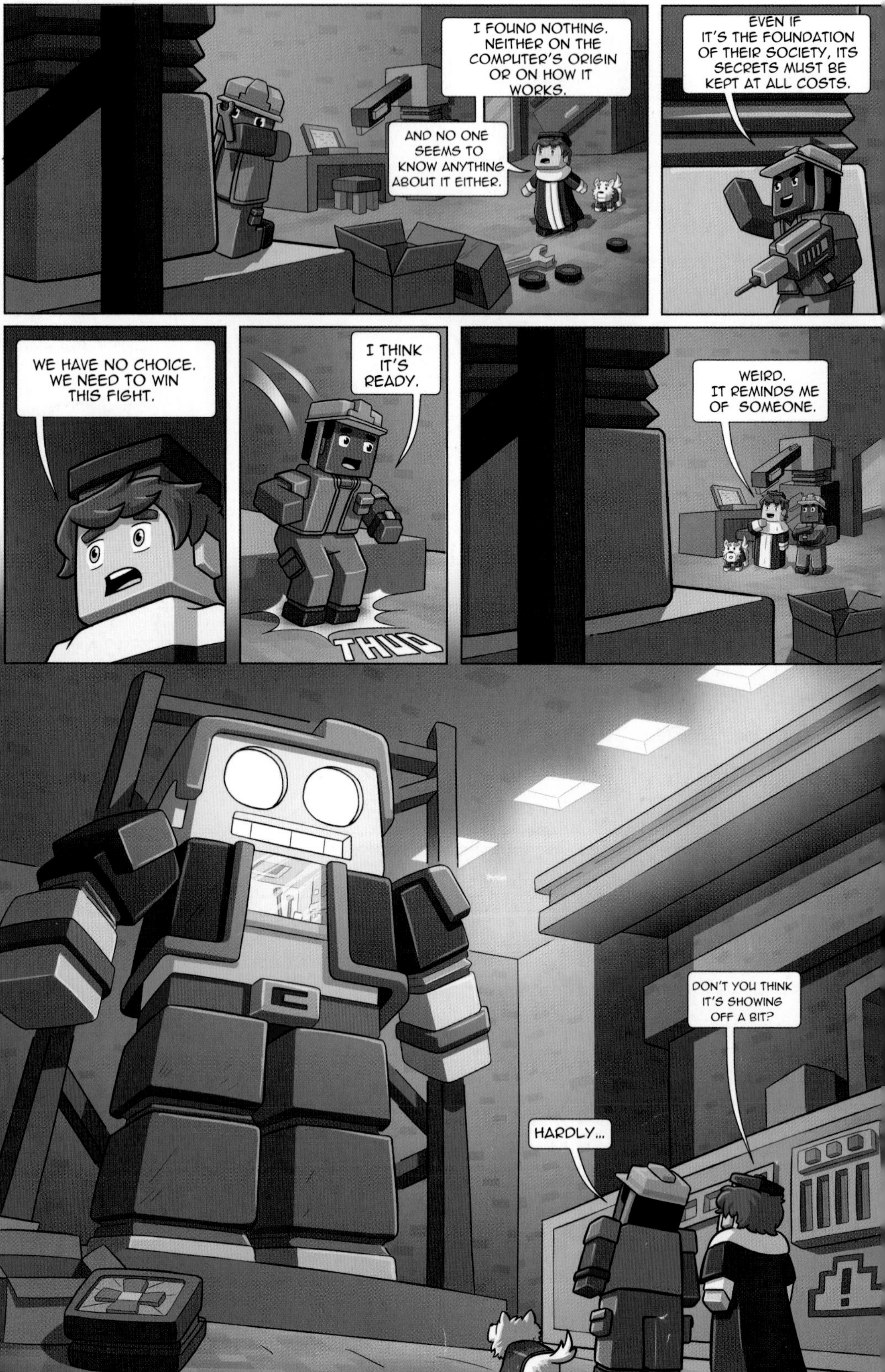
I FOUND NOTHING. NEITHER ON THE COMPUTER'S ORIGIN OR ON HOW IT WORKS.
AND NO ONE SEEMS TO KNOW ANYTHING ABOUT IT EITHER.
EVEN IF IT'S THE FOUNDATION OF THEIR SOCIETY, ITS SECRETS MUST BE KEPT AT ALL COSTS.
WE HAVE NO CHOICE. WE NEED TO WIN THIS FIGHT.
I THINK IT'S READY.
THUD
WEIRD. IT REMINDS ME OF SOMEONE.
DON'T YOU THINK IT'S SHOWING OFF A BIT?
HARDLY...

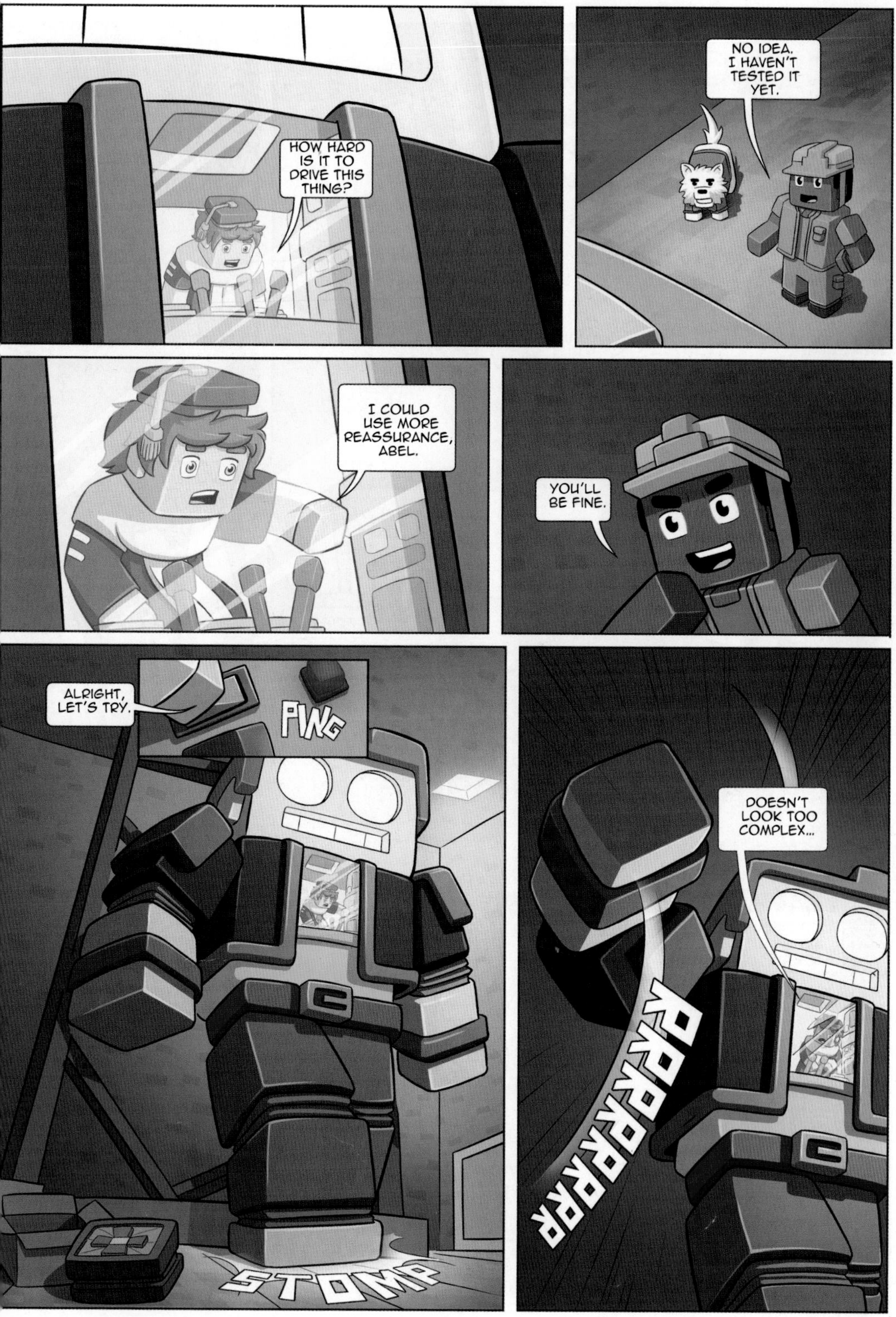
HOW HARD IS IT TO DRIVE THIS THING?
NO IDEA. I HAVEN'T TESTED IT YET.
I COULD USE MORE REASSURANCE, ABEL.
YOU'LL BE FINE.
ALRIGHT, LET'S TRY.
PING
STOMP
DOESN'T LOOK TOO COMPLEX...
RRRRRRRR

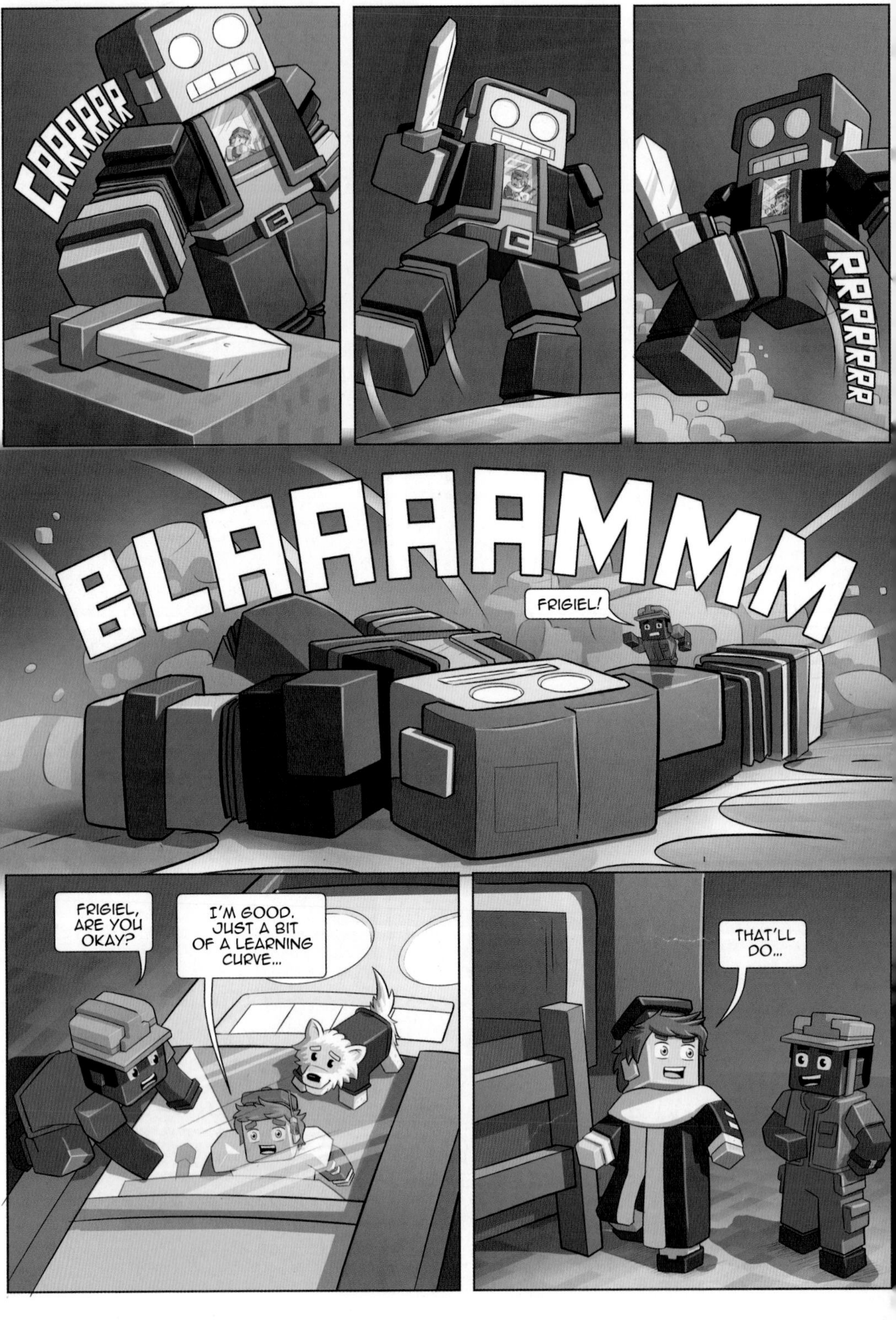
CRRRRRR
RRRRRRR
BLAAAAMMM
FRIGIEL!
FRIGIEL, ARE YOU OKAY?
I'M GOOD. JUST A BIT OF A LEARNING CURVE...
THAT'LL DO...

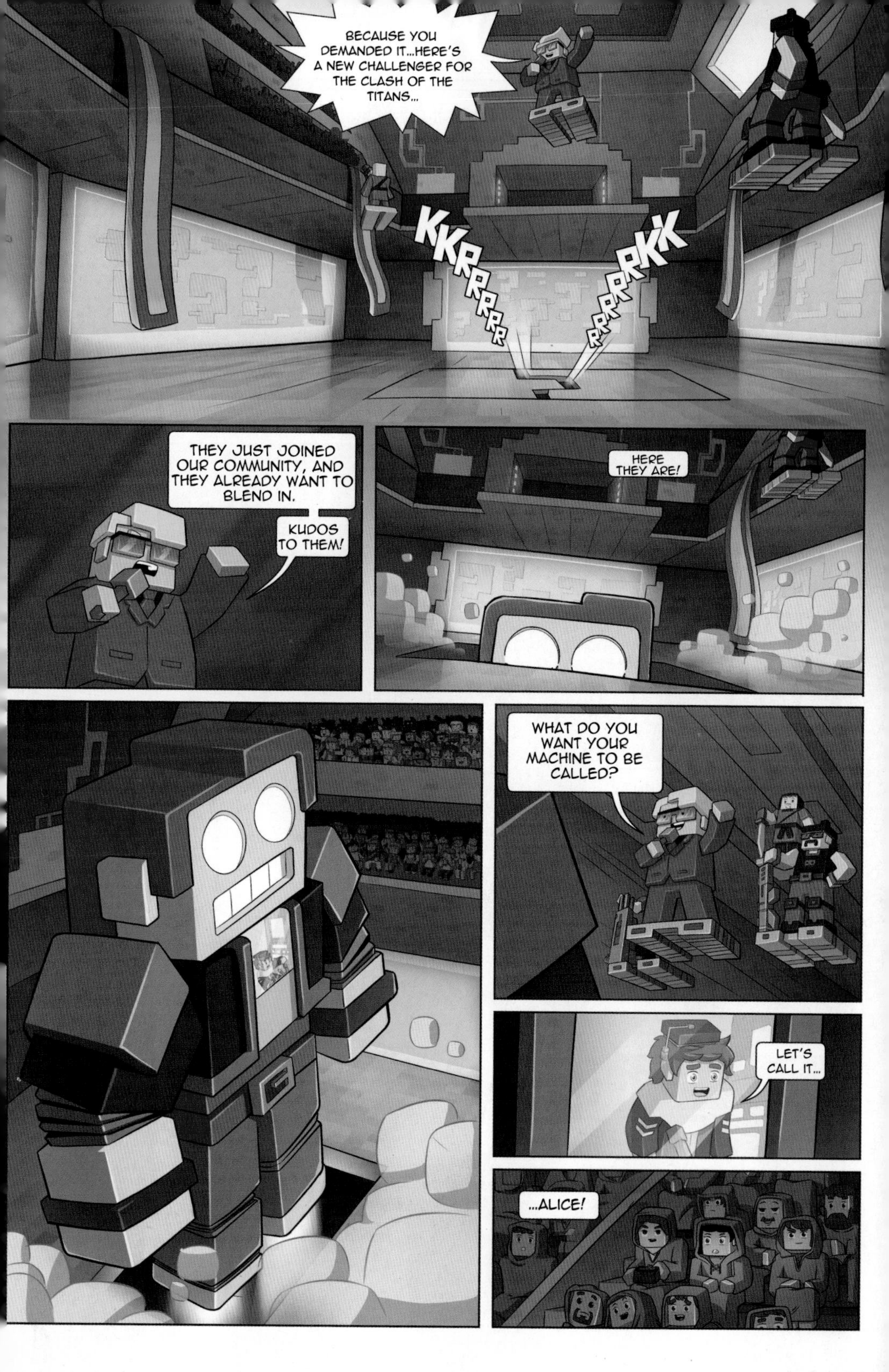
BECAUSE YOU DEMANDED IT...HERE'S A NEW CHALLENGER FOR THE CLASH OF THE TITANS...
KKRRRRR
RRRRRKK
THEY JUST JOINED OUR COMMUNITY, AND THEY ALREADY WANT TO BLEND IN.
KUDOS TO THEM!
HERE THEY ARE!
WHAT DO YOU WANT YOUR MACHINE TO BE CALLED?
LET'S CALL IT...
...ALICE!

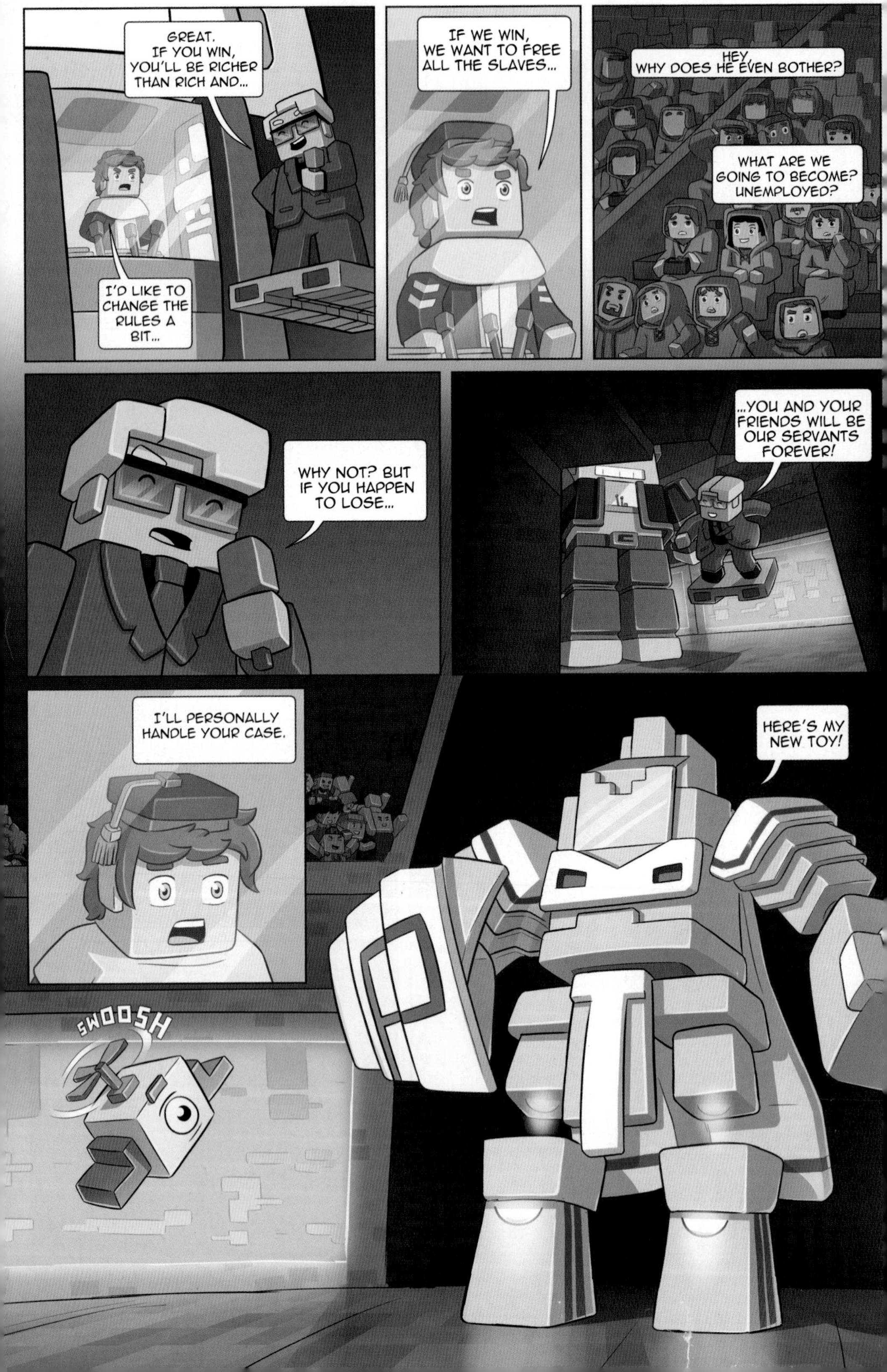
GREAT. IF YOU WIN, YOU'LL BE RICHER THAN RICH AND...
I'D LIKE TO CHANGE THE RULES A BIT...
IF WE WIN, WE WANT TO FREE ALL THE SLAVES...
HEY, WHY DOES HE EVEN BOTHER?
WHAT ARE WE GOING TO BECOME? UNEMPLOYED?
WHY NOT? BUT IF YOU HAPPEN TO LOSE...
...YOU AND YOUR FRIENDS WILL BE OUR SERVANTS FOREVER!
I'LL PERSONALLY HANDLE YOUR CASE.
HERE'S MY NEW TOY!
SWOOSH

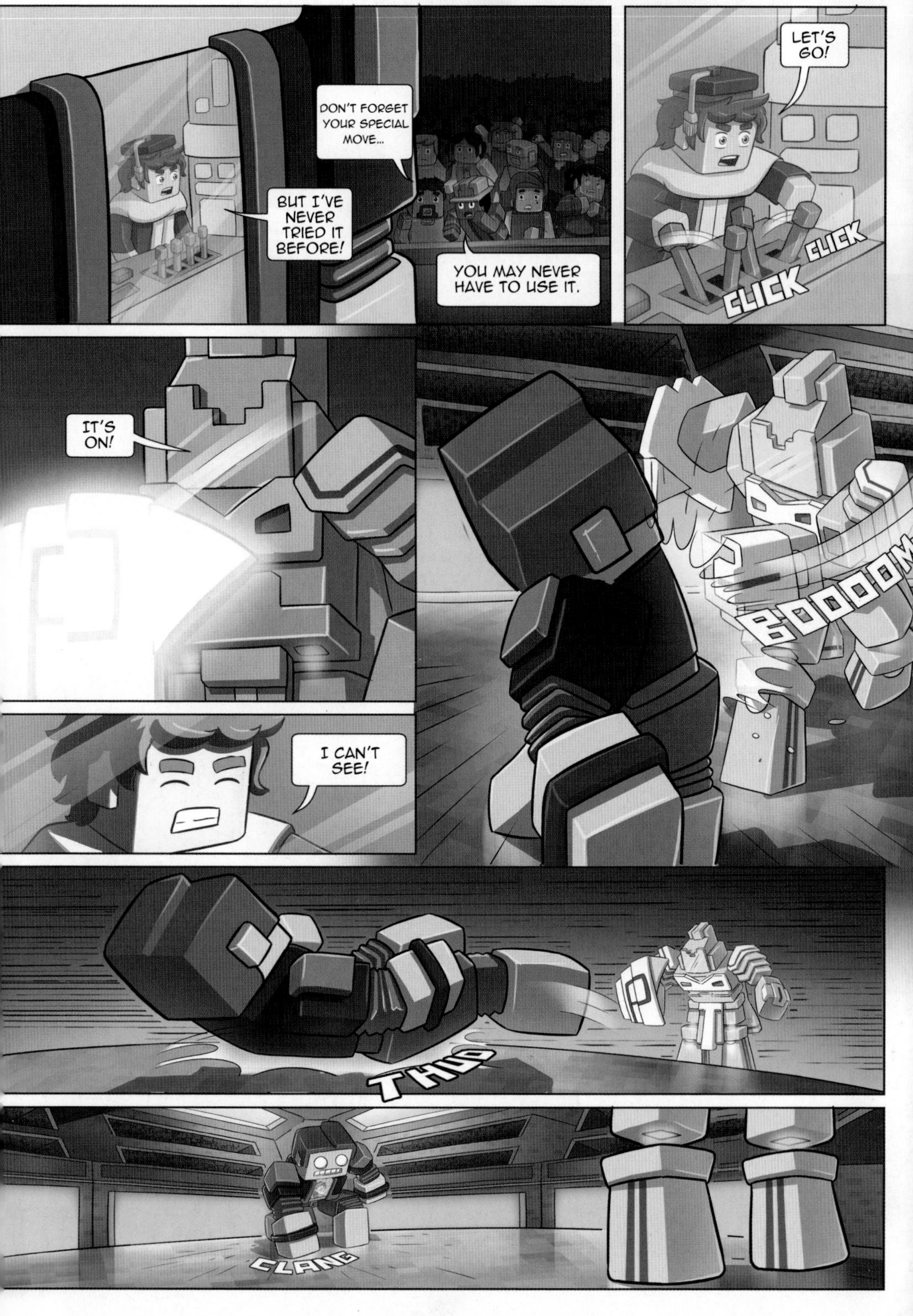
DON'T FORGET YOUR SPECIAL MOVE...
BUT I'VE NEVER TRIED IT BEFORE!
YOU MAY NEVER HAVE TO USE IT.
LET'S GO!
CLICK CLICK
CLICK
IT'S ON!
BOOOOM
I CAN'T SEE!
THUD
CLANG

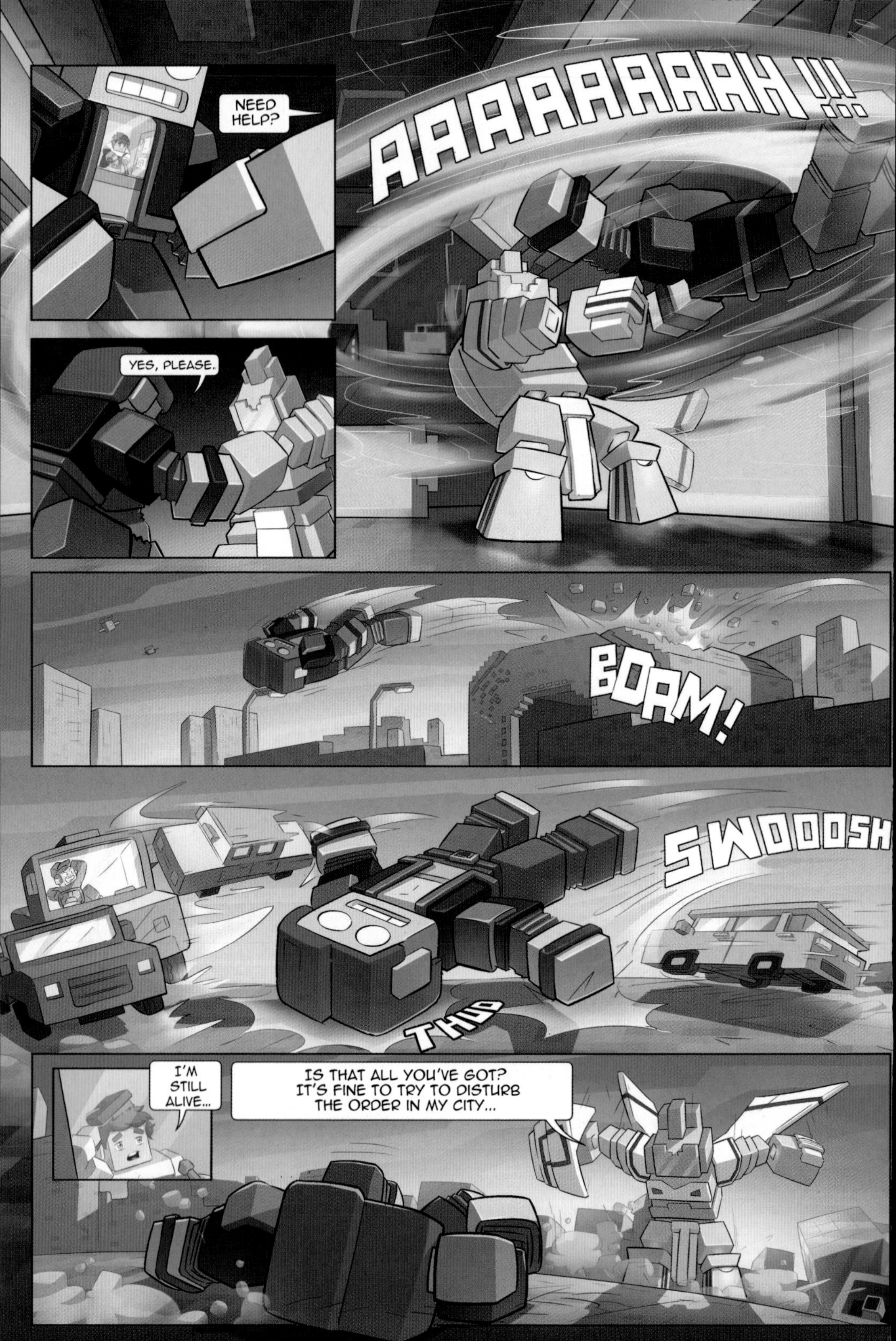
NEED HELP?
AAAAAAAAAH!!!
YES, PLEASE.
BOAM!
SWOOOSH
THUD
I'M STILL ALIVE...
IS THAT ALL YOU'VE GOT? IT'S FINE TO TRY TO DISTURB THE ORDER IN MY CITY...

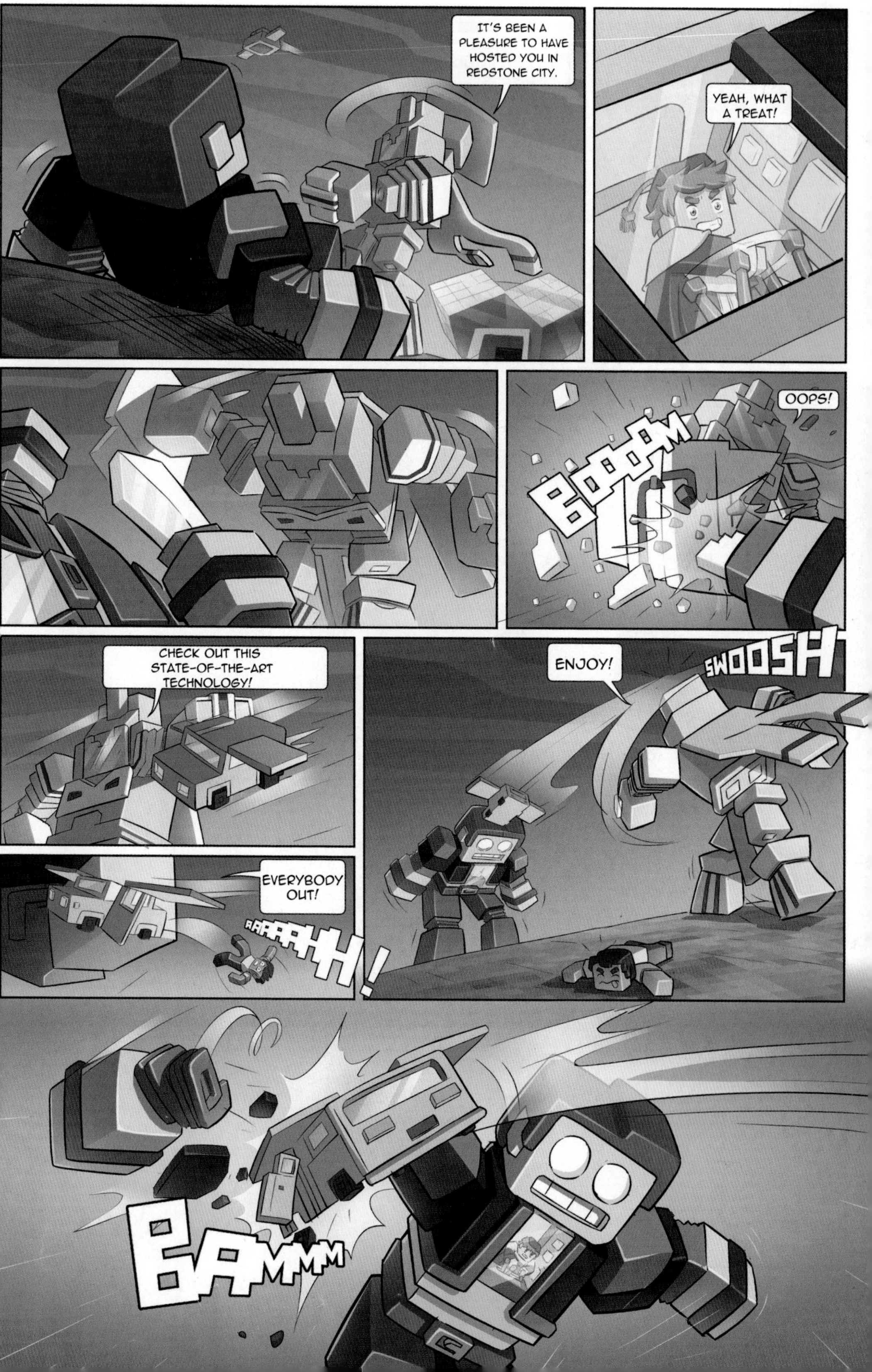
IT'S BEEN A PLEASURE TO HAVE HOSTED YOU IN REDSTONE CITY.
YEAH, WHAT A TREAT!
BOOOM
OOPS!
CHECK OUT THIS STATE-OF-THE-ART TECHNOLOGY!
ENJOY!
SWOOSH
EVERYBODY OUT!
AAAAAHH!
BAMMM

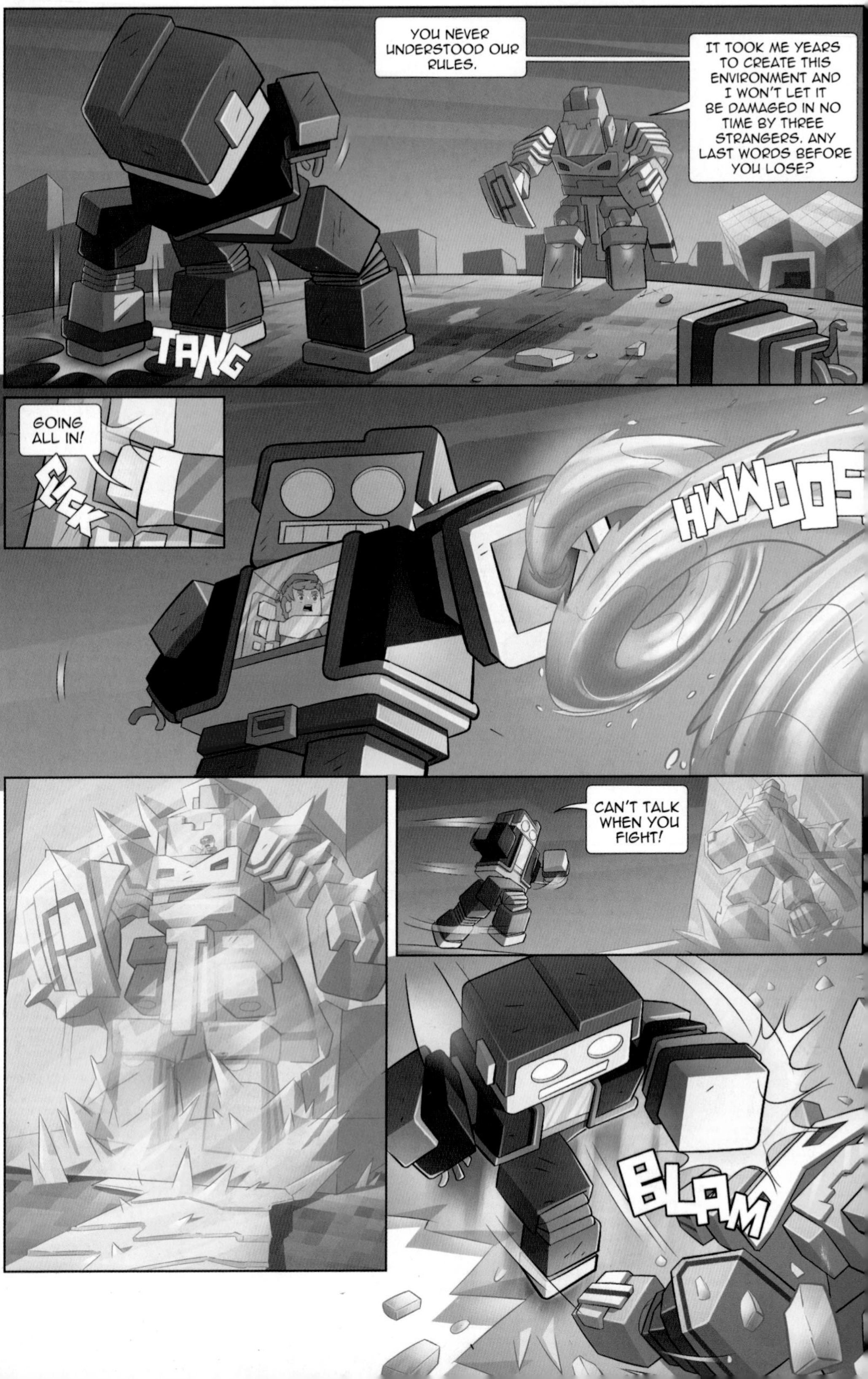
YOU NEVER UNDERSTOOD OUR RULES.
IT TOOK ME YEARS TO CREATE THIS ENVIRONMENT AND I WON'T LET IT BE DAMAGED IN NO TIME BY THREE STRANGERS. ANY LAST WORDS BEFORE YOU LOSE?
TANG
GOING ALL IN!
CLICK
HWWOOSH
CAN'T TALK WHEN YOU FIGHT!
BLAM

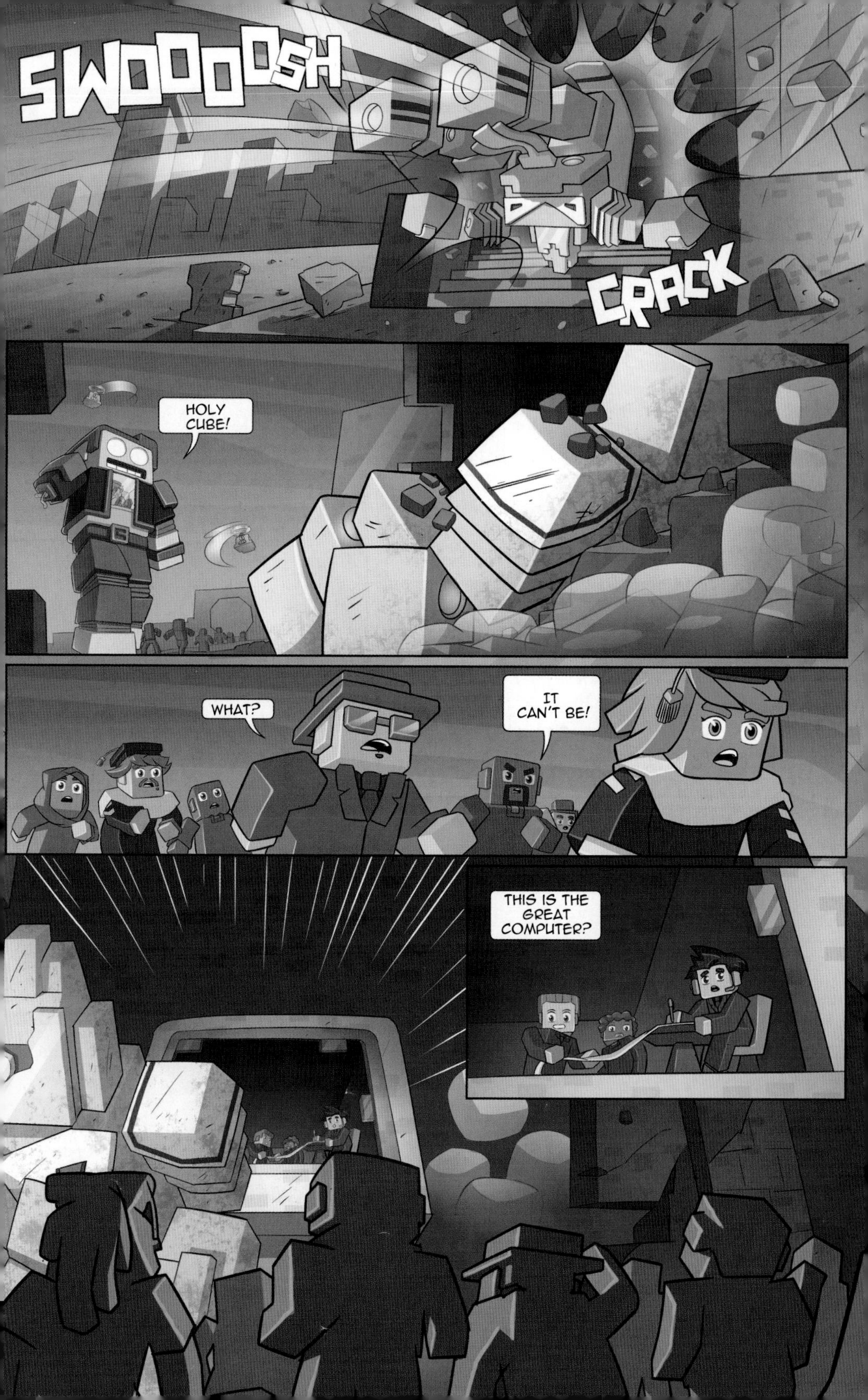
SWOOOOSH
CRACK
HOLY CUBE!
WHAT?
IT CAN'T BE!
THIS IS THE GREAT COMPUTER?

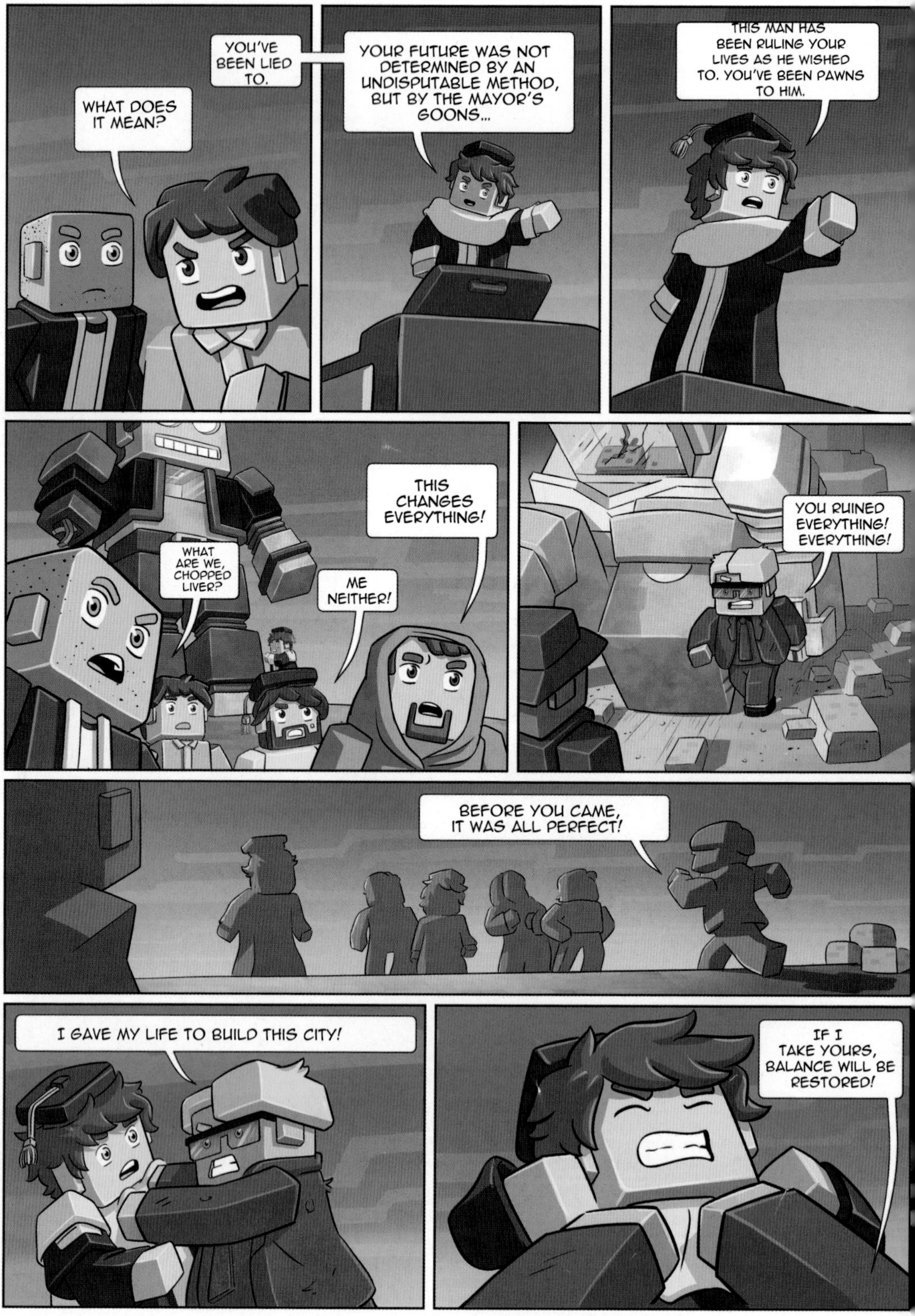
WHAT DOES IT MEAN?
YOU'VE BEEN LIED TO.
YOUR FUTURE WAS NOT DETERMINED BY AN UNDISPUTABLE METHOD, BUT BY THE MAYOR'S GOONS...
THIS MAN HAS BEEN RULING YOUR LIVES AS HE WISHED TO. YOU'VE BEEN PAWNS TO HIM.
THIS CHANGES EVERYTHING!
WHAT ARE WE, CHOPPED LIVER?
ME NEITHER!
YOU RUINED EVERYTHING! EVERYTHING!
BEFORE YOU CAME, IT WAS ALL PERFECT!
I GAVE MY LIFE TO BUILD THIS CITY!
IF I TAKE YOURS, BALANCE WILL BE RESTORED!

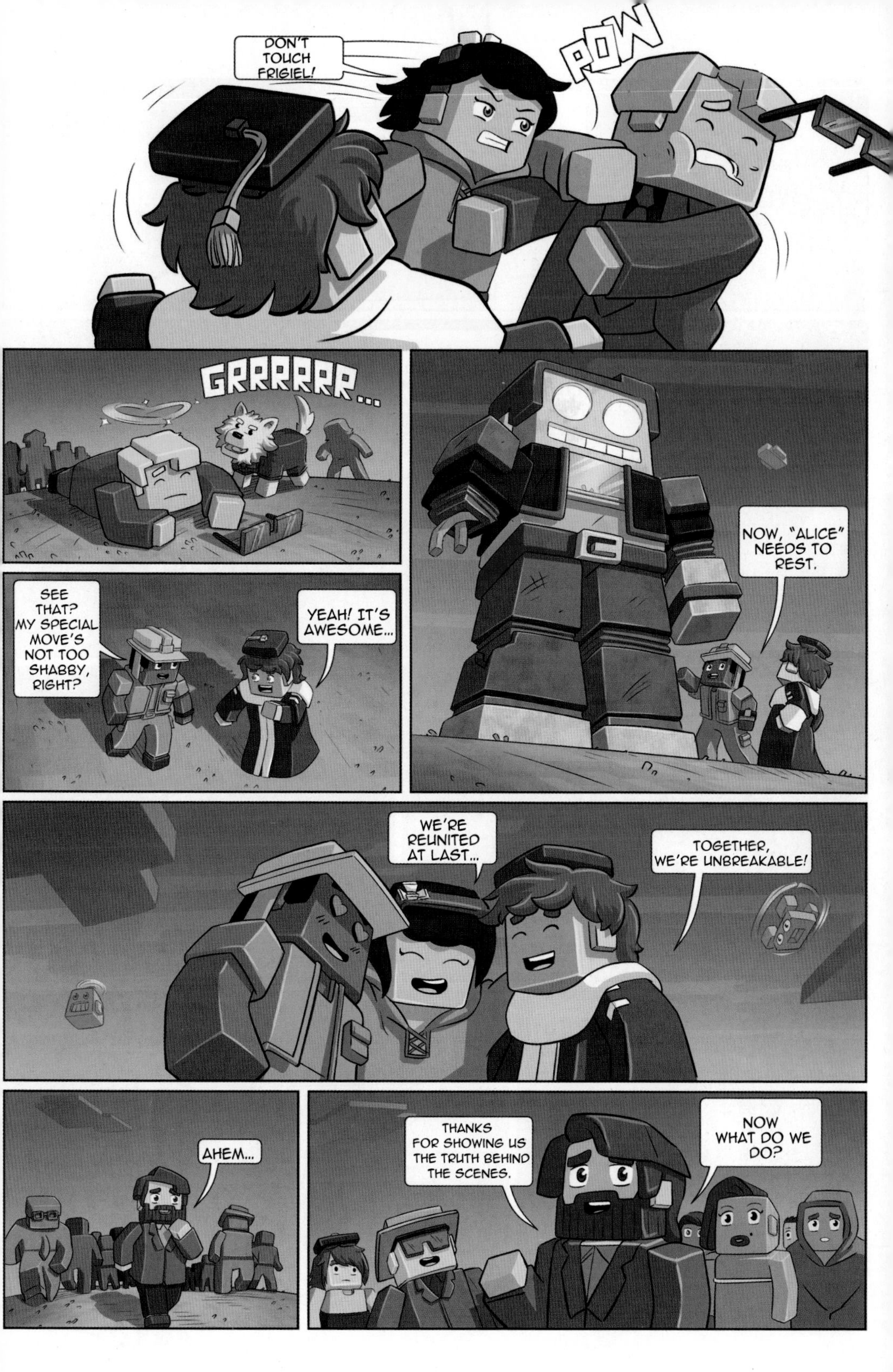
DON'T TOUCH FRIGIEL!
POW
GRRRRRR...
SEE THAT? MY SPECIAL MOVE'S NOT TOO SHABBY, RIGHT?
YEAH! IT'S AWESOME...
NOW, "ALICE" NEEDS TO REST.
WE'RE REUNITED AT LAST...
TOGETHER, WE'RE UNBREAKABLE!
AHEM...
THANKS FOR SHOWING US THE TRUTH BEHIND THE SCENES.
NOW WHAT DO WE DO?

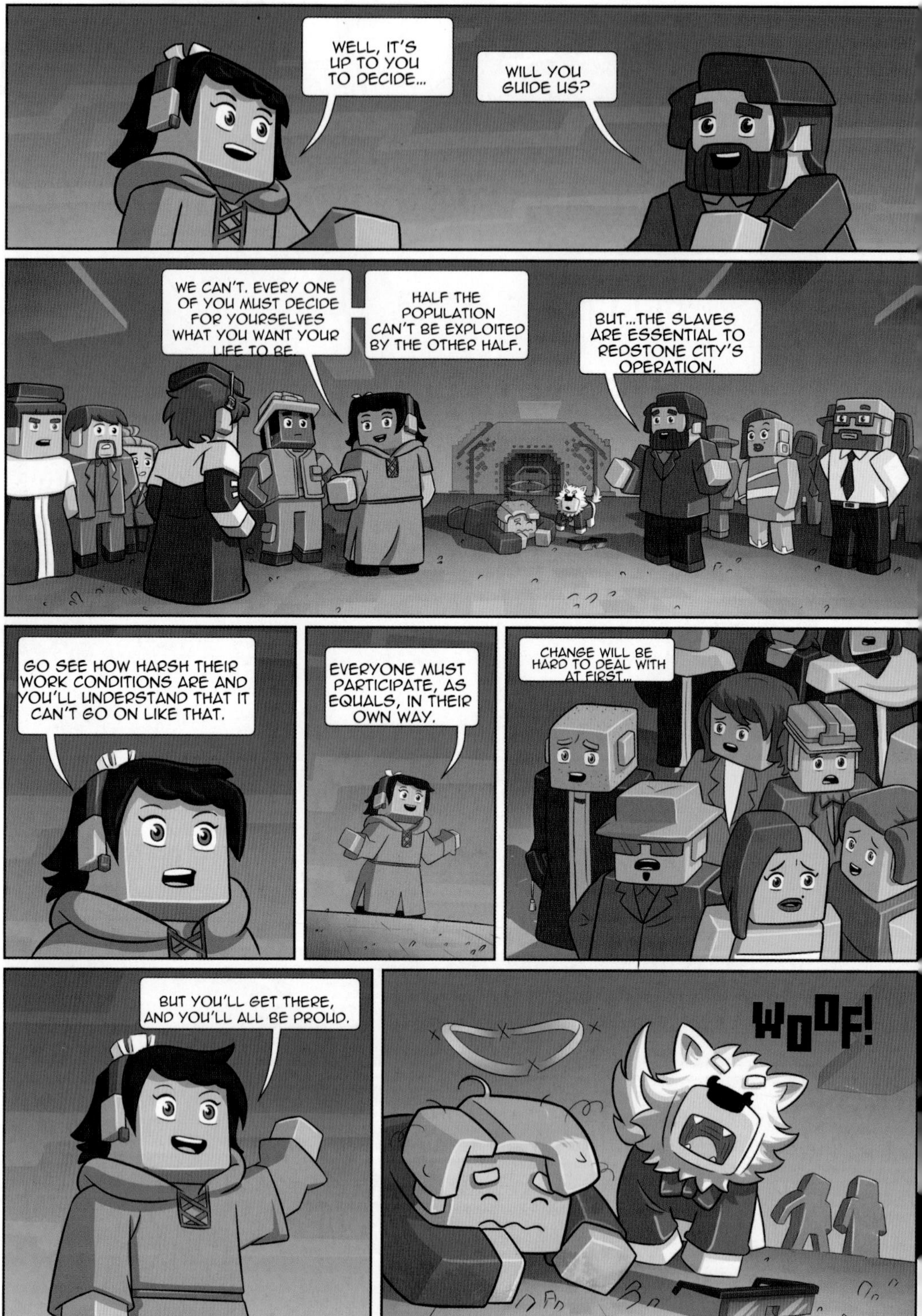
WELL, IT'S UP TO YOU TO DECIDE...
WILL YOU GUIDE US?
WE CAN'T. EVERY ONE OF YOU MUST DECIDE FOR YOURSELVES WHAT YOU WANT YOUR LIFE TO BE.
HALF THE POPULATION CAN'T BE EXPLOITED BY THE OTHER HALF.
BUT...THE SLAVES ARE ESSENTIAL TO REDSTONE CITY'S OPERATION.
GO SEE HOW HARSH THEIR WORK CONDITIONS ARE AND YOU'LL UNDERSTAND THAT IT CAN'T GO ON LIKE THAT.
EVERYONE MUST PARTICIPATE, AS EQUALS, IN THEIR OWN WAY.
CHANGE WILL BE HARD TO DEAL WITH AT FIRST...
BUT YOU'LL GET THERE, AND YOU'LL ALL BE PROUD.
WOOF!

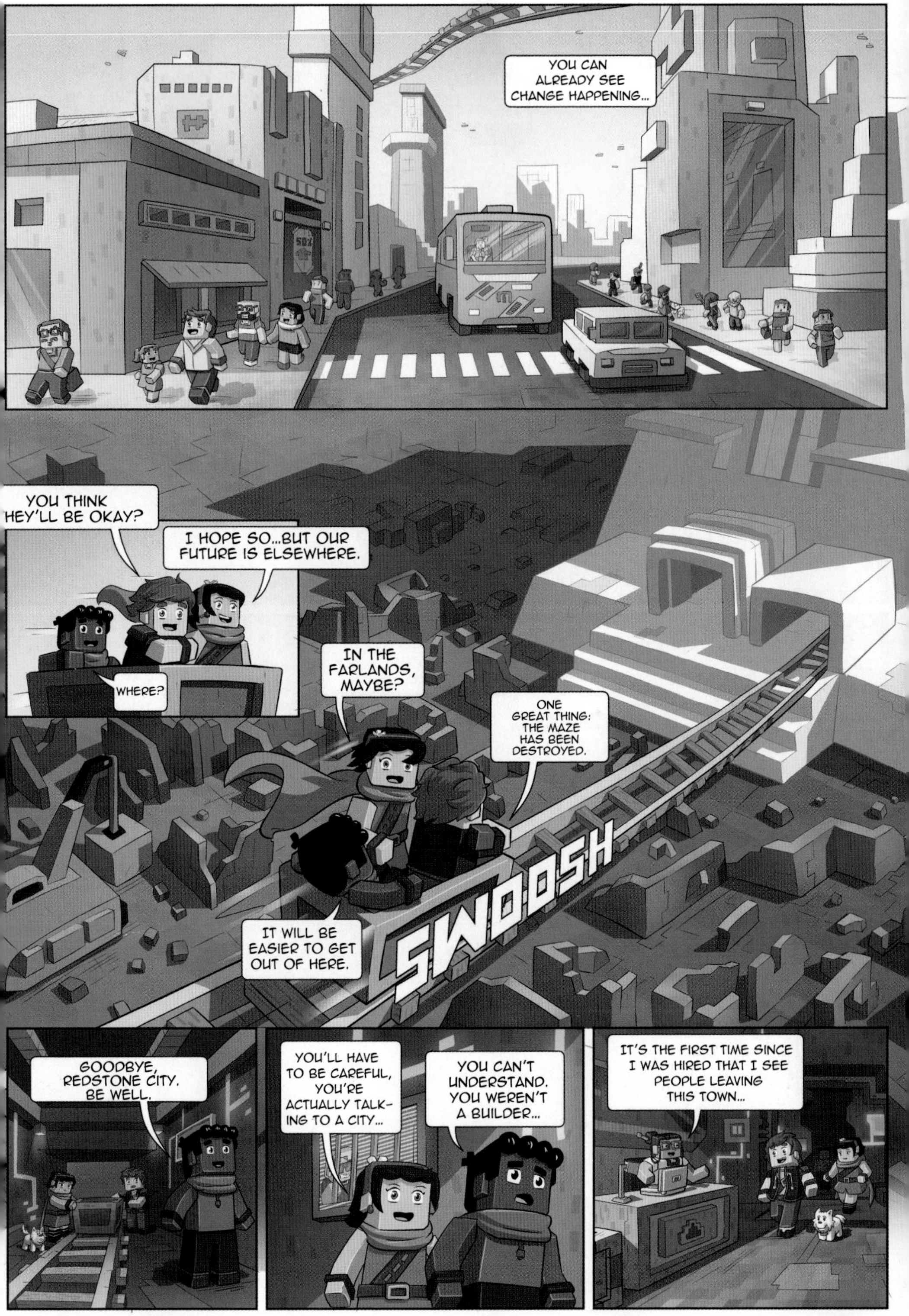
YOU CAN ALREADY SEE CHANGE HAPPENING...
YOU THINK HEY'LL BE OKAY?
I HOPE SO...BUT OUR FUTURE IS ELSEWHERE.
WHERE?
IN THE FARLANDS, MAYBE?
ONE GREAT THING: THE MAZE HAS BEEN DESTROYED.
IT WILL BE EASIER TO GET OUT OF HERE.
SWOOSH
GOODBYE, REDSTONE CITY. BE WELL.
YOU'LL HAVE TO BE CAREFUL, YOU'RE ACTUALLY TALKING TO A CITY...
YOU CAN'T UNDERSTAND. YOU WEREN'T A BUILDER...
IT'S THE FIRST TIME SINCE I WAS HIRED THAT I SEE PEOPLE LEAVING THIS TOWN...

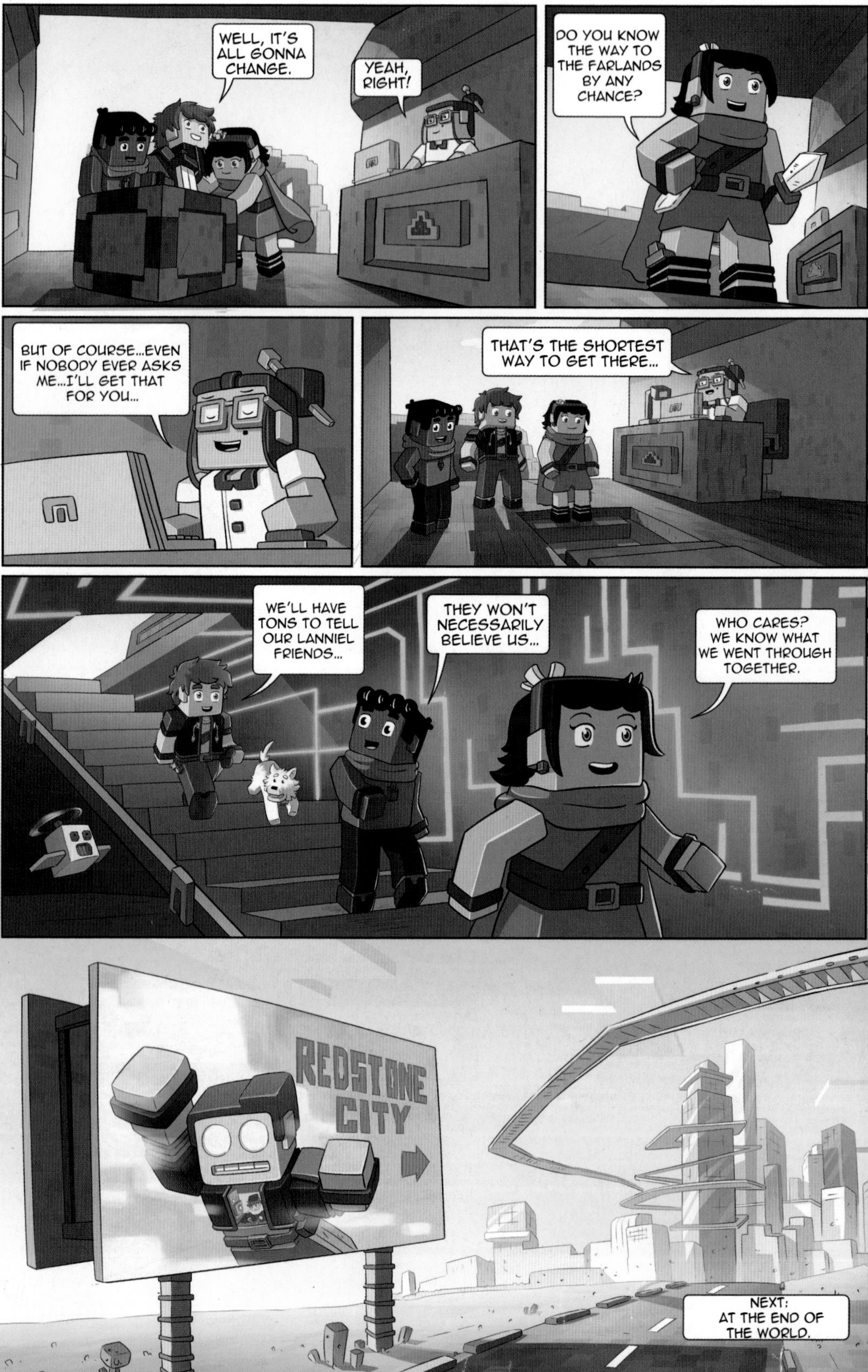
WELL, IT'S ALL GONNA CHANGE.
YEAH, RIGHT!
DO YOU KNOW THE WAY TO THE FARLANDS BY ANY CHANCE?
BUT OF COURSE...EVEN IF NOBODY EVER ASKS ME...I'LL GET THAT FOR YOU...
THAT'S THE SHORTEST WAY TO GET THERE...
WE'LL HAVE TONS TO TELL OUR LANNIEL FRIENDS...
THEY WON'T NECESSARILY BELIEVE US...
WHO CARES? WE KNOW WHAT WE WENT THROUGH TOGETHER.
REDSTONE CITY
NEXT: AT THE END OF THE WORLD.

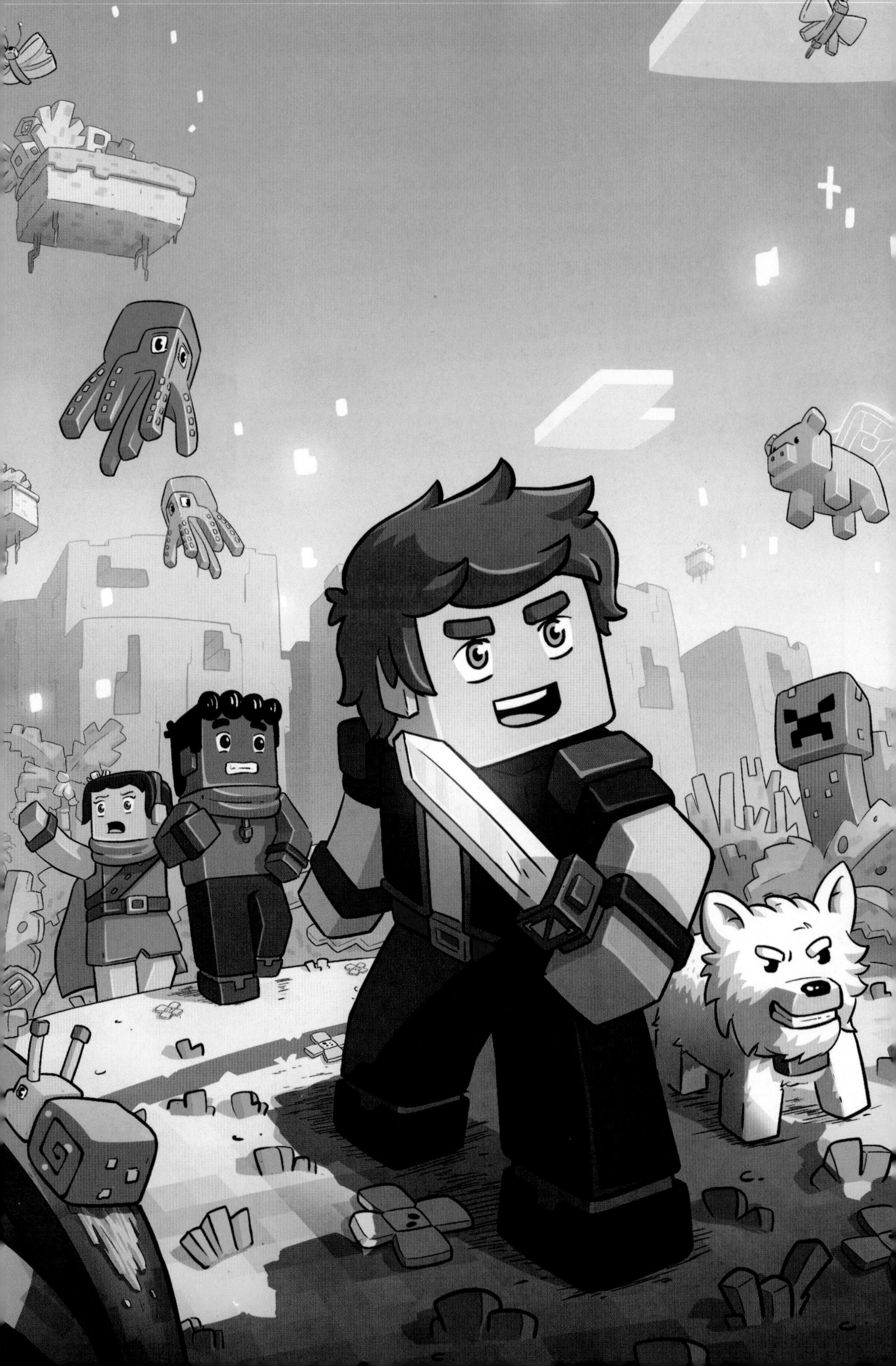

Dramatis Personae

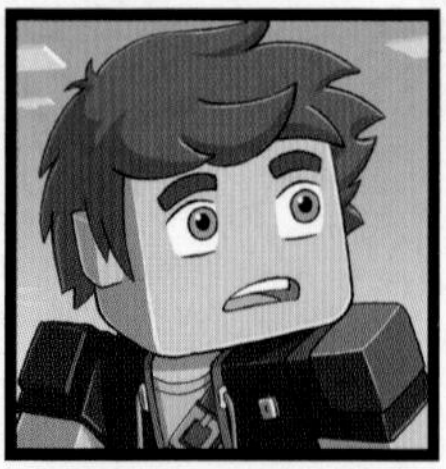

■ Frigiel

A brave sorcerer's apprentice ever-ready to give his all for his friends. He dreams of one day becoming a true adventurer. His chance to discover the world begins today...

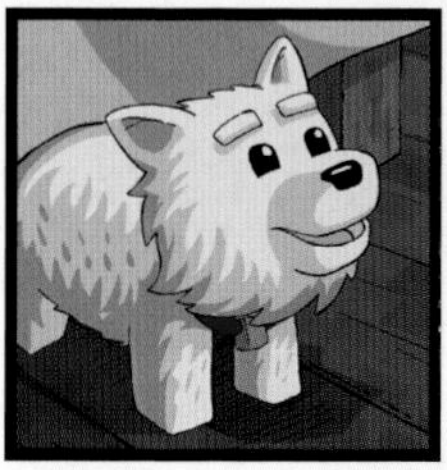

■ Fluffy

Frigiel's faithful canine companion, as cuddly with his master as he is bitey with the bad guys.

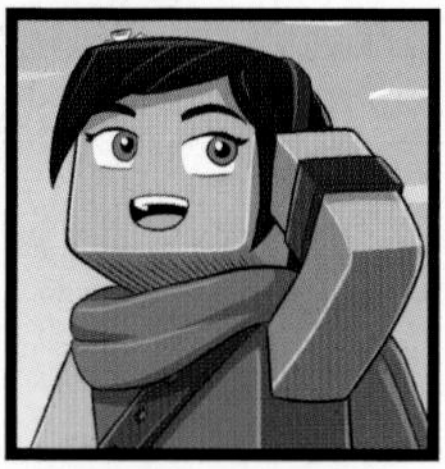

■ Alice

Proud and passionate, this thief-in-training keeps her secrets close to her heart...

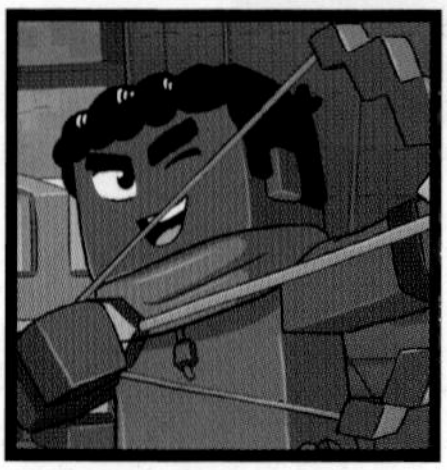

■ Abel

A clever builder, and a somewhat mocking friend, he doesn't always see the irony of the situation.

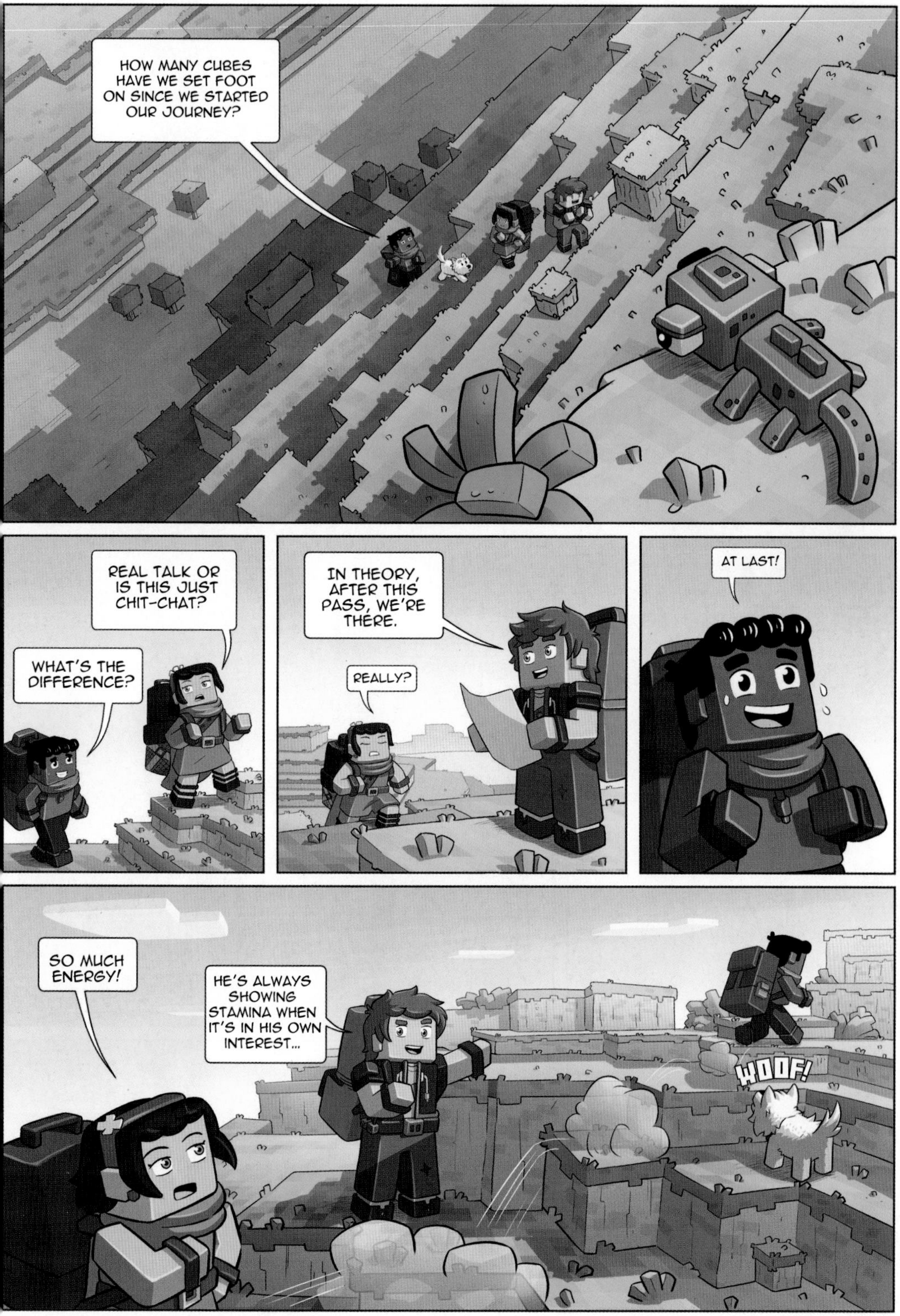
HOW MANY CUBES HAVE WE SET FOOT ON SINCE WE STARTED OUR JOURNEY?
REAL TALK OR IS THIS JUST CHIT-CHAT?
WHAT'S THE DIFFERENCE?
IN THEORY, AFTER THIS PASS, WE'RE THERE.
REALLY?
AT LAST!
SO MUCH ENERGY!
HE'S ALWAYS SHOWING STAMINA WHEN IT'S IN HIS OWN INTEREST...
WOOF!

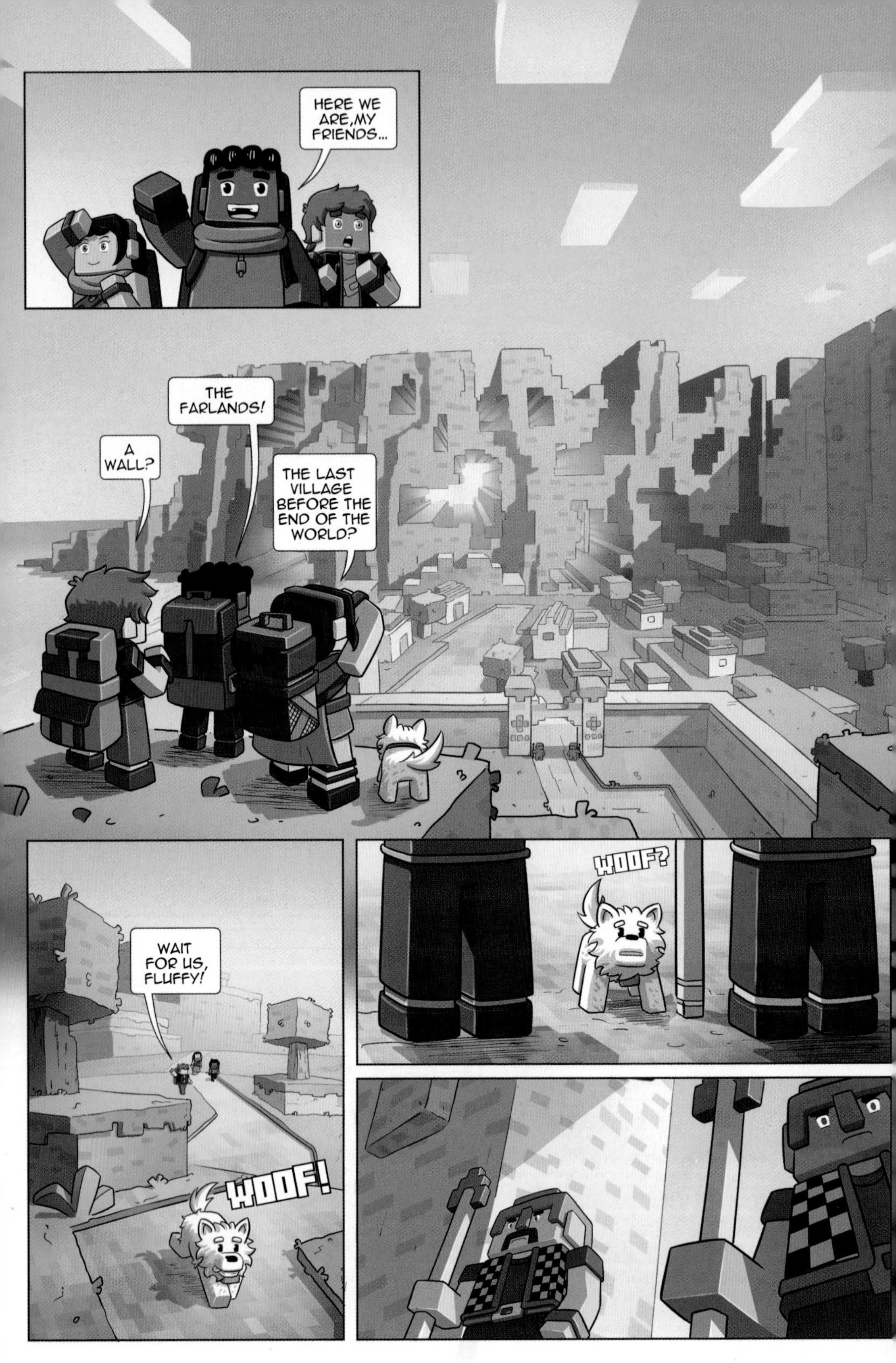
HERE WE ARE, MY FRIENDS...
THE FARLANDS!
A WALL?
THE LAST VILLAGE BEFORE THE END OF THE WORLD?
WAIT FOR US, FLUFFY!
WOOF!
WOOF?

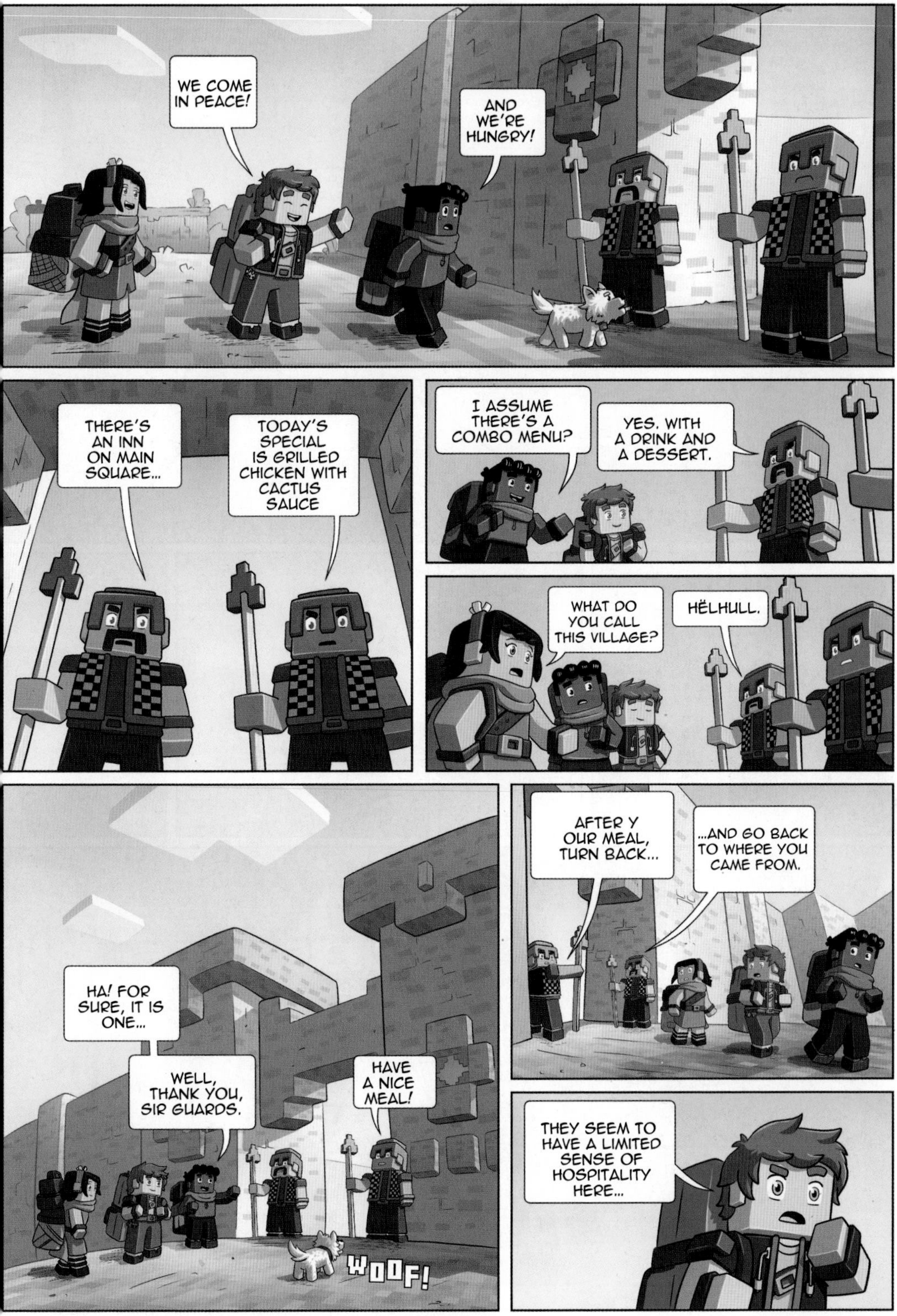
WE COME IN PEACE!
AND WE'RE HUNGRY!
THERE'S AN INN ON MAIN SQUARE...
TODAY'S SPECIAL IS GRILLED CHICKEN WITH CACTUS SAUCE
I ASSUME THERE'S A COMBO MENU?
YES. WITH A DRINK AND A DESSERT.
WHAT DO YOU CALL THIS VILLAGE?
HËLHULL.
HA! FOR SURE, IT IS ONE...
WELL, THANK YOU, SIR GUARDS.
HAVE A NICE MEAL!
WOOF!
AFTER Y OUR MEAL, TURN BACK...
...AND GO BACK TO WHERE YOU CAME FROM.
THEY SEEM TO HAVE A LIMITED SENSE OF HOSPITALITY HERE...

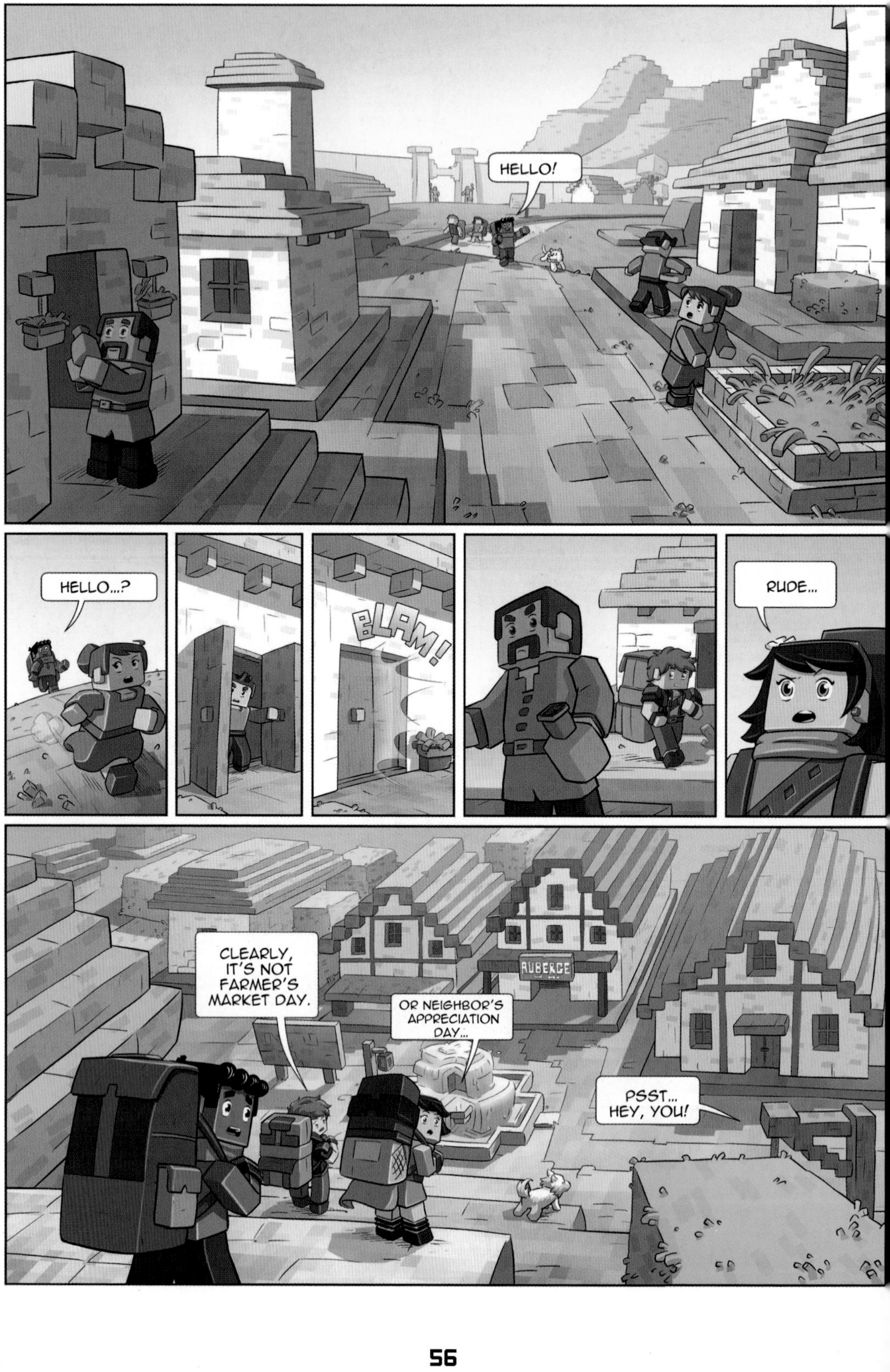
HELLO!
HELLO...?
BLAM!
RUDE...
CLEARLY, IT'S NOT FARMER'S MARKET DAY.
AUBERGE
OR NEIGHBOR'S APPRECIATION DAY...
PSST... HEY, YOU!

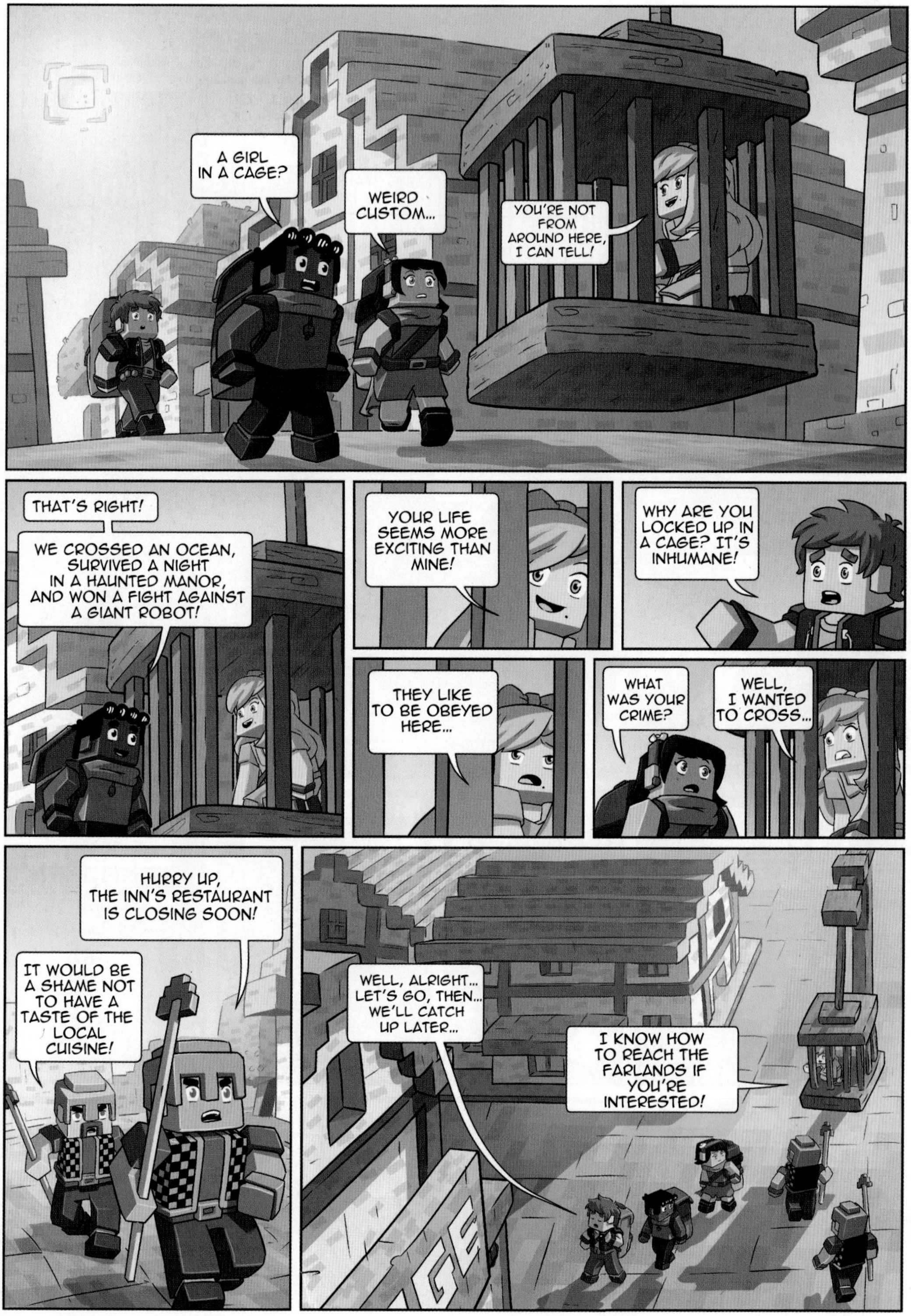

A GIRL IN A CAGE?
WEIRD CUSTOM...
YOU'RE NOT FROM AROUND HERE, I CAN TELL!
THAT'S RIGHT!
WE CROSSED AN OCEAN, SURVIVED A NIGHT IN A HAUNTED MANOR, AND WON A FIGHT AGAINST A GIANT ROBOT!
YOUR LIFE SEEMS MORE EXCITING THAN MINE!
WHY ARE YOU LOCKED UP IN A CAGE? IT'S INHUMANE!
THEY LIKE TO BE OBEYED HERE...
WHAT WAS YOUR CRIME?
WELL, I WANTED TO CROSS...
HURRY UP, THE INN'S RESTAURANT IS CLOSING SOON!
IT WOULD BE A SHAME NOT TO HAVE A TASTE OF THE LOCAL CUISINE!
WELL, ALRIGHT... LET'S GO, THEN... WE'LL CATCH UP LATER...
I KNOW HOW TO REACH THE FARLANDS IF YOU'RE INTERESTED!

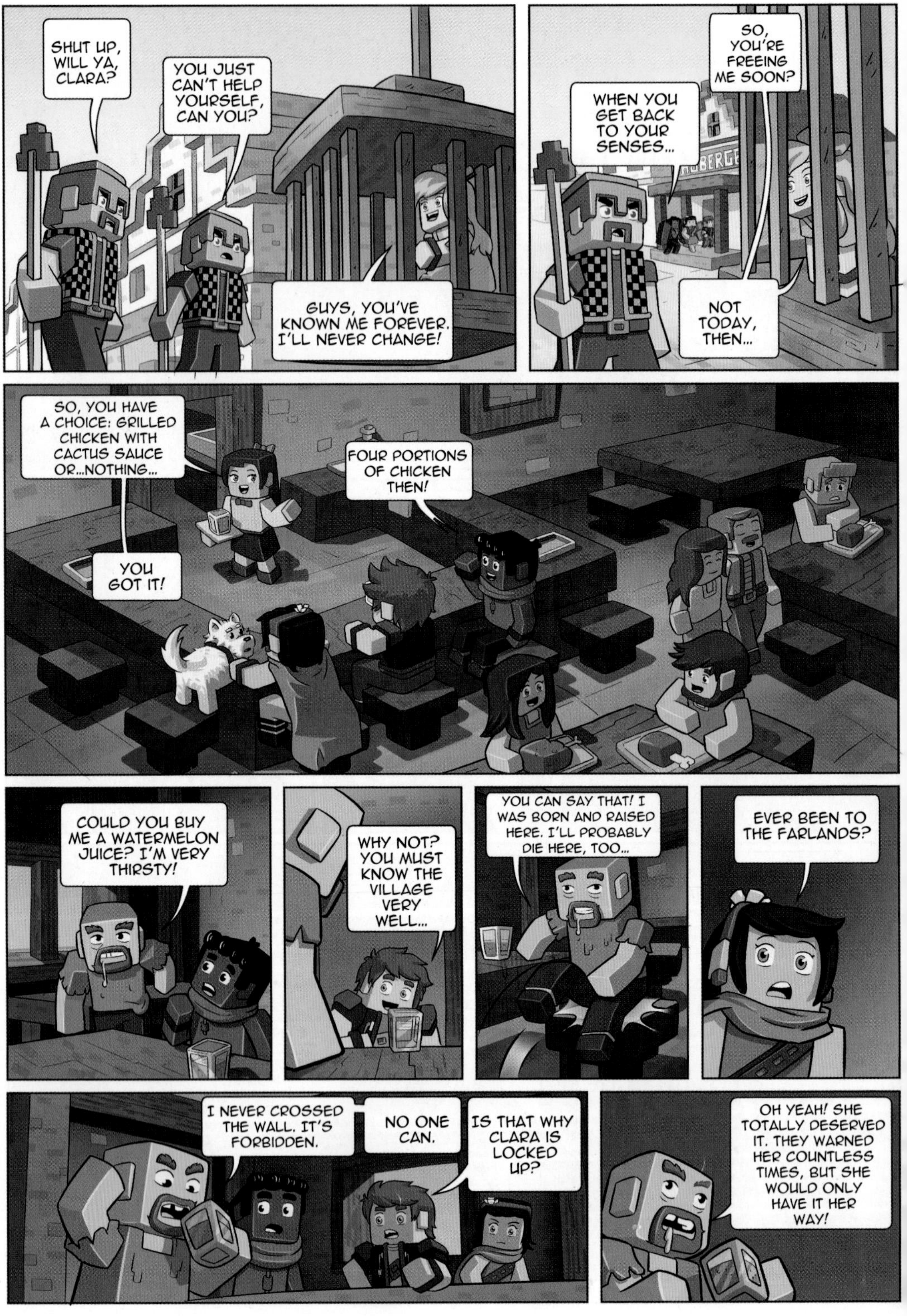
SHUT UP, WILL YA, CLARA?
YOU JUST CAN'T HELP YOURSELF, CAN YOU?
GUYS, YOU'VE KNOWN ME FOREVER. I'LL NEVER CHANGE!
SO, YOU'RE FREEING ME SOON?
WHEN YOU GET BACK TO YOUR SENSES...
NOT TODAY, THEN...
SO, YOU HAVE A CHOICE: GRILLED CHICKEN WITH CACTUS SAUCE OR...NOTHING...
FOUR PORTIONS OF CHICKEN THEN!
YOU GOT IT!
COULD YOU BUY ME A WATERMELON JUICE? I'M VERY THIRSTY!
WHY NOT? YOU MUST KNOW THE VILLAGE VERY WELL...
YOU CAN SAY THAT! I WAS BORN AND RAISED HERE. I'LL PROBABLY DIE HERE, TOO...
EVER BEEN TO THE FARLANDS?
I NEVER CROSSED THE WALL. IT'S FORBIDDEN.
NO ONE CAN.
IS THAT WHY CLARA IS LOCKED UP?
OH YEAH! SHE TOTALLY DESERVED IT. THEY WARNED HER COUNTLESS TIMES, BUT SHE WOULD ONLY HAVE IT HER WAY!

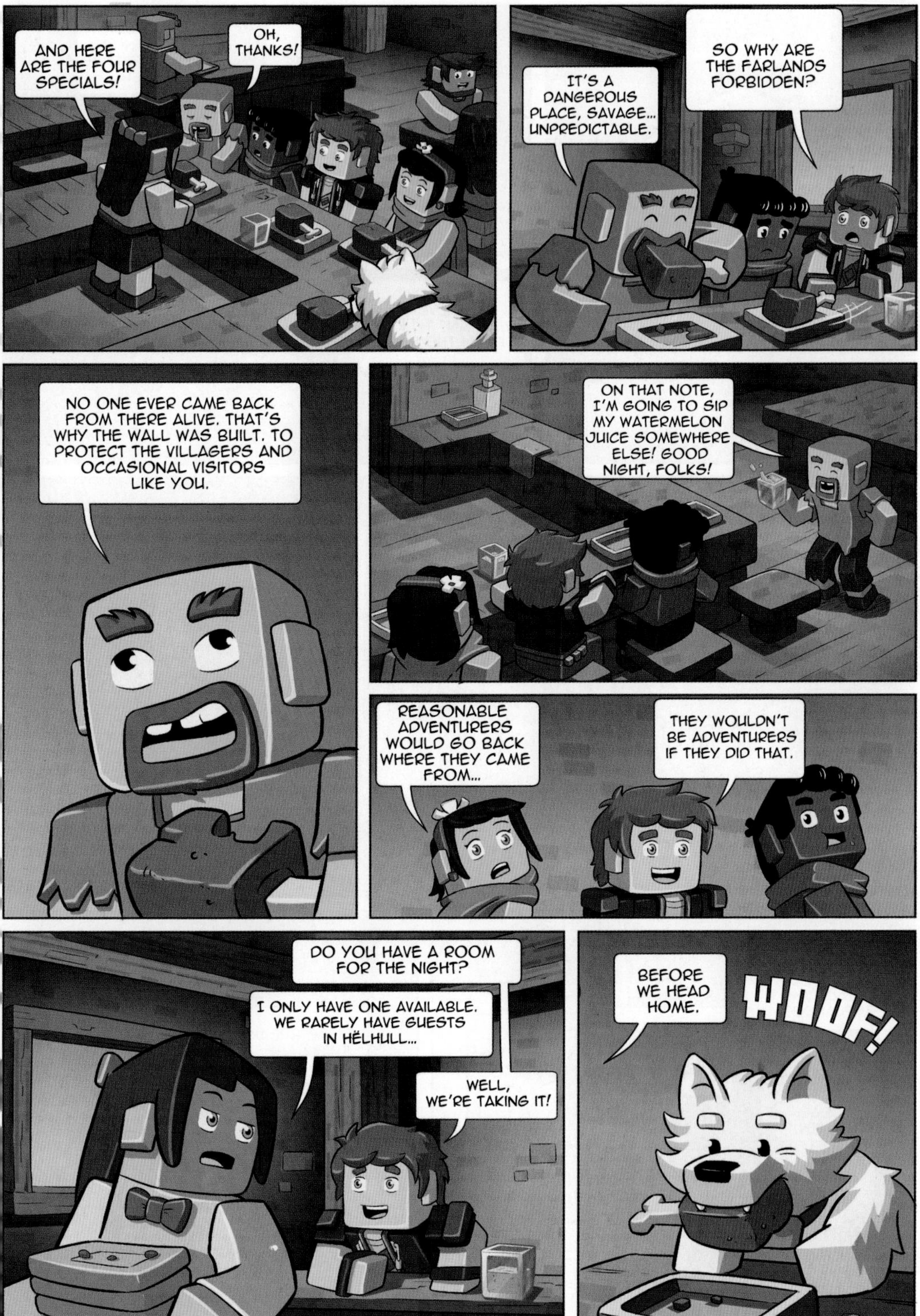
AND HERE ARE THE FOUR SPECIALS!
OH, THANKS!
SO WHY ARE THE FARLANDS FORBIDDEN?
IT'S A DANGEROUS PLACE, SAVAGE... UNPREDICTABLE.
NO ONE EVER CAME BACK FROM THERE ALIVE. THAT'S WHY THE WALL WAS BUILT. TO PROTECT THE VILLAGERS AND OCCASIONAL VISITORS LIKE YOU.
ON THAT NOTE, I'M GOING TO SIP MY WATERMELON JUICE SOMEWHERE ELSE! GOOD NIGHT, FOLKS!
REASONABLE ADVENTURERS WOULD GO BACK WHERE THEY CAME FROM...
THEY WOULDN'T BE ADVENTURERS IF THEY DID THAT.
DO YOU HAVE A ROOM FOR THE NIGHT?
I ONLY HAVE ONE AVAILABLE. WE RARELY HAVE GUESTS IN HËLHULL...
WELL, WE'RE TAKING IT!
BEFORE WE HEAD HOME.
WOOF!

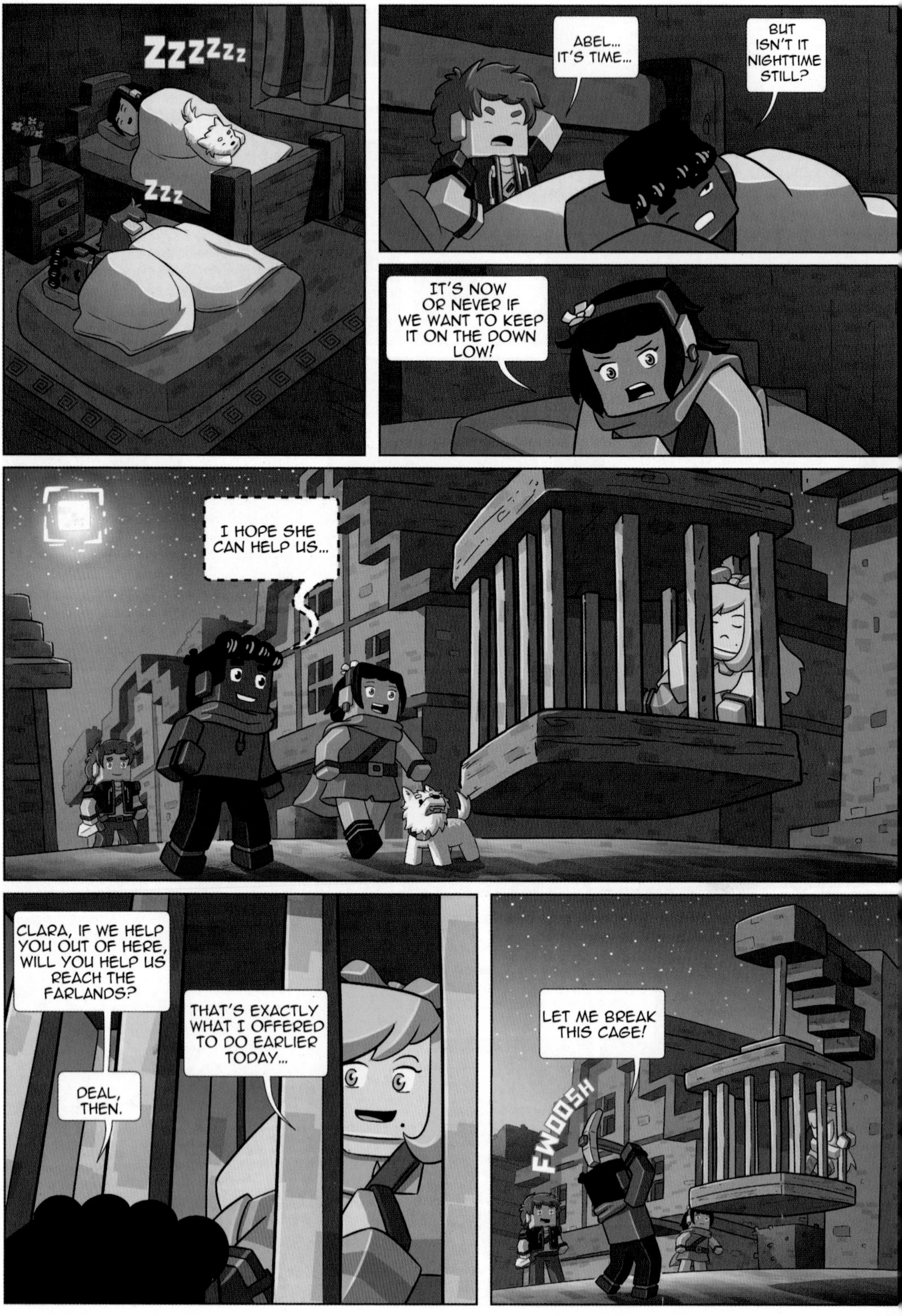
ZZZZzz
ZZz
ABEL... IT'S TIME...
BUT ISN'T IT NIGHTTIME STILL?
IT'S NOW OR NEVER IF WE WANT TO KEEP IT ON THE DOWN LOW!
I HOPE SHE CAN HELP US...
CLARA, IF WE HELP YOU OUT OF HERE, WILL YOU HELP US REACH THE FARLANDS?
DEAL, THEN.
THAT'S EXACTLY WHAT I OFFERED TO DO EARLIER TODAY...
LET ME BREAK THIS CAGE!
FWOOSH

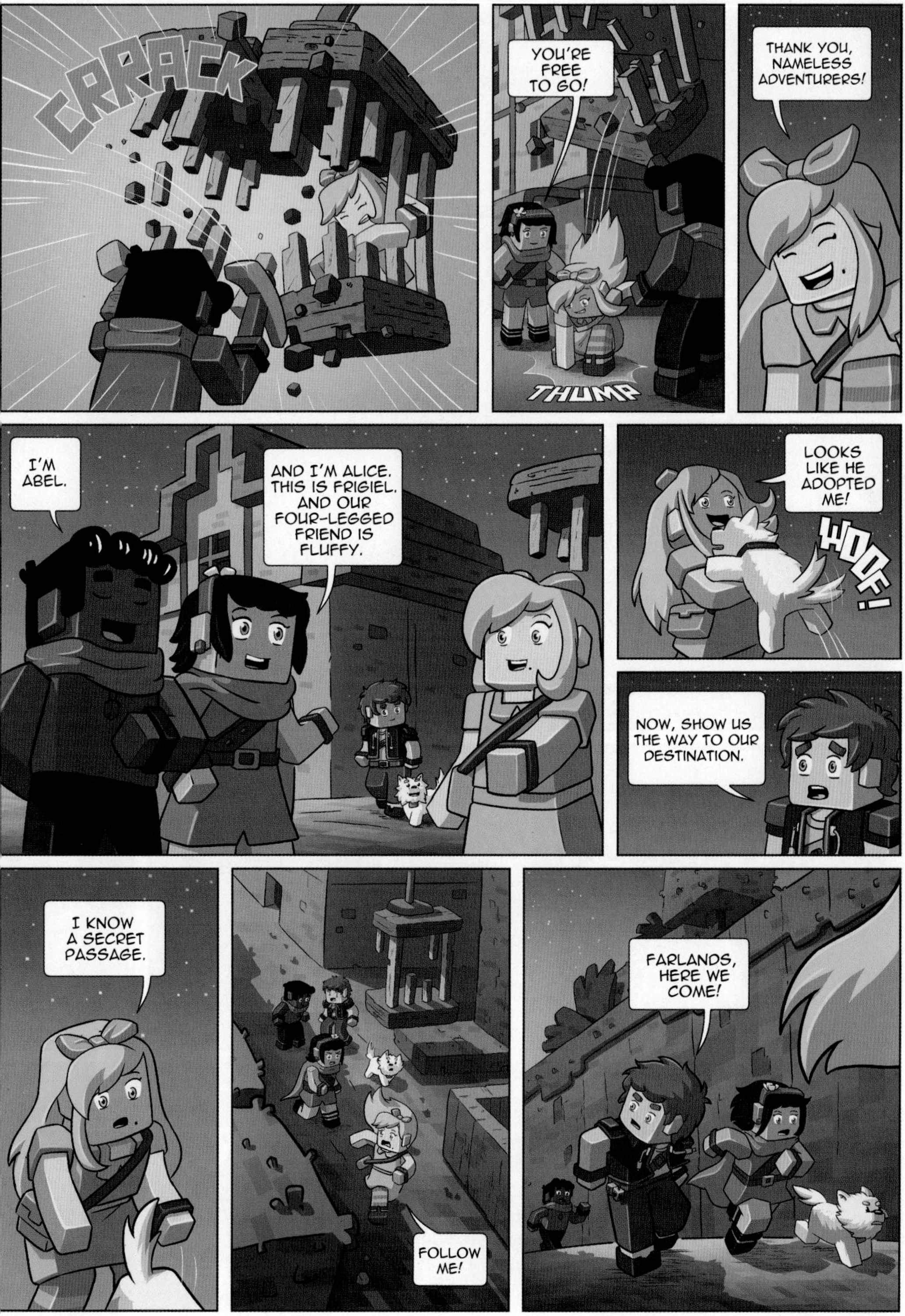
CRRACK
YOU'RE FREE TO GO!
THUMP
THANK YOU, NAMELESS ADVENTURERS!
I'M ABEL.
AND I'M ALICE. THIS IS FRIGIEL. AND OUR FOUR-LEGGED FRIEND IS FLUFFY.
LOOKS LIKE HE ADOPTED ME!
WOOF!
NOW, SHOW US THE WAY TO OUR DESTINATION.
I KNOW A SECRET PASSAGE.
FOLLOW ME!
FARLANDS, HERE WE COME!

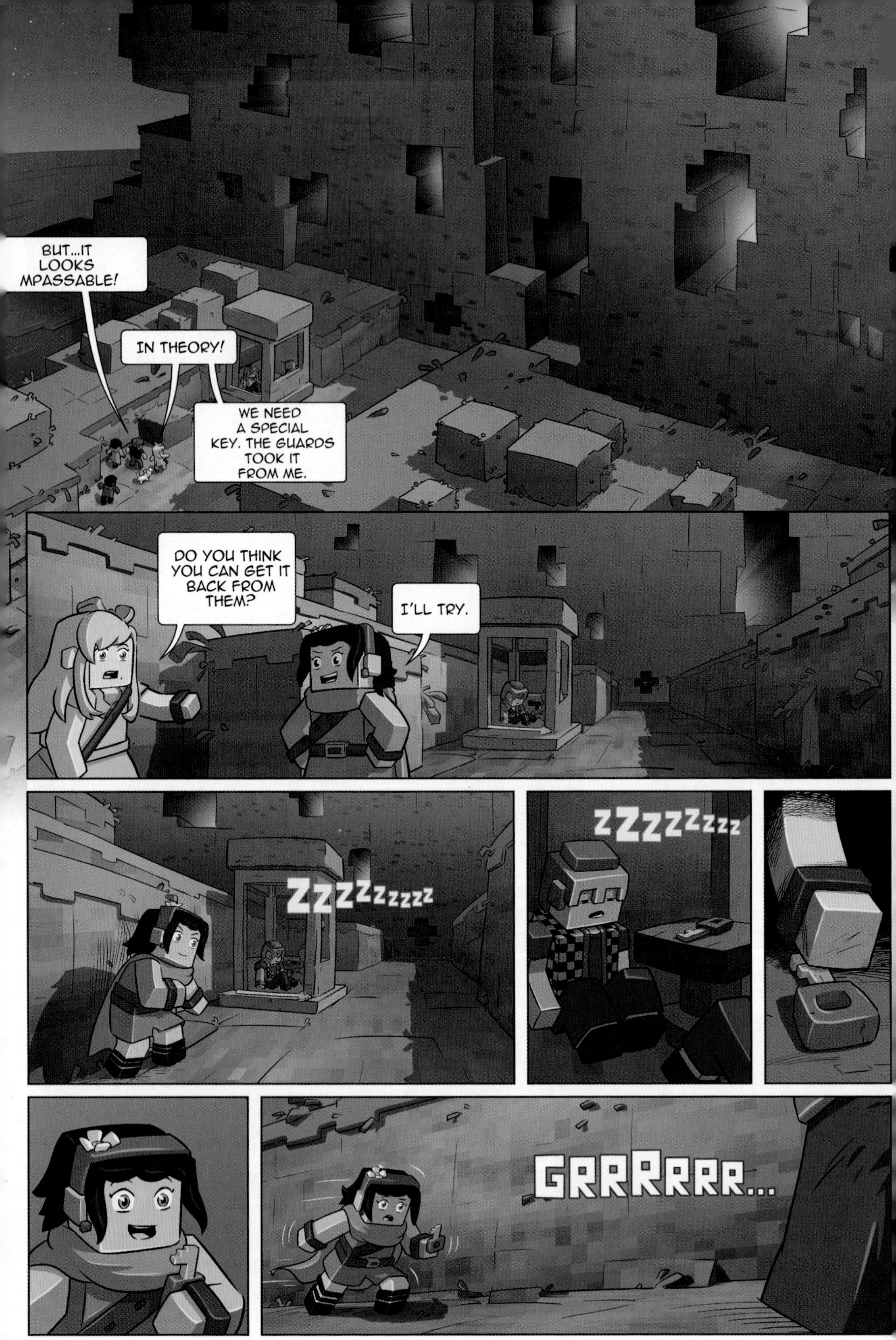
BUT...IT LOOKS MPASSABLE!
IN THEORY!
WE NEED A SPECIAL KEY. THE GUARDS TOOK IT FROM ME.
DO YOU THINK YOU CAN GET IT BACK FROM THEM?
I'LL TRY.
ZZZZzzzz
zZZZzzz
GRRRrrr...

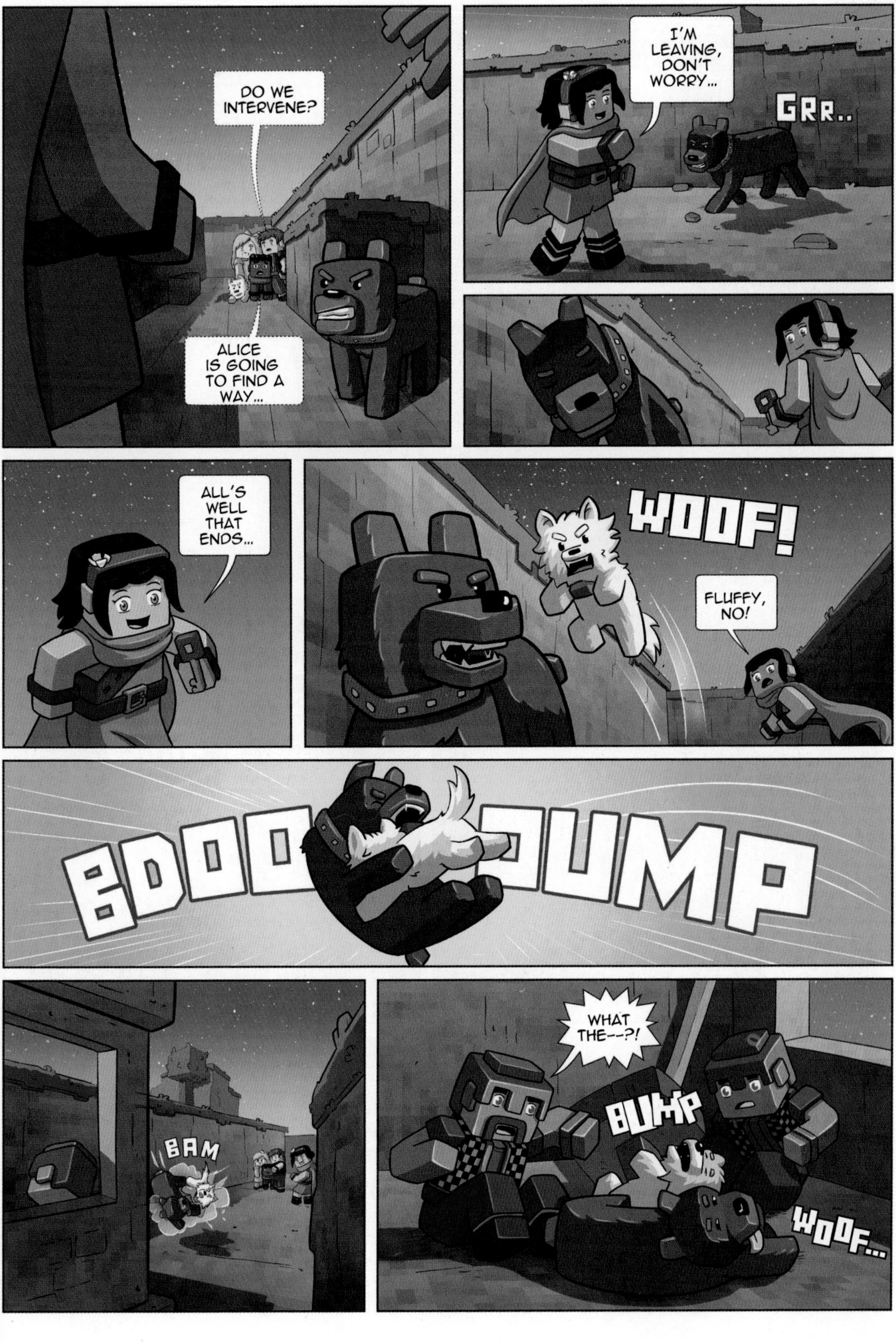
DO WE INTERVENE?
ALICE IS GOING TO FIND A WAY...
I'M LEAVING, DON'T WORRY...
GRR..
ALL'S WELL THAT ENDS...
WOOF!
FLUFFY, NO!
BDOOOOUMP
BAM
WHAT THE--?!
BUMP
WOOF...

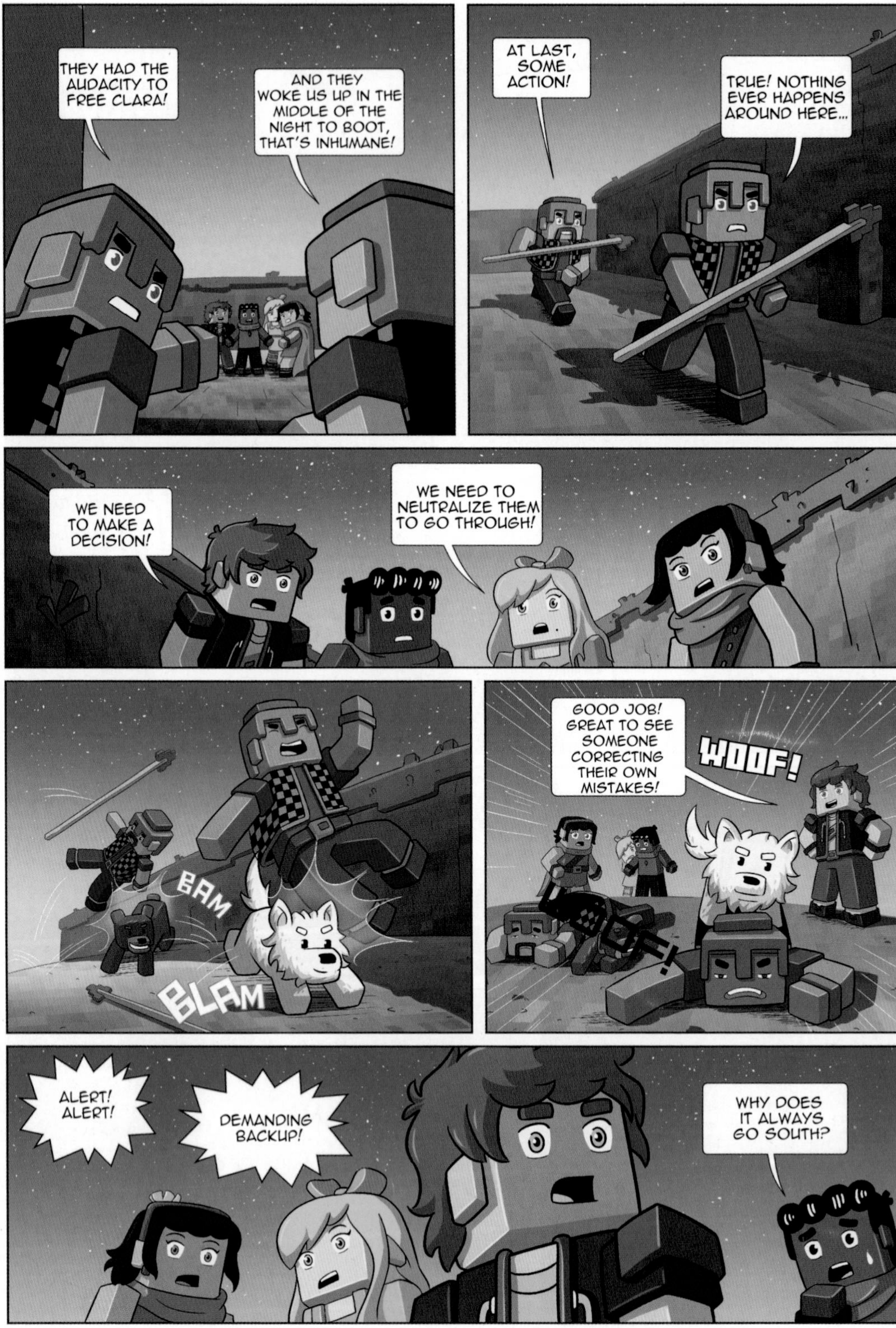
THEY HAD THE AUDACITY TO FREE CLARA!
AND THEY WOKE US UP IN THE MIDDLE OF THE NIGHT TO BOOT, THAT'S INHUMANE!
AT LAST, SOME ACTION!
TRUE! NOTHING EVER HAPPENS AROUND HERE...
WE NEED TO MAKE A DECISION!
WE NEED TO NEUTRALIZE THEM TO GO THROUGH!
BAM
BLAM
GOOD JOB! GREAT TO SEE SOMEONE CORRECTING THEIR OWN MISTAKES!
WOOF!
ALERT! ALERT!
DEMANDING BACKUP!
WHY DOES IT ALWAYS GO SOUTH?

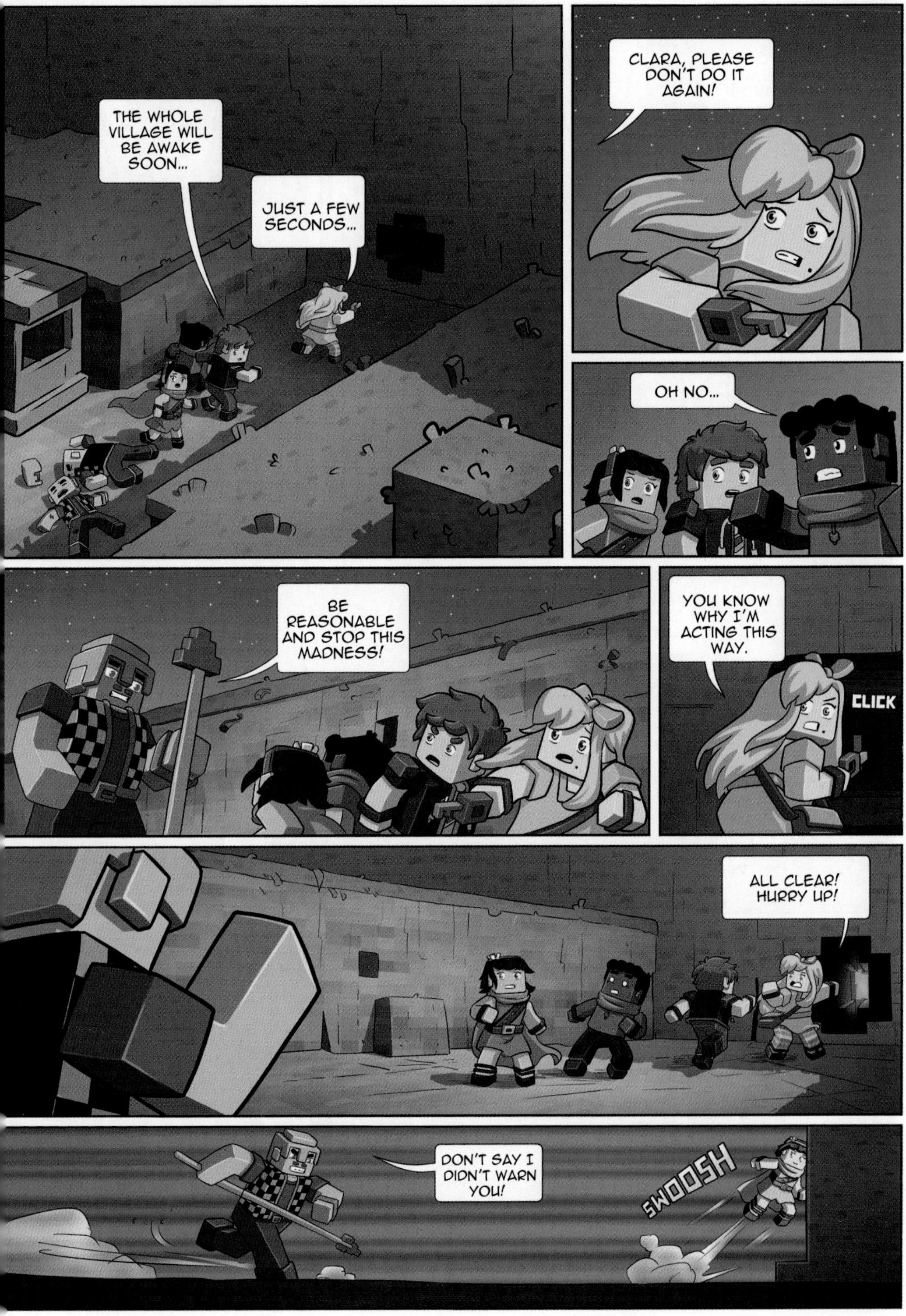
THE WHOLE VILLAGE WILL BE AWAKE SOON...
JUST A FEW SECONDS...
CLARA, PLEASE DON'T DO IT AGAIN!
OH NO...
BE REASONABLE AND STOP THIS MADNESS!
YOU KNOW WHY I'M ACTING THIS WAY.
CLICK
ALL CLEAR! HURRY UP!
DON'T SAY I DIDN'T WARN YOU!
SWOOSH

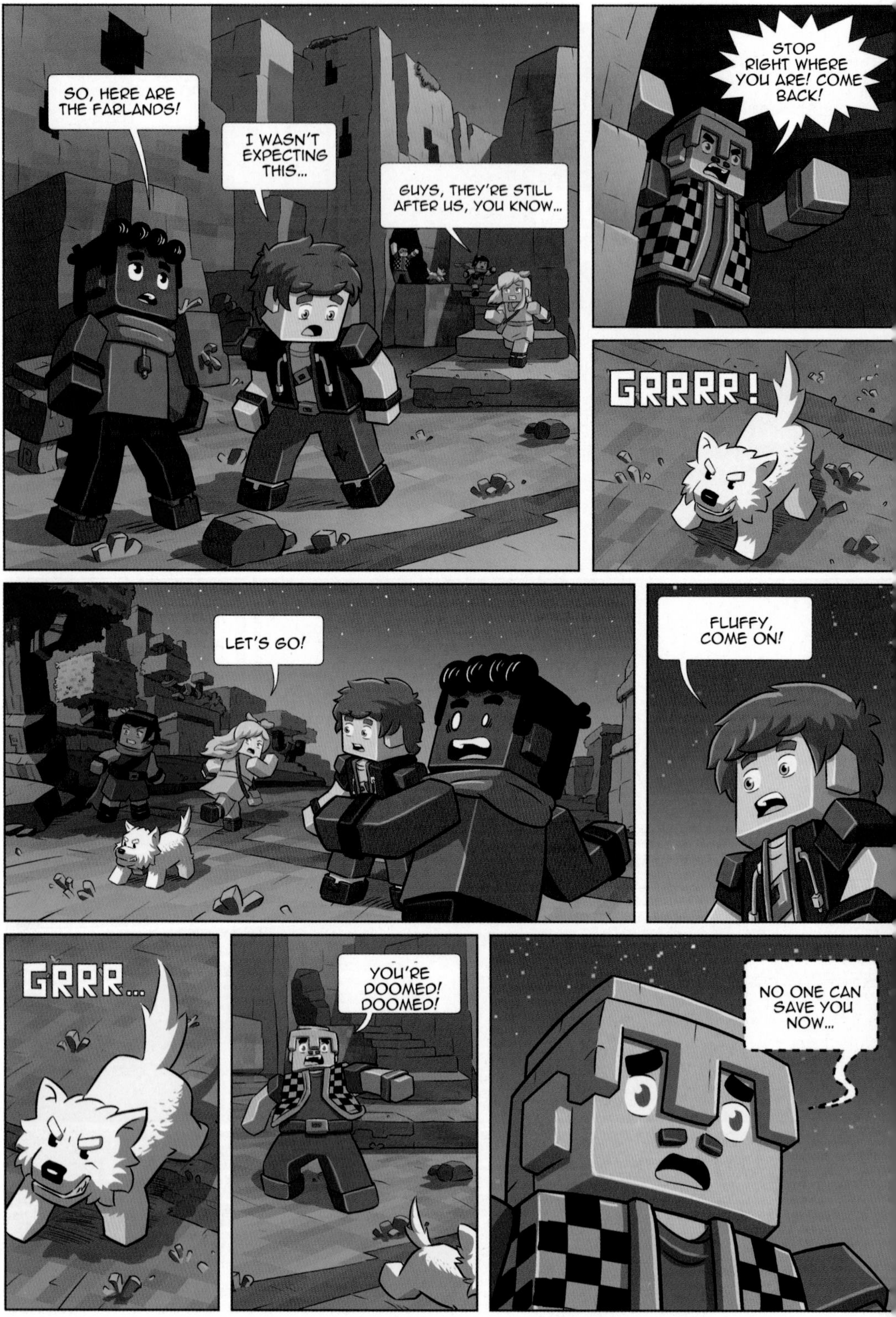
SO, HERE ARE THE FARLANDS!
I WASN'T EXPECTING THIS...
GUYS, THEY'RE STILL AFTER US, YOU KNOW...
STOP RIGHT WHERE YOU ARE! COME BACK!
GRRRR!
LET'S GO!
FLUFFY, COME ON!
GRRR...
YOU'RE DOOMED! DOOMED!
NO ONE CAN SAVE YOU NOW...

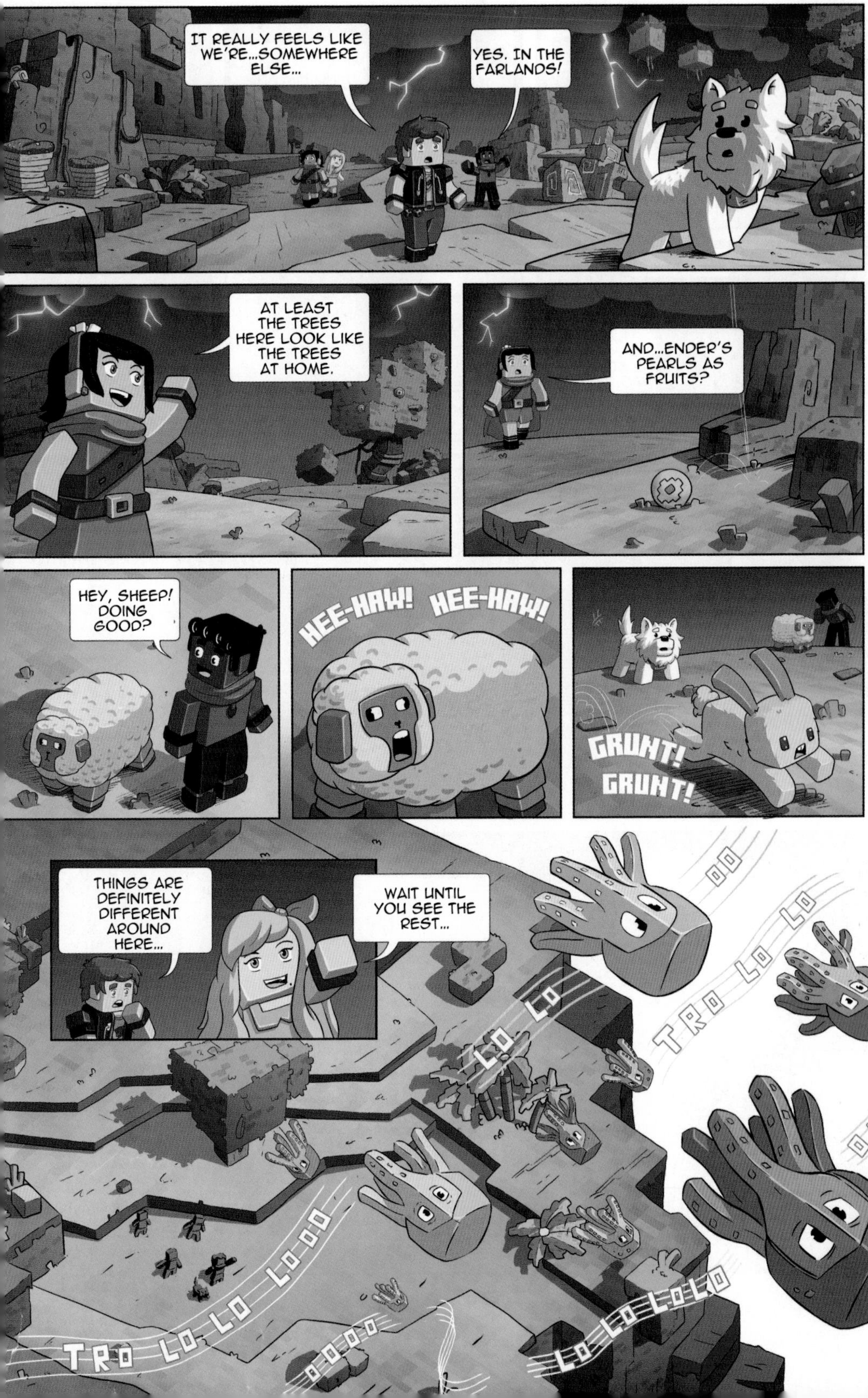
IT REALLY FEELS LIKE WE'RE...SOMEWHERE ELSE...
YES. IN THE FARLANDS!
AT LEAST THE TREES HERE LOOK LIKE THE TREES AT HOME.
AND...ENDER'S PEARLS AS FRUITS?
HEY, SHEEP! DOING GOOD?
HEE-HAW! HEE-HAW!
GRUNT! GRUNT!
THINGS ARE DEFINITELY DIFFERENT AROUND HERE...
WAIT UNTIL YOU SEE THE REST...
TRO LO LO LO LO OOOO
TRO LO LO OO
LO LO
LO LO LO LO LO

ARE FLYING OCTOPUSES SCARING YOU THAT MUCH?

NOT AT ALL, BUT I'M WORRIED FOR KREOSOT...

HEE-HAW!

KREO WHAT?

HE'S A KID FROM THE VILLAGE. HE WANTED TO SEE WHAT WAS BEYOND THE WALL...

...AND HE DISAPPEARED. I WAS PREVENTED FROM SEARCHING FOR HIM.

WE'RE GOING TO FIND HIM AND BRING HIM BACK. PROMISE!

I DON'T HAVE ANY WEAPONS, JUST THESE TWO HEALING POTIONS THEY HAVEN'T TAKEN FROM ME.

MIGHT PROVE USEFUL DOWN THE ROAD... IN THE MEANTIME...

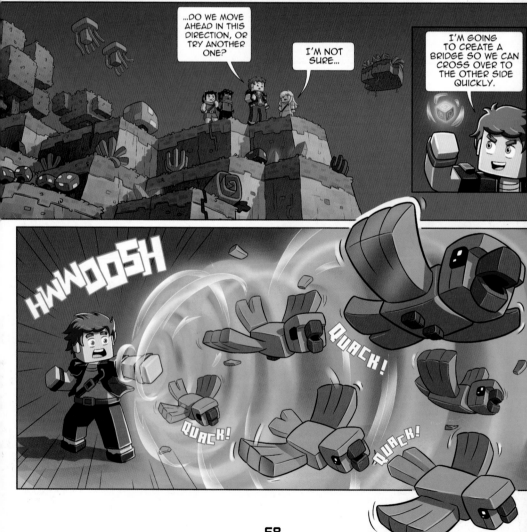

...DO WE MOVE AHEAD IN THIS DIRECTION, OR TRY ANOTHER ONE?

I'M NOT SURE...

I'M GOING TO CREATE A BRIDGE SO WE CAN CROSS OVER TO THE OTHER SIDE QUICKLY.

HWWOOSH

QUACK!

QUACK!

QUACK!

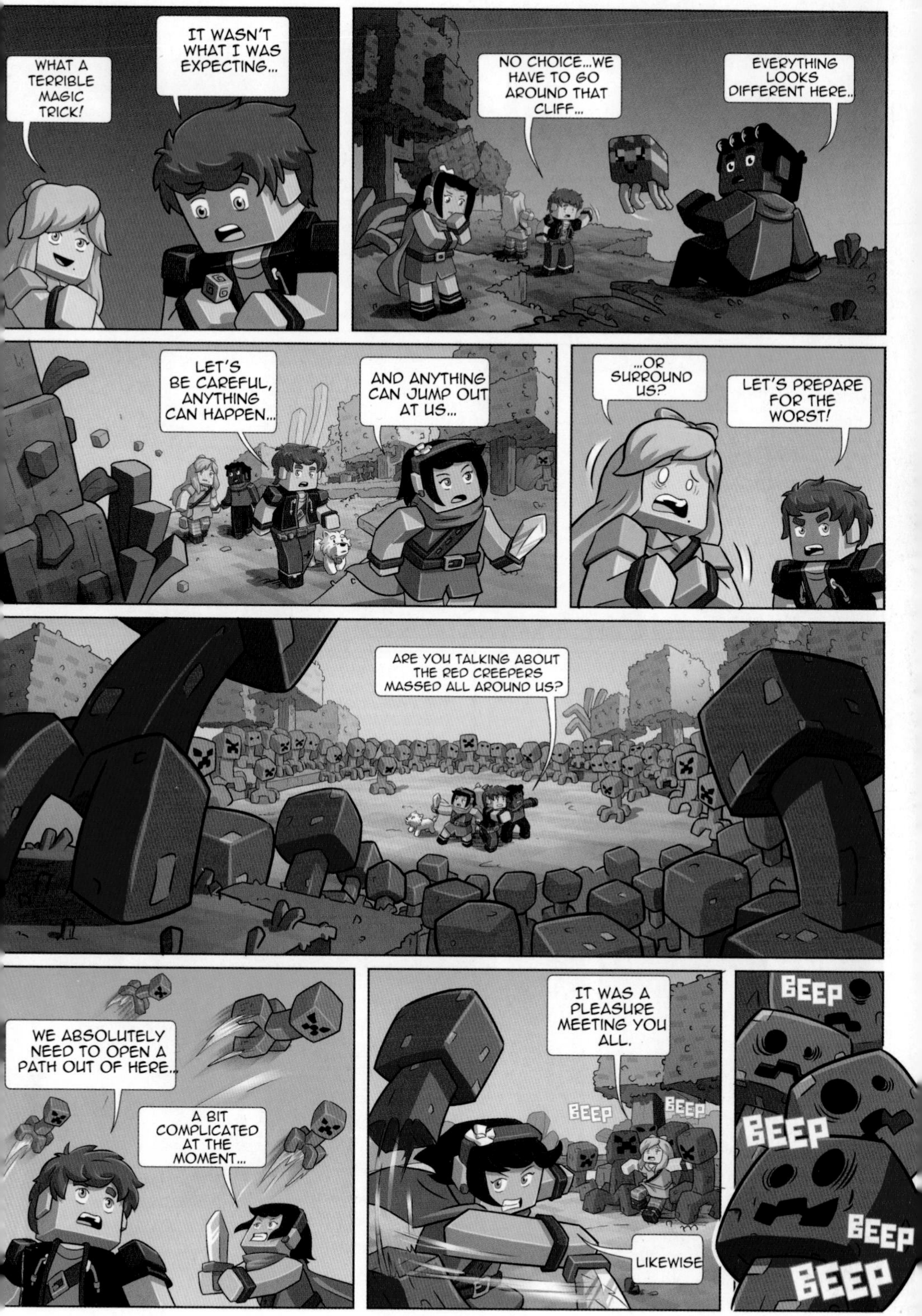
WHAT A TERRIBLE MAGIC TRICK!
IT WASN'T WHAT I WAS EXPECTING...
NO CHOICE...WE HAVE TO GO AROUND THAT CLIFF...
EVERYTHING LOOKS DIFFERENT HERE...
LET'S BE CAREFUL, ANYTHING CAN HAPPEN...
AND ANYTHING CAN JUMP OUT AT US...
...OR SURROUND US?
LET'S PREPARE FOR THE WORST!
ARE YOU TALKING ABOUT THE RED CREEPERS MASSED ALL AROUND US?
WE ABSOLUTELY NEED TO OPEN A PATH OUT OF HERE...
A BIT COMPLICATED AT THE MOMENT...
IT WAS A PLEASURE MEETING YOU ALL.
BEEP
BEEP
LIKEWISE
BEEP
BEEP
BEEP
BEEP

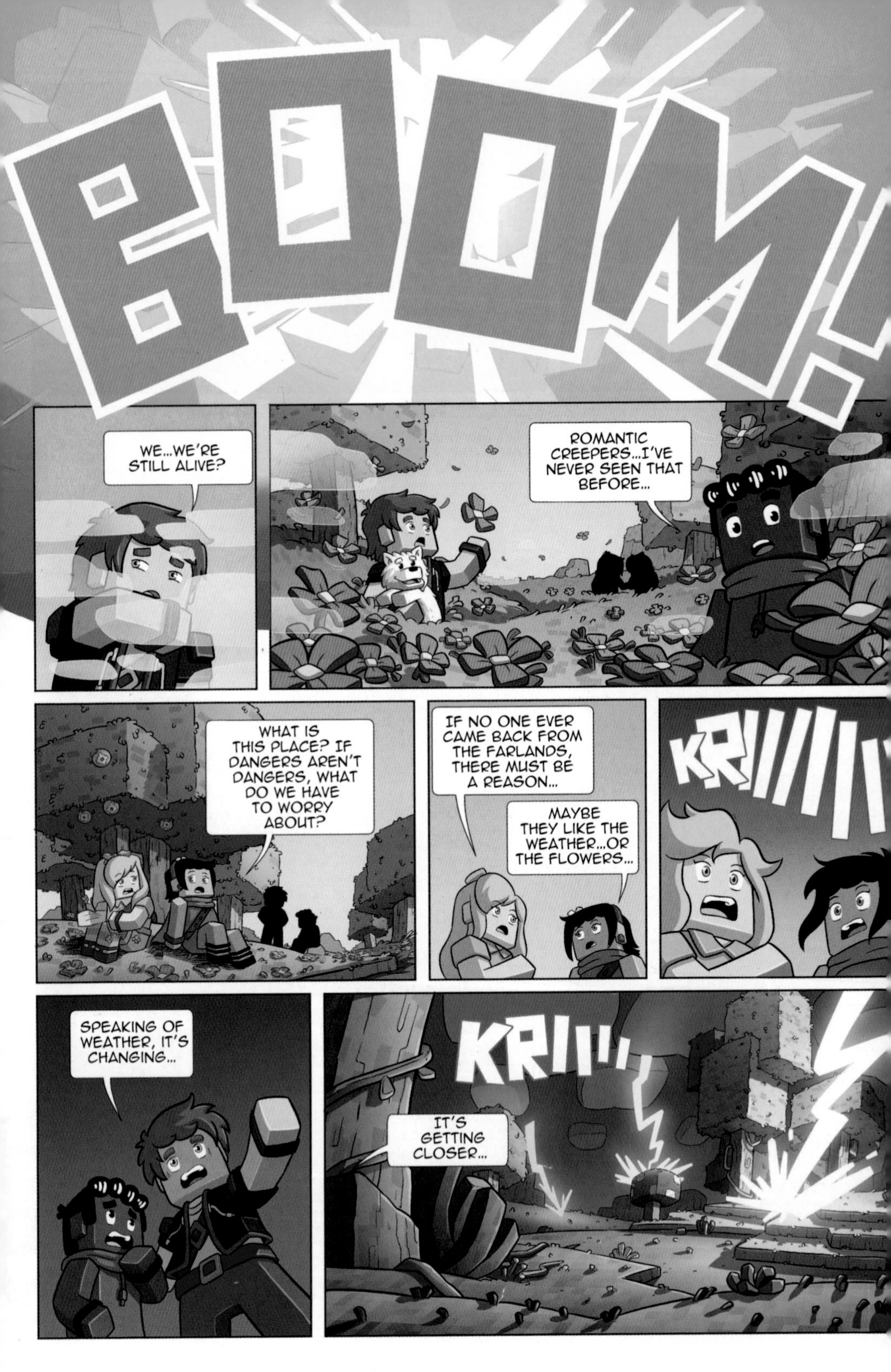
BOOM!
WE...WE'RE STILL ALIVE?
ROMANTIC CREEPERS...I'VE NEVER SEEN THAT BEFORE...
WHAT IS THIS PLACE? IF DANGERS AREN'T DANGERS, WHAT DO WE HAVE TO WORRY ABOUT?
IF NO ONE EVER CAME BACK FROM THE FARLANDS, THERE MUST BE A REASON...
MAYBE THEY LIKE THE WEATHER...OR THE FLOWERS...
KRIIIIII
SPEAKING OF WEATHER, IT'S CHANGING...
KRIIII
IT'S GETTING CLOSER...

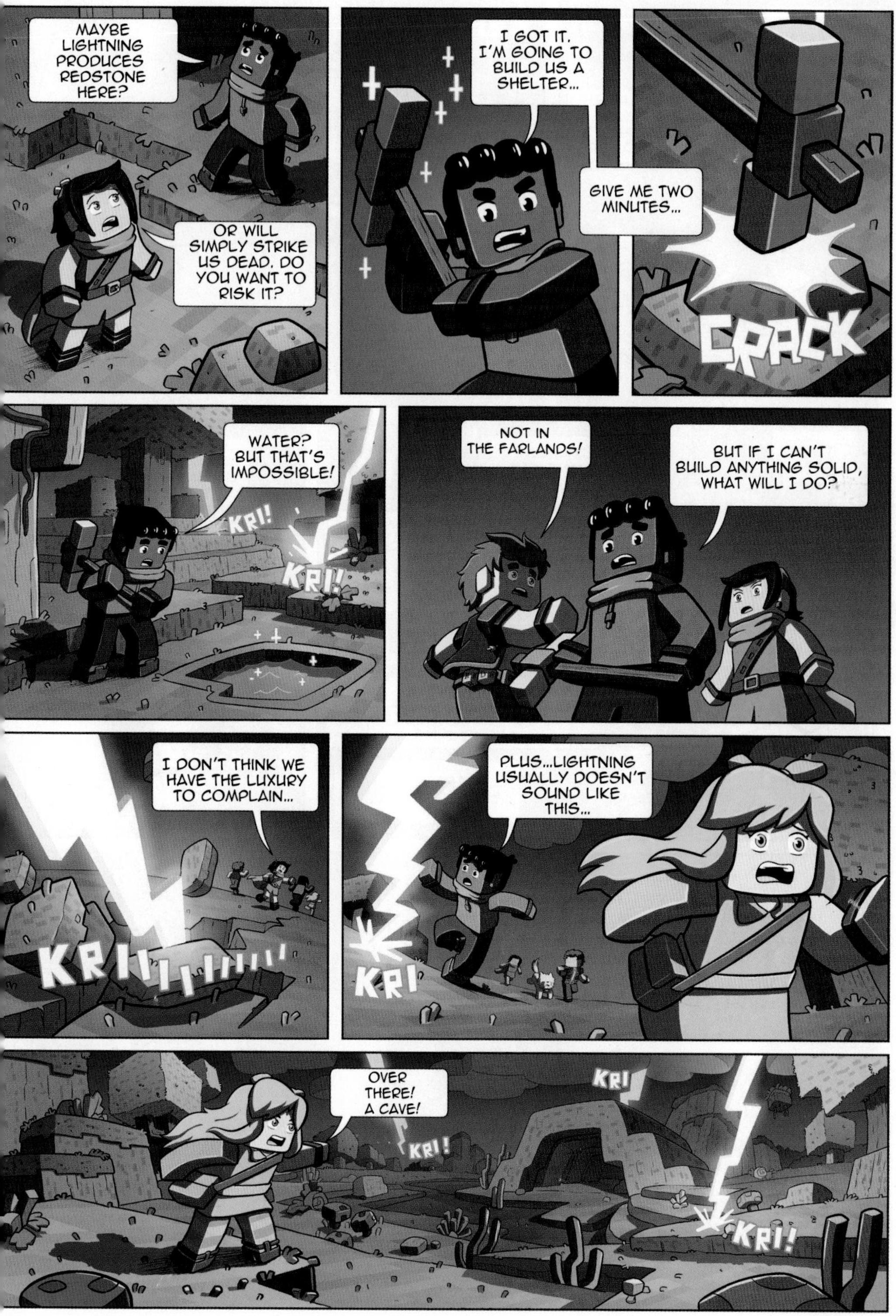
MAYBE LIGHTNING PRODUCES REDSTONE HERE?
OR WILL SIMPLY STRIKE US DEAD. DO YOU WANT TO RISK IT?
I GOT IT. I'M GOING TO BUILD US A SHELTER...
GIVE ME TWO MINUTES...
CRACK
WATER? BUT THAT'S IMPOSSIBLE!
KRI!
KRI!
NOT IN THE FARLANDS!
BUT IF I CAN'T BUILD ANYTHING SOLID, WHAT WILL I DO?
I DON'T THINK WE HAVE THE LUXURY TO COMPLAIN...
KRIIIIIIIII
PLUS...LIGHTNING USUALLY DOESN'T SOUND LIKE THIS...
KRI
OVER THERE! A CAVE!
KRI!
KRI!
KRI!

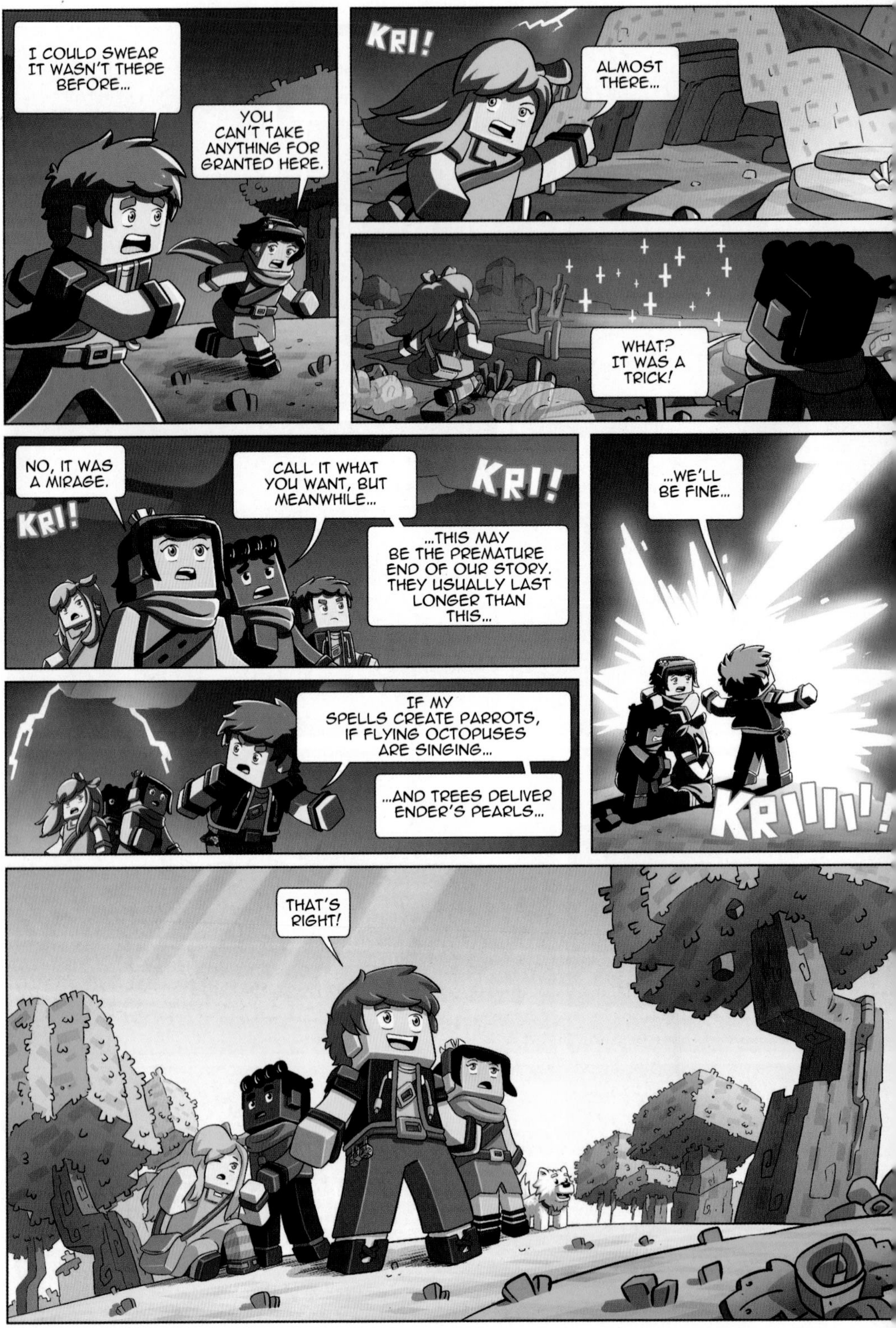
I COULD SWEAR IT WASN'T THERE BEFORE...
YOU CAN'T TAKE ANYTHING FOR GRANTED HERE.
KRI!
ALMOST THERE...
WHAT? IT WAS A TRICK!
NO, IT WAS A MIRAGE.
KRI!
CALL IT WHAT YOU WANT, BUT MEANWHILE...
KRI!
...THIS MAY BE THE PREMATURE END OF OUR STORY. THEY USUALLY LAST LONGER THAN THIS...
IF MY SPELLS CREATE PARROTS, IF FLYING OCTOPUSES ARE SINGING...
...AND TREES DELIVER ENDER'S PEARLS...
...WE'LL BE FINE...
KRIIIII!
THAT'S RIGHT!

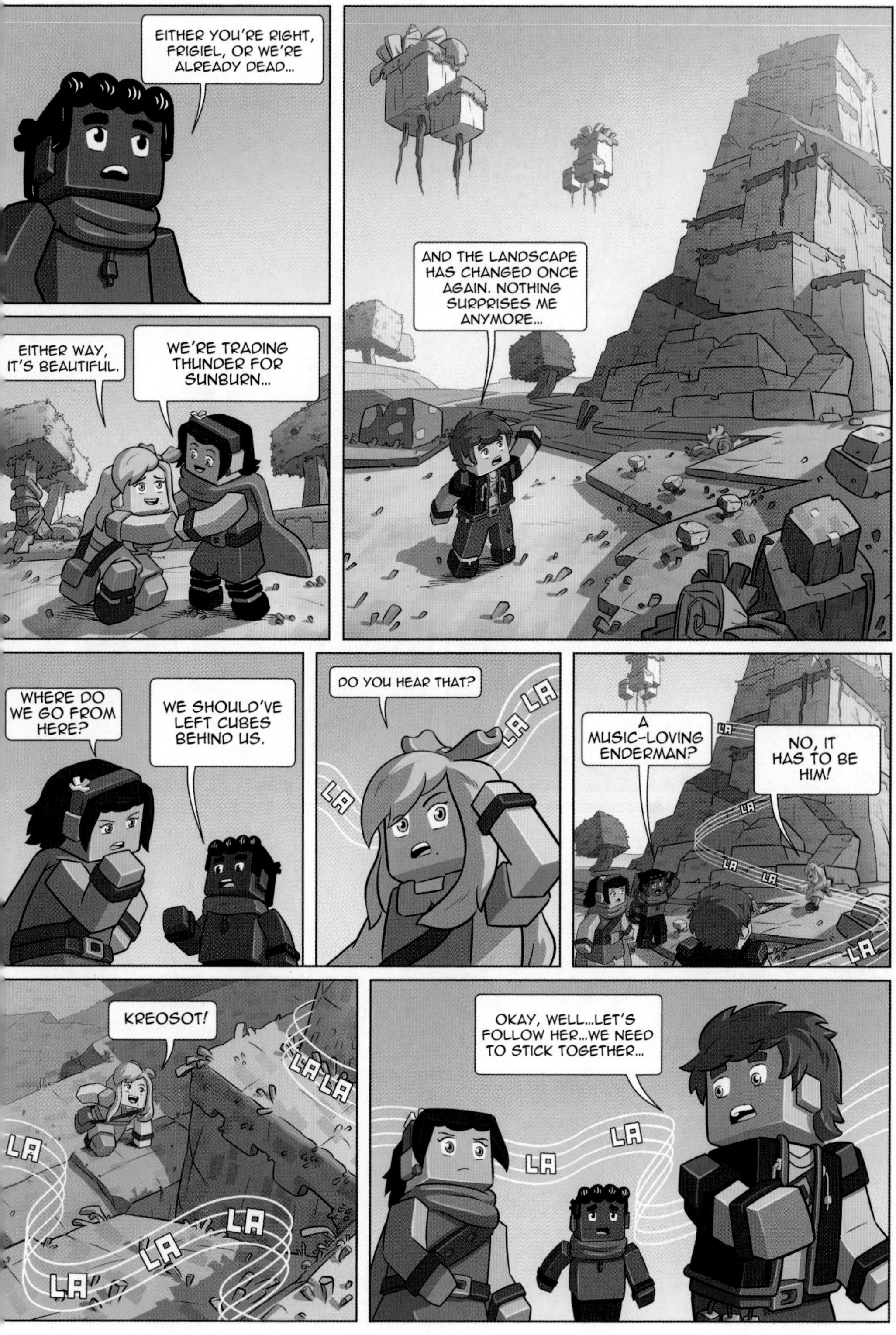
EITHER YOU'RE RIGHT, FRIGIEL, OR WE'RE ALREADY DEAD...
AND THE LANDSCAPE HAS CHANGED ONCE AGAIN. NOTHING SURPRISES ME ANYMORE...
EITHER WAY, IT'S BEAUTIFUL.
WE'RE TRADING THUNDER FOR SUNBURN...
WHERE DO WE GO FROM HERE?
WE SHOULD'VE LEFT CUBES BEHIND US.
DO YOU HEAR THAT?
LA LA
LA
A MUSIC-LOVING ENDERMAN?
NO, IT HAS TO BE HIM!
LA
LA
LA
LA
LA
KREOSOT!
LA LA
LA
LA
LA
LA
OKAY, WELL...LET'S FOLLOW HER...WE NEED TO STICK TOGETHER...
LA
LA

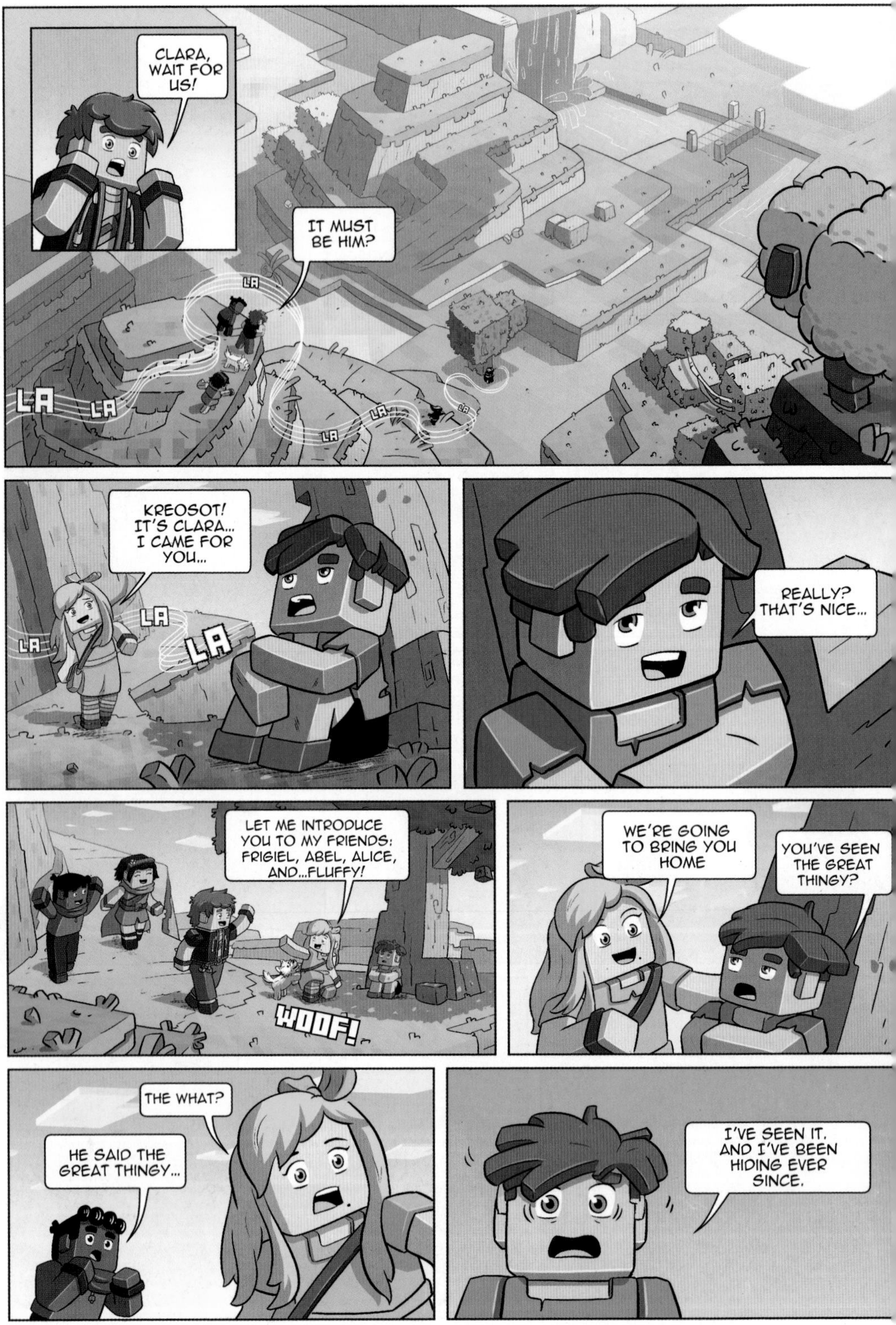
CLARA, WAIT FOR US!
IT MUST BE HIM?
LA
LA
LA
LA
LA
LA
LA
KREOSOT! IT'S CLARA... I CAME FOR YOU...
LA
LA
LA
REALLY? THAT'S NICE...
LET ME INTRODUCE YOU TO MY FRIENDS: FRIGIEL, ABEL, ALICE, AND...FLUFFY!
WOOF!
WE'RE GOING TO BRING YOU HOME
YOU'VE SEEN THE GREAT THINGY?
THE WHAT?
HE SAID THE GREAT THINGY...
I'VE SEEN IT. AND I'VE BEEN HIDING EVER SINCE.

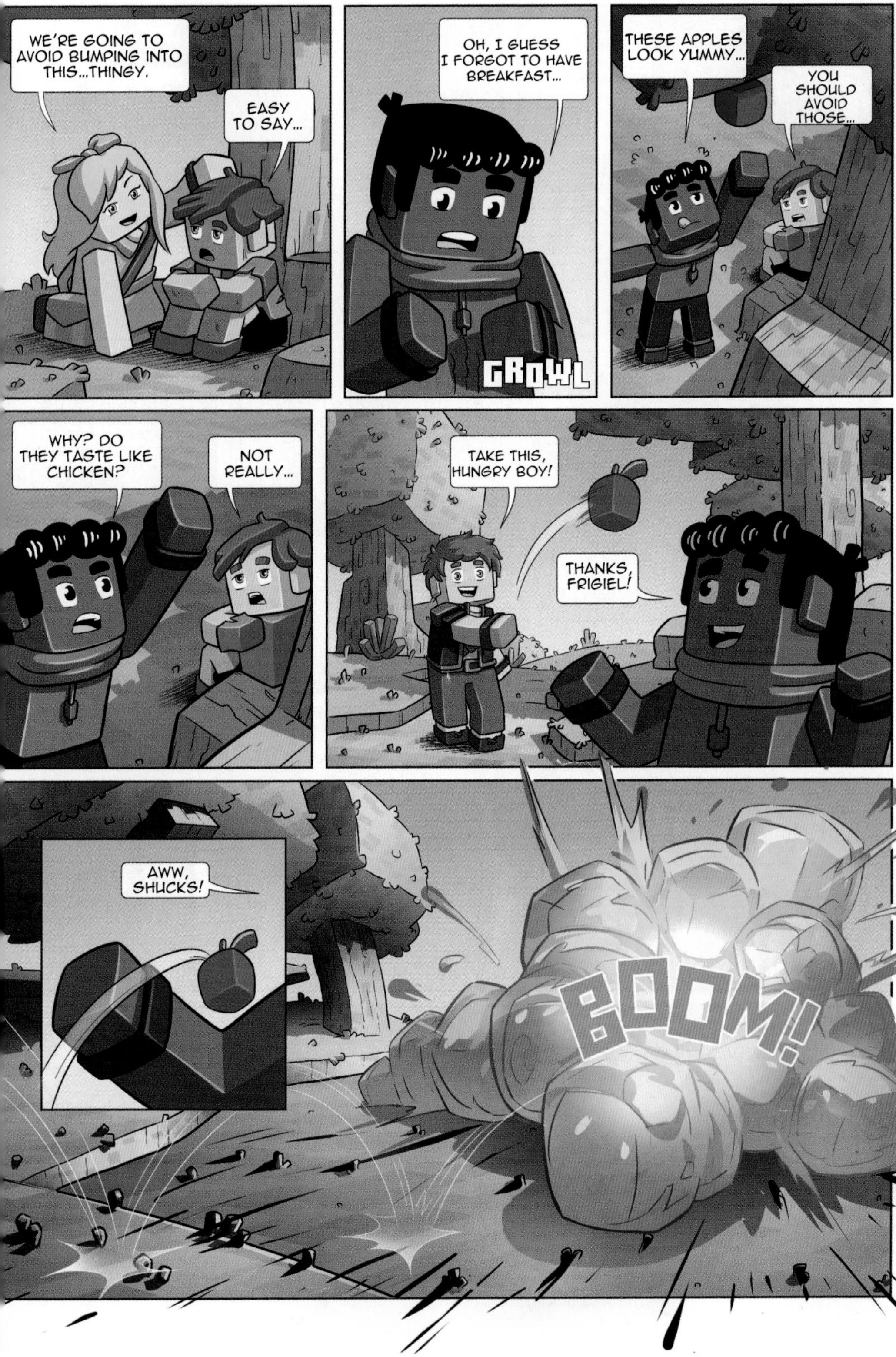
WE'RE GOING TO AVOID BUMPING INTO THIS...THINGY.
EASY TO SAY...
OH, I GUESS I FORGOT TO HAVE BREAKFAST...
GROWL
THESE APPLES LOOK YUMMY...
YOU SHOULD AVOID THOSE...
WHY? DO THEY TASTE LIKE CHICKEN?
NOT REALLY...
TAKE THIS, HUNGRY BOY!
THANKS, FRIGIEL!
AWW, SHUCKS!
BOOM!

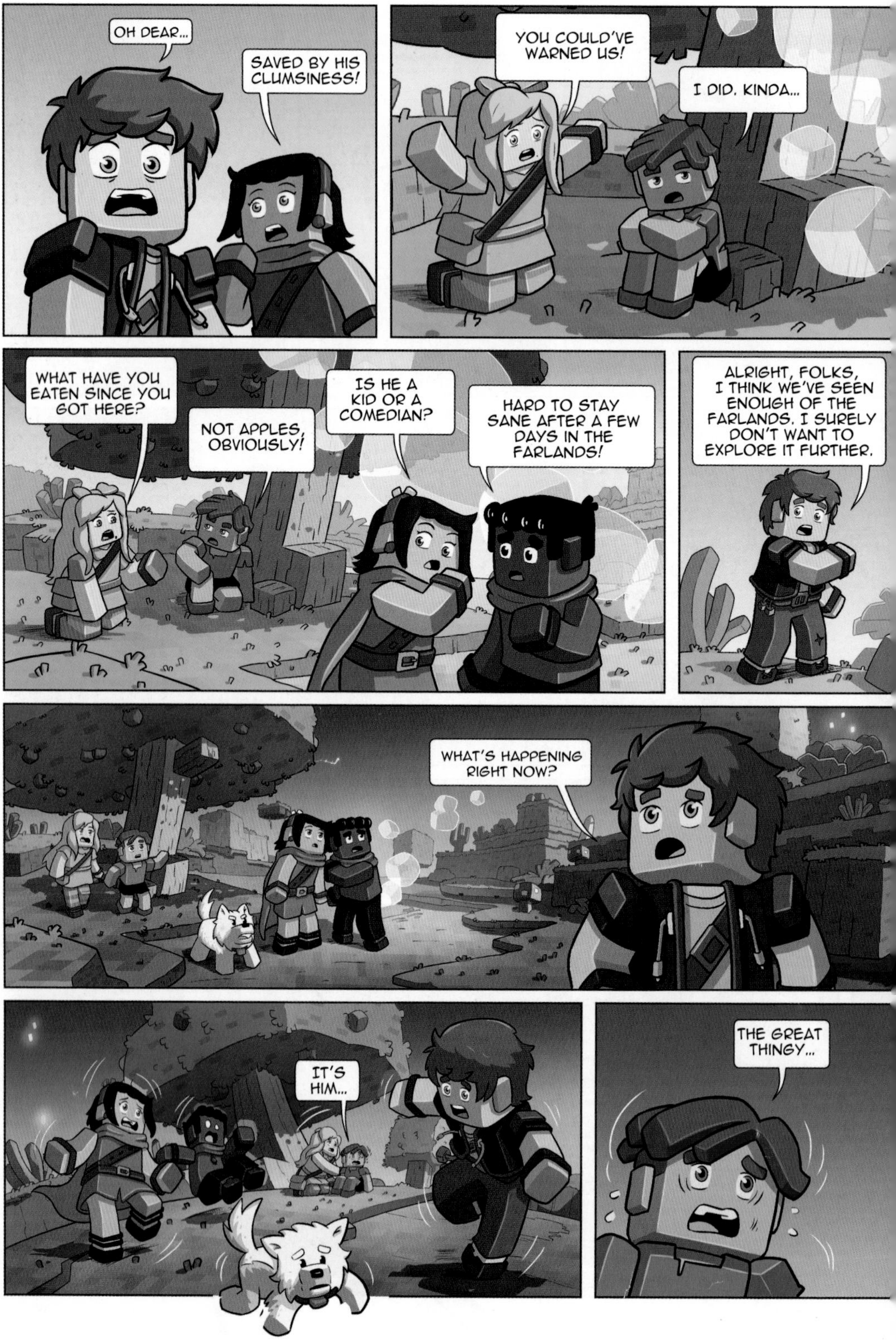
OH DEAR...
SAVED BY HIS CLUMSINESS!
YOU COULD'VE WARNED US!
I DID, KINDA...
WHAT HAVE YOU EATEN SINCE YOU GOT HERE?
NOT APPLES, OBVIOUSLY!
IS HE A KID OR A COMEDIAN?
HARD TO STAY SANE AFTER A FEW DAYS IN THE FARLANDS!
ALRIGHT, FOLKS, I THINK WE'VE SEEN ENOUGH OF THE FARLANDS. I SURELY DON'T WANT TO EXPLORE IT FURTHER.
WHAT'S HAPPENING RIGHT NOW?
IT'S HIM...
THE GREAT THINGY...

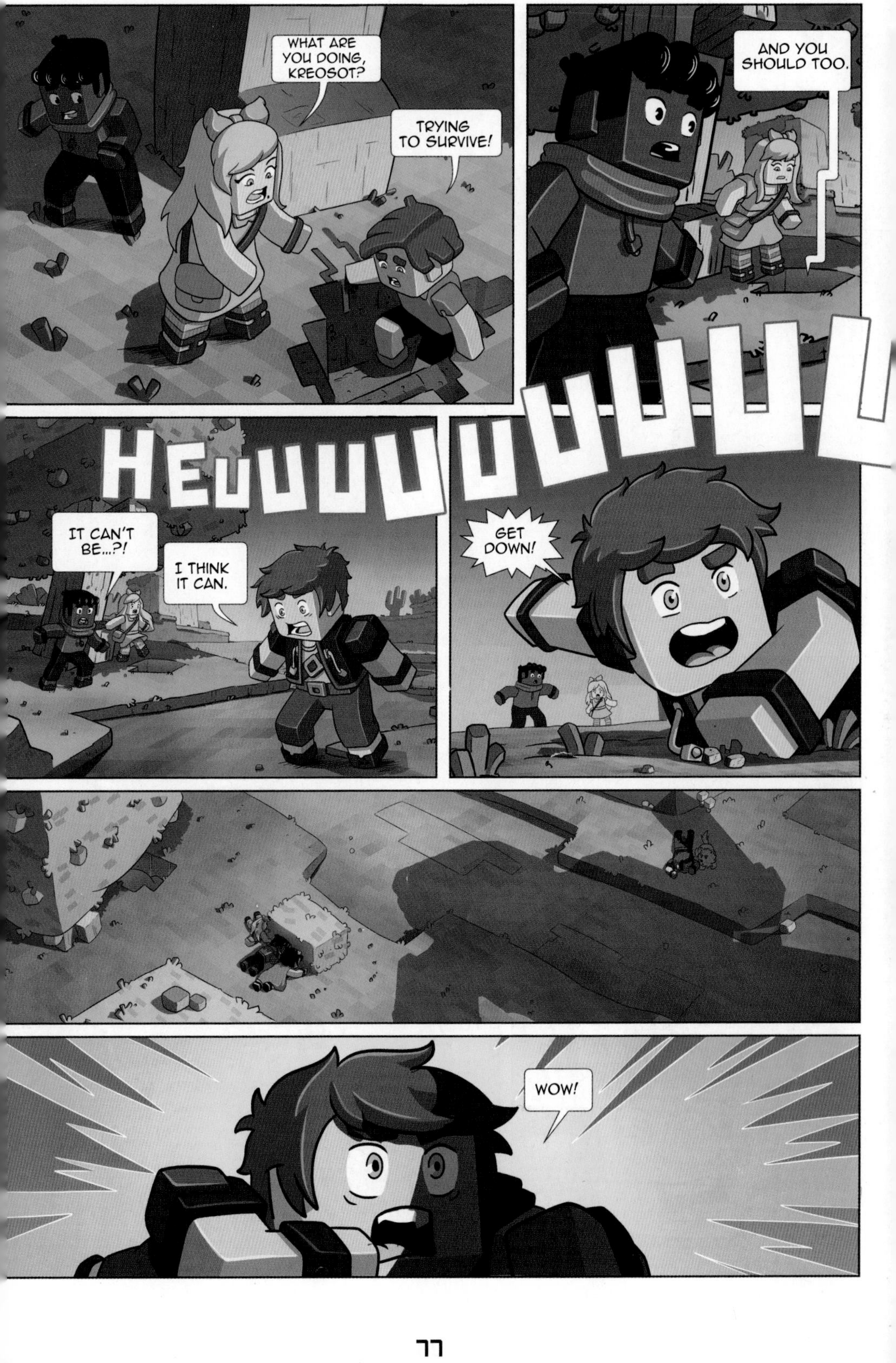
WHAT ARE YOU DOING, KREOSOT?
TRYING TO SURVIVE!
AND YOU SHOULD TOO.
HEUUUUUUUUUUUU
IT CAN'T BE...?!
I THINK IT CAN.
GET DOWN!
WOW!

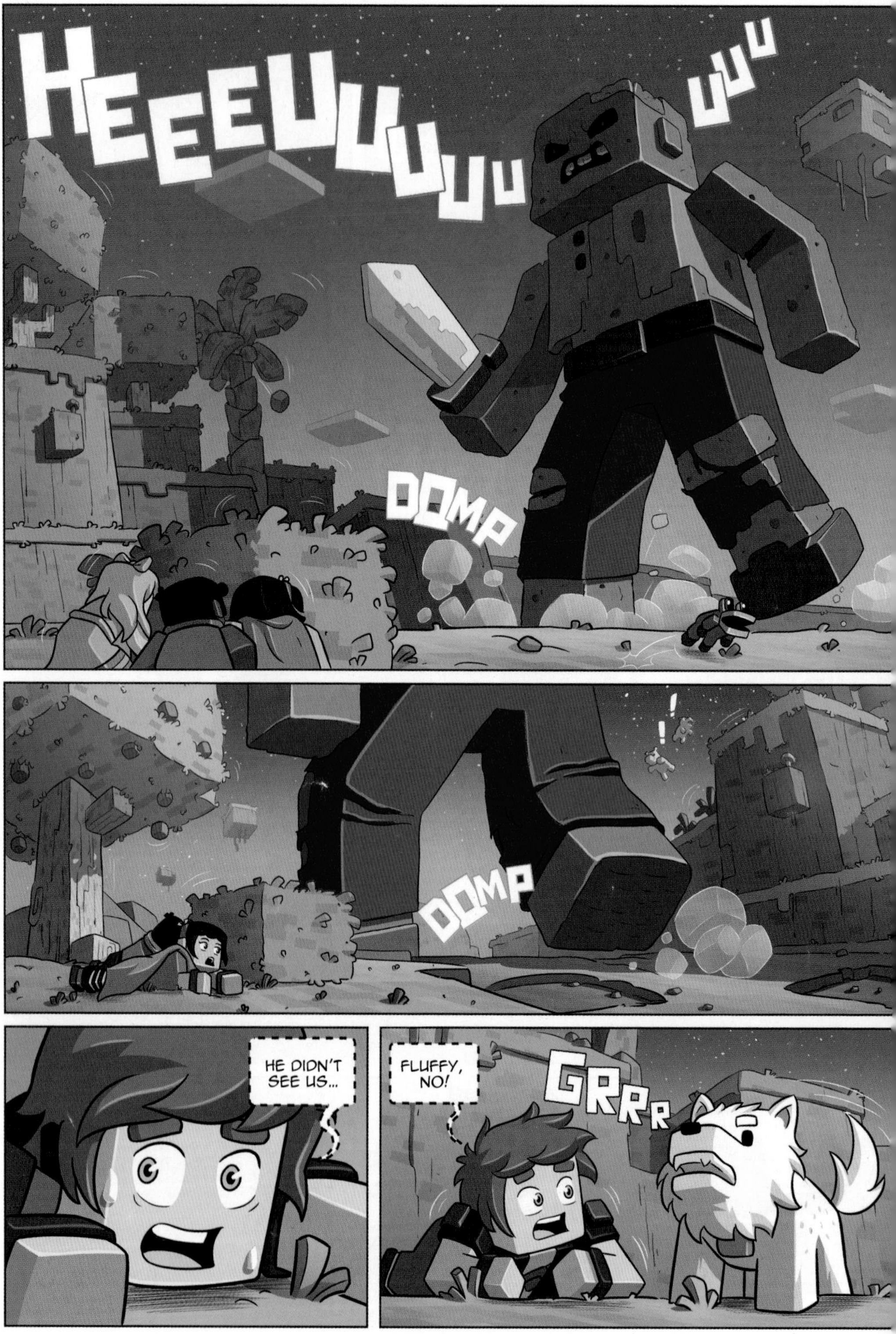
HEEEUUUUUUuuuu
DOMP
DOMP
HE DIDN'T SEE US...
FLUFFY, NO!
GRRR

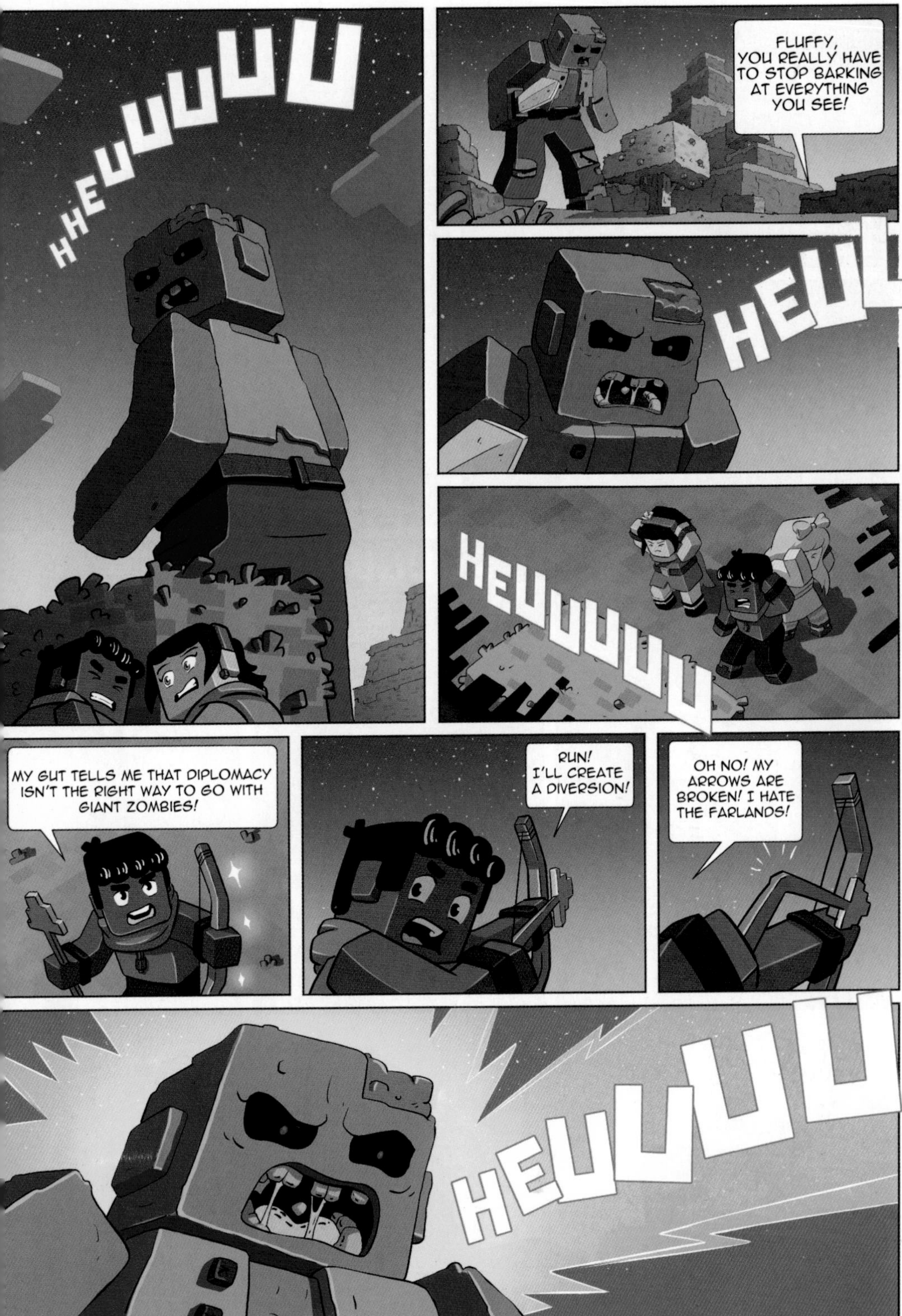
HHEUUUUUU
FLUFFY, YOU REALLY HAVE TO STOP BARKING AT EVERYTHING YOU SEE!
HEUU
HEUUUUUU
MY GUT TELLS ME THAT DIPLOMACY ISN'T THE RIGHT WAY TO GO WITH GIANT ZOMBIES!
RUN! I'LL CREATE A DIVERSION!
OH NO! MY ARROWS ARE BROKEN! I HATE THE FARLANDS!
HEUUUUU

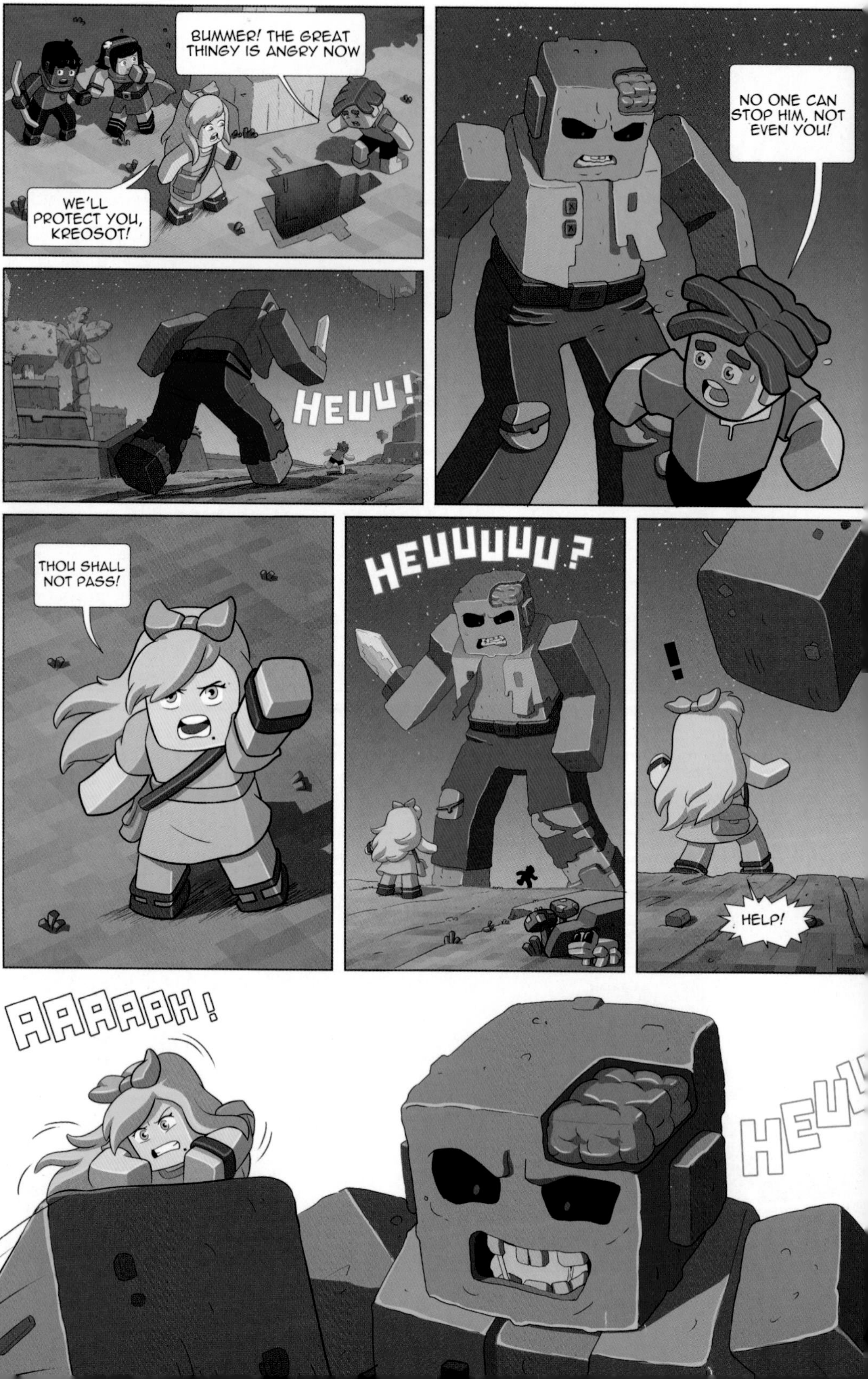
BUMMER! THE GREAT THINGY IS ANGRY NOW
WE'LL PROTECT YOU, KREOSOT!
NO ONE CAN STOP HIM, NOT EVEN YOU!
HEUU!
THOU SHALL NOT PASS!
HEUUUUUU?
!
HELP!
AAAAAH!

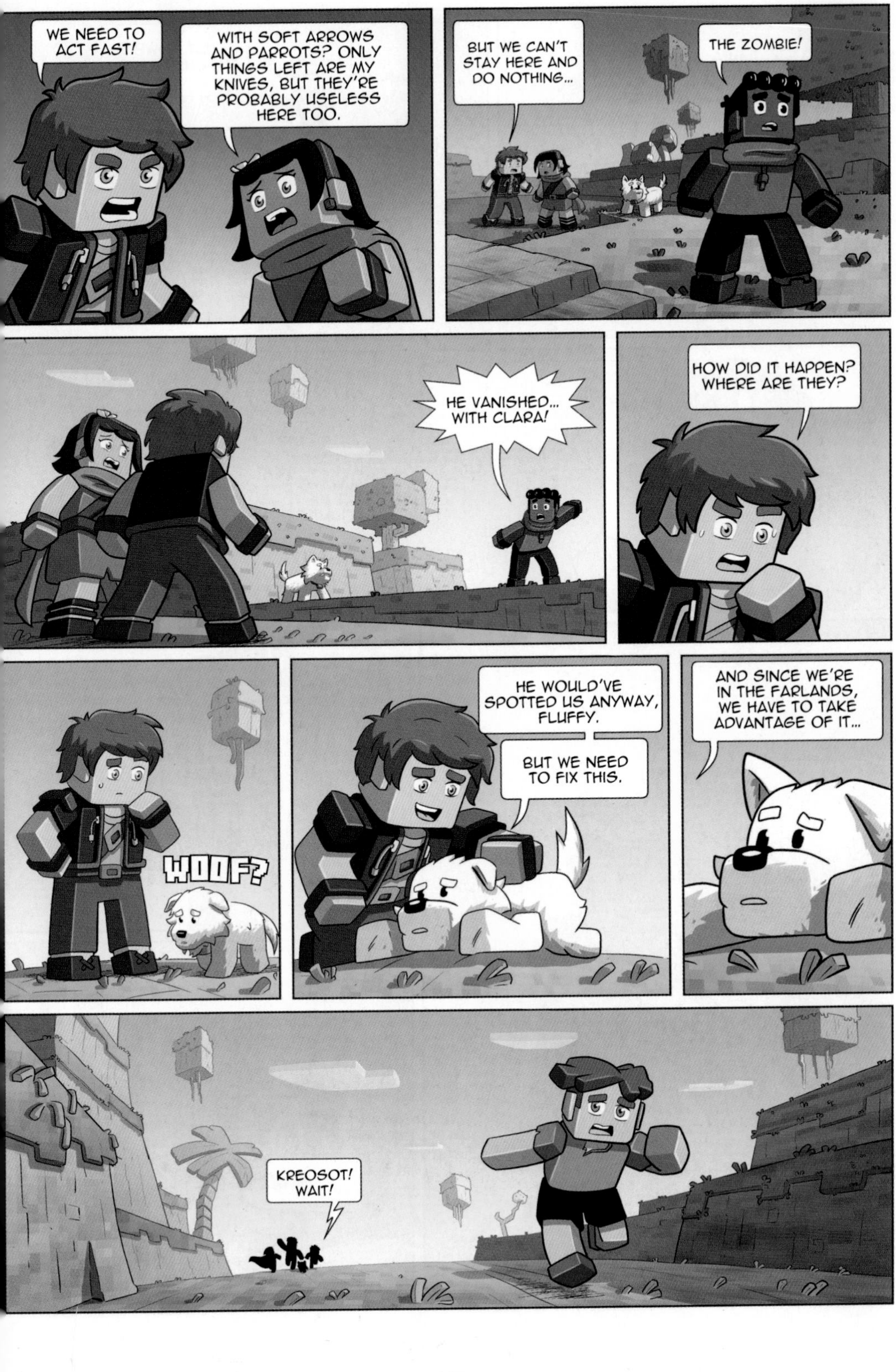
WE NEED TO ACT FAST!
WITH SOFT ARROWS AND PARROTS? ONLY THINGS LEFT ARE MY KNIVES, BUT THEY'RE PROBABLY USELESS HERE TOO.
BUT WE CAN'T STAY HERE AND DO NOTHING...
THE ZOMBIE!
HE VANISHED... WITH CLARA!
HOW DID IT HAPPEN? WHERE ARE THEY?
WOOF?
HE WOULD'VE SPOTTED US ANYWAY, FLUFFY.
BUT WE NEED TO FIX THIS.
AND SINCE WE'RE IN THE FARLANDS, WE HAVE TO TAKE ADVANTAGE OF IT...
KREOSOT! WAIT!

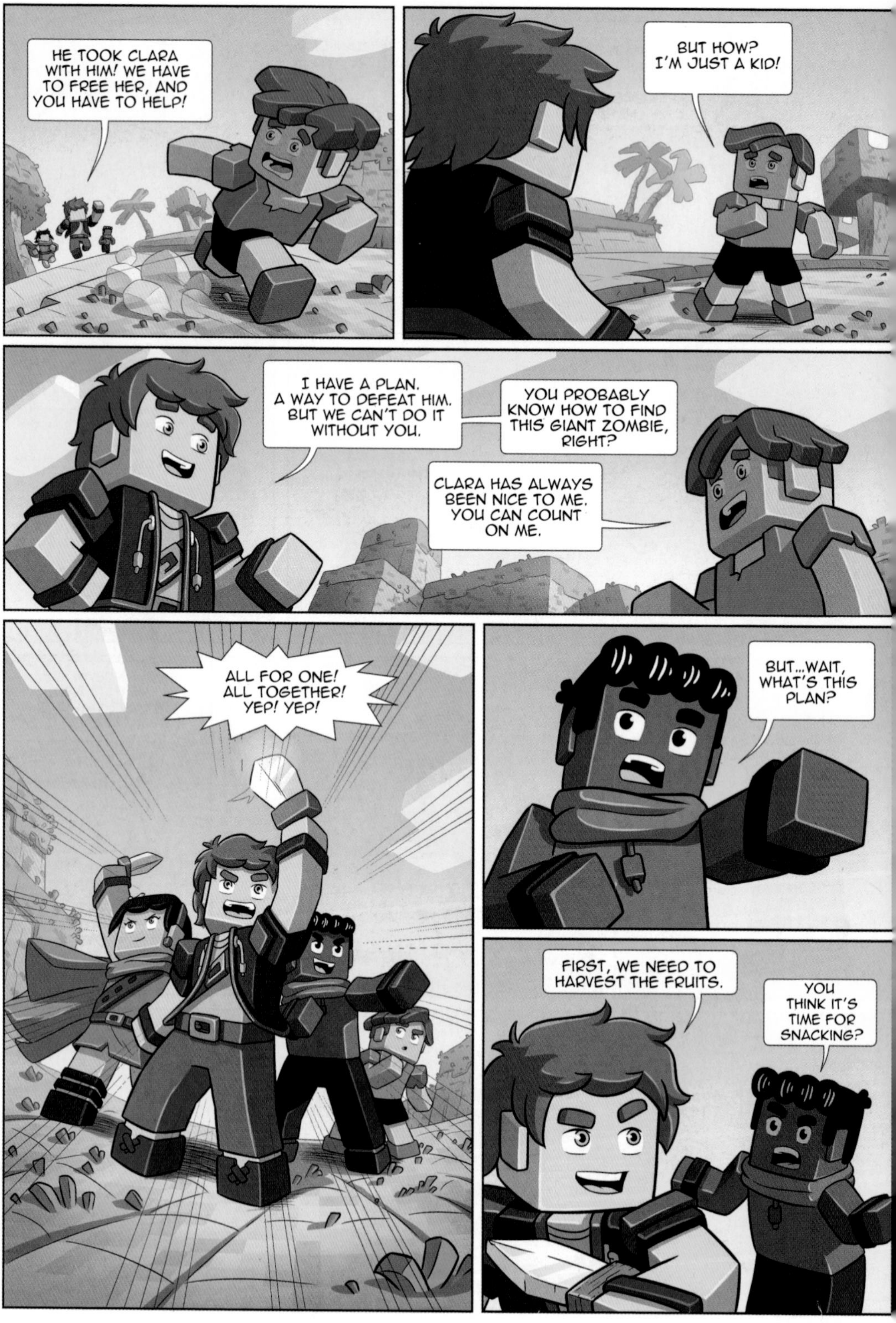
HE TOOK CLARA WITH HIM! WE HAVE TO FREE HER, AND YOU HAVE TO HELP!
BUT HOW? I'M JUST A KID!
I HAVE A PLAN. A WAY TO DEFEAT HIM. BUT WE CAN'T DO IT WITHOUT YOU.
YOU PROBABLY KNOW HOW TO FIND THIS GIANT ZOMBIE, RIGHT?
CLARA HAS ALWAYS BEEN NICE TO ME. YOU CAN COUNT ON ME.
ALL FOR ONE! ALL TOGETHER! YEP! YEP!
BUT...WAIT, WHAT'S THIS PLAN?
FIRST, WE NEED TO HARVEST THE FRUITS.
YOU THINK IT'S TIME FOR SNACKING?

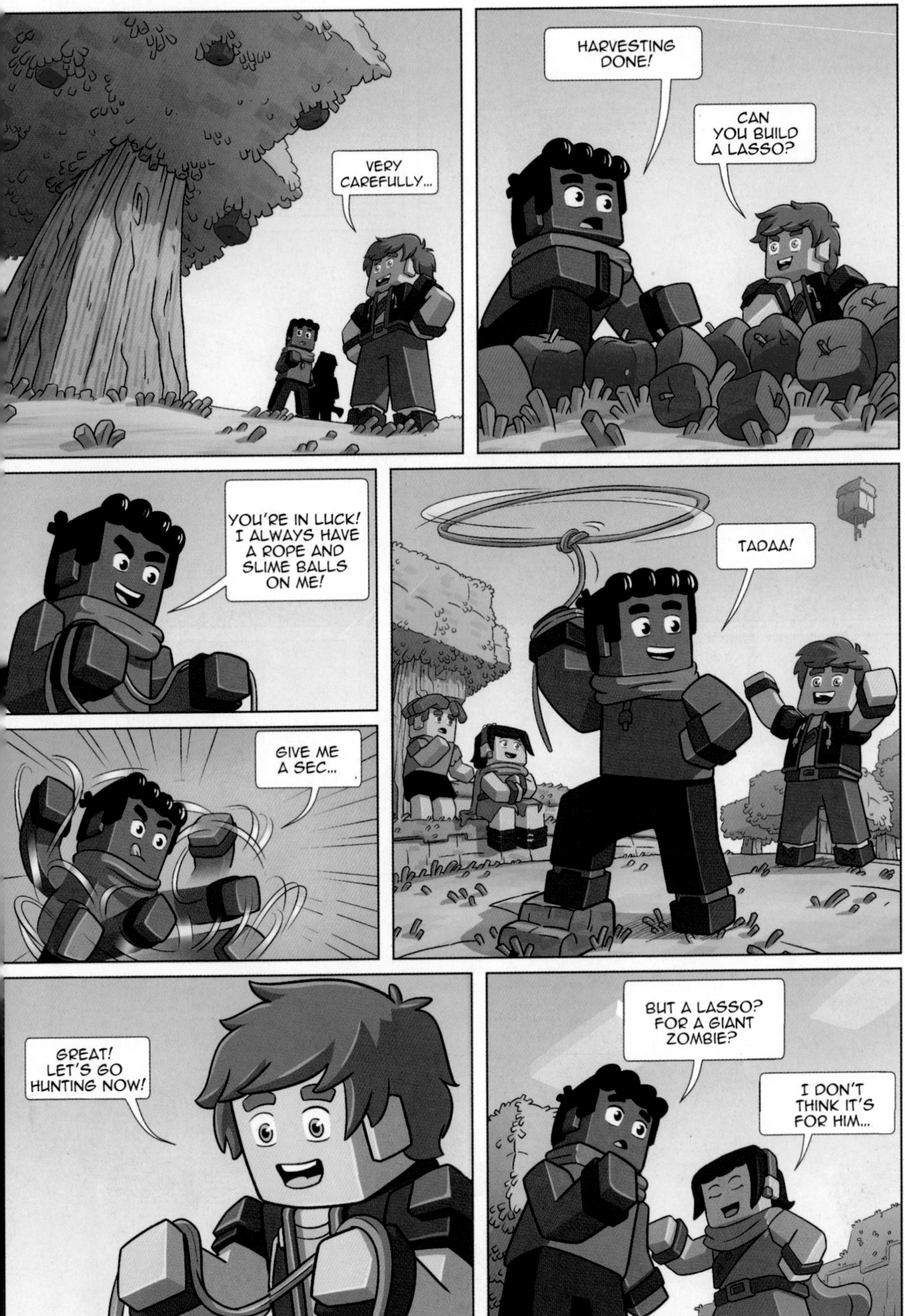
VERY CAREFULLY...
HARVESTING DONE!
CAN YOU BUILD A LASSO?
YOU'RE IN LUCK! I ALWAYS HAVE A ROPE AND SLIME BALLS ON ME!
GIVE ME A SEC...
TADAA!
GREAT! LET'S GO HUNTING NOW!
BUT A LASSO? FOR A GIANT ZOMBIE?
I DON'T THINK IT'S FOR HIM...

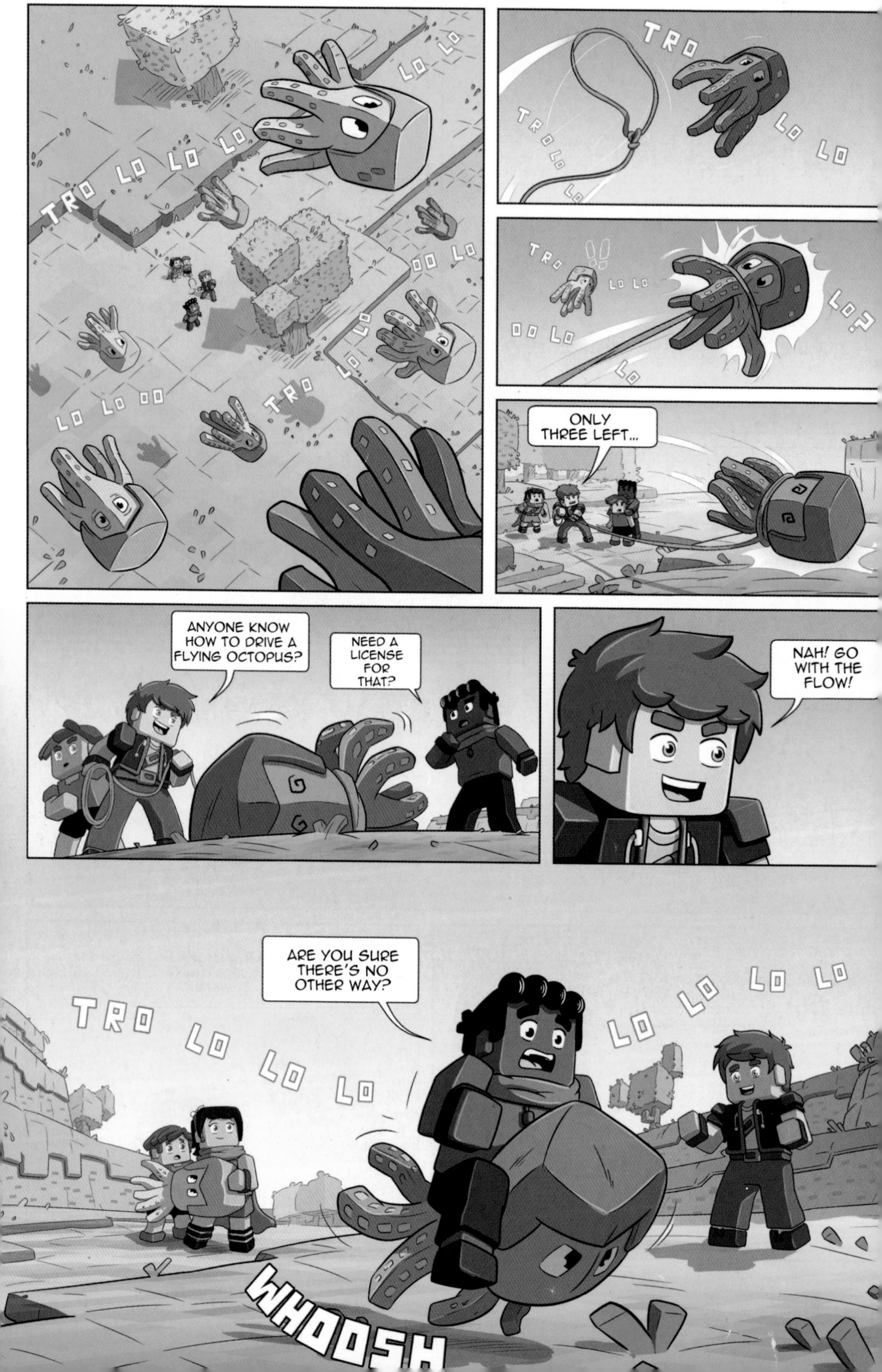
TRO LO LO LO
LO LO
OO LO
LO LO OO
TRO LO LO
TRO
TRO LO LO
LO LO
TRO
LO LO
OO LO
LO
LO?
ONLY THREE LEFT...
ANYONE KNOW HOW TO DRIVE A FLYING OCTOPUS?
NEED A LICENSE FOR THAT?
NAH! GO WITH THE FLOW!
ARE YOU SURE THERE'S NO OTHER WAY?
TRO LO LO LO
LO LO LO LO
WHOOSH

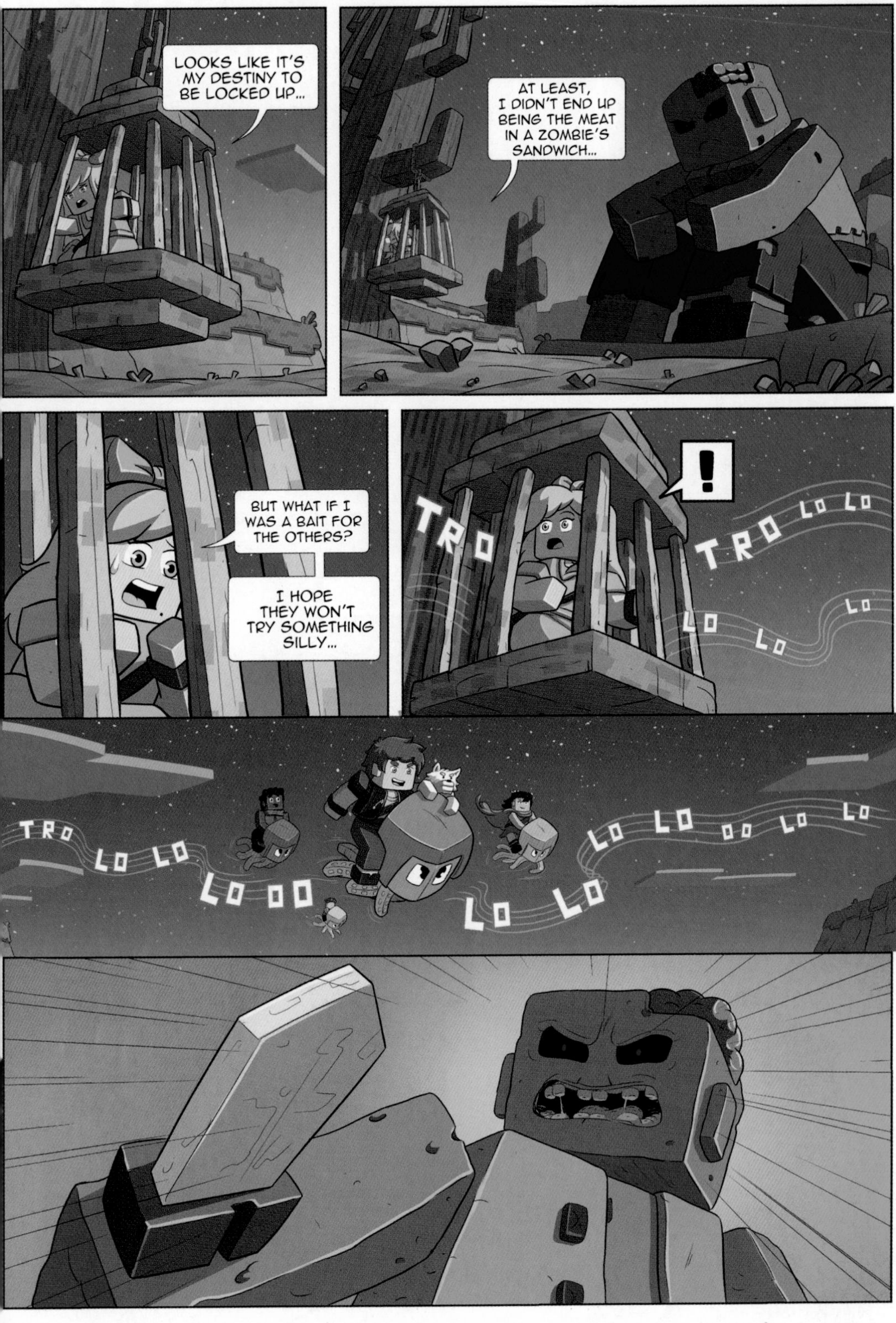
LOOKS LIKE IT'S MY DESTINY TO BE LOCKED UP...
AT LEAST, I DIDN'T END UP BEING THE MEAT IN A ZOMBIE'S SANDWICH...
BUT WHAT IF I WAS A BAIT FOR THE OTHERS?
I HOPE THEY WON'T TRY SOMETHING SILLY...
TRO
!
TRO LO LO
LO LO LO
TRO LO LO LO OO
LO LO LO LO OO LO LO

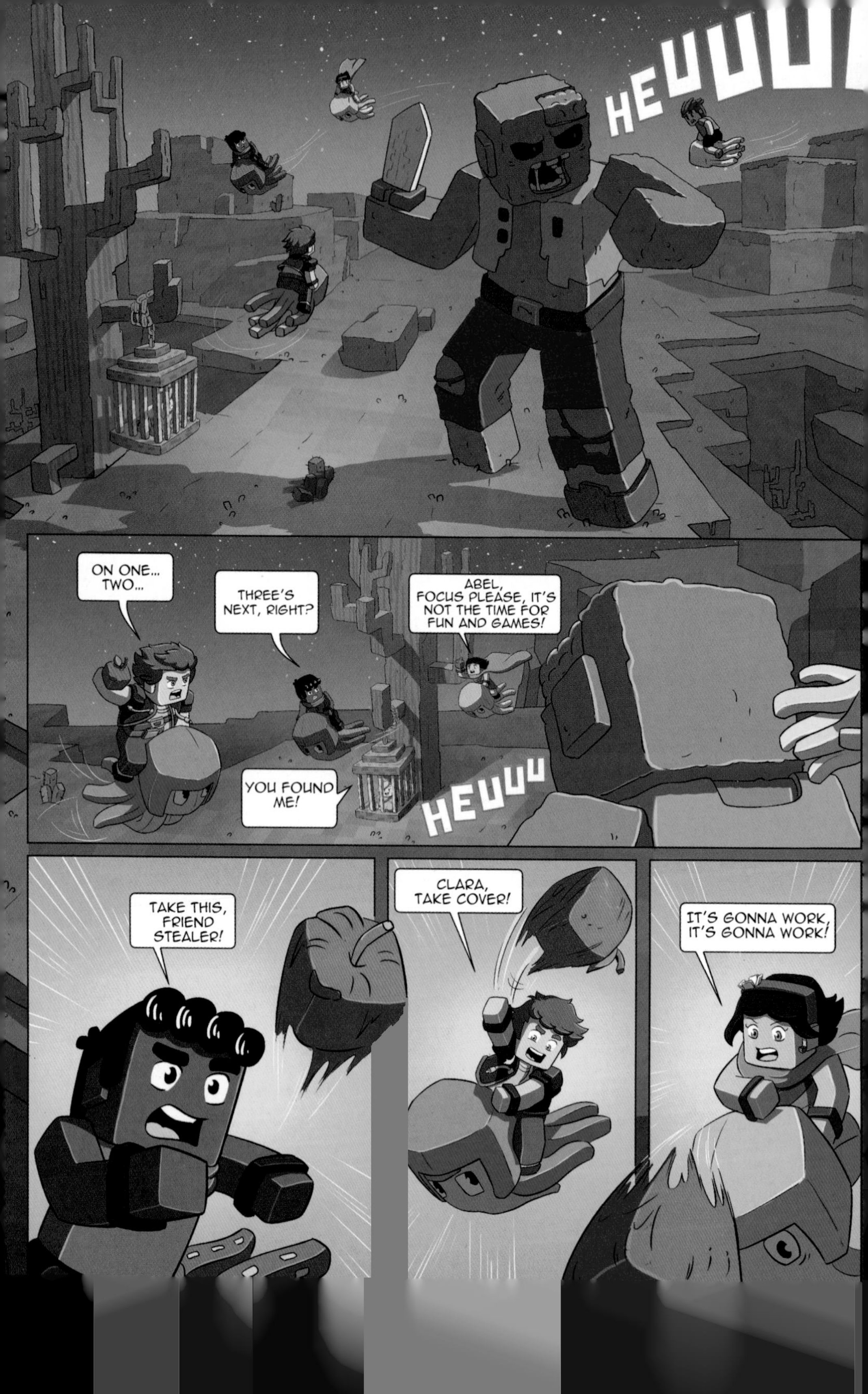

HEUUUU
ON ONE... TWO...
THREE'S NEXT, RIGHT?
ABEL, FOCUS PLEASE, IT'S NOT THE TIME FOR FUN AND GAMES!
YOU FOUND ME!
HEUUU
TAKE THIS, FRIEND STEALER!
CLARA, TAKE COVER!
IT'S GONNA WORK, IT'S GONNA WORK!

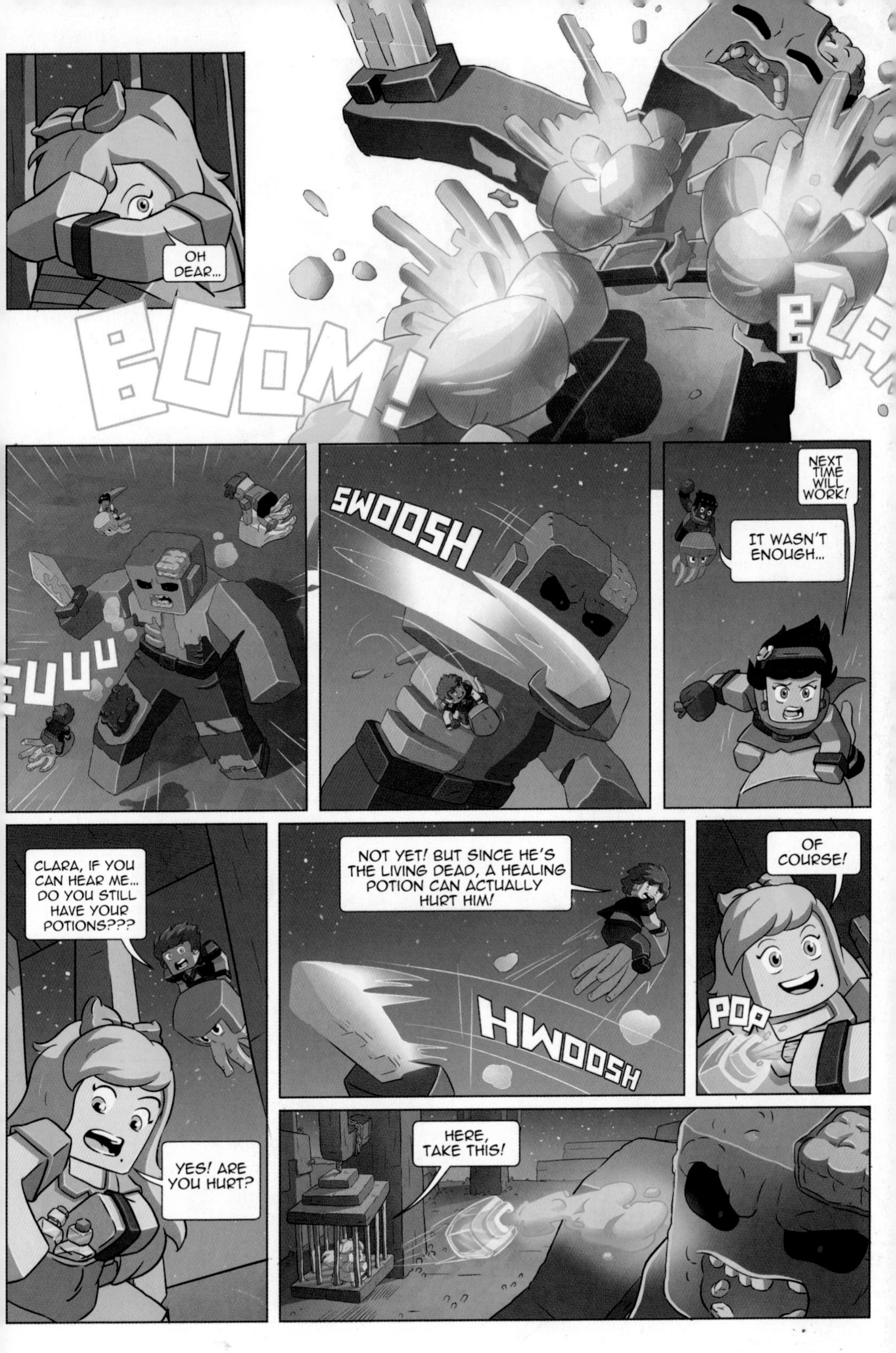

OH DEAR...
BOOM!
BLAM
FUUU
SWOOSH
NEXT TIME WILL WORK!
IT WASN'T ENOUGH...
CLARA, IF YOU CAN HEAR ME... DO YOU STILL HAVE YOUR POTIONS???
YES! ARE YOU HURT?
NOT YET! BUT SINCE HE'S THE LIVING DEAD, A HEALING POTION CAN ACTUALLY HURT HIM!
HWOOSH
OF COURSE!
POP
HERE, TAKE THIS!

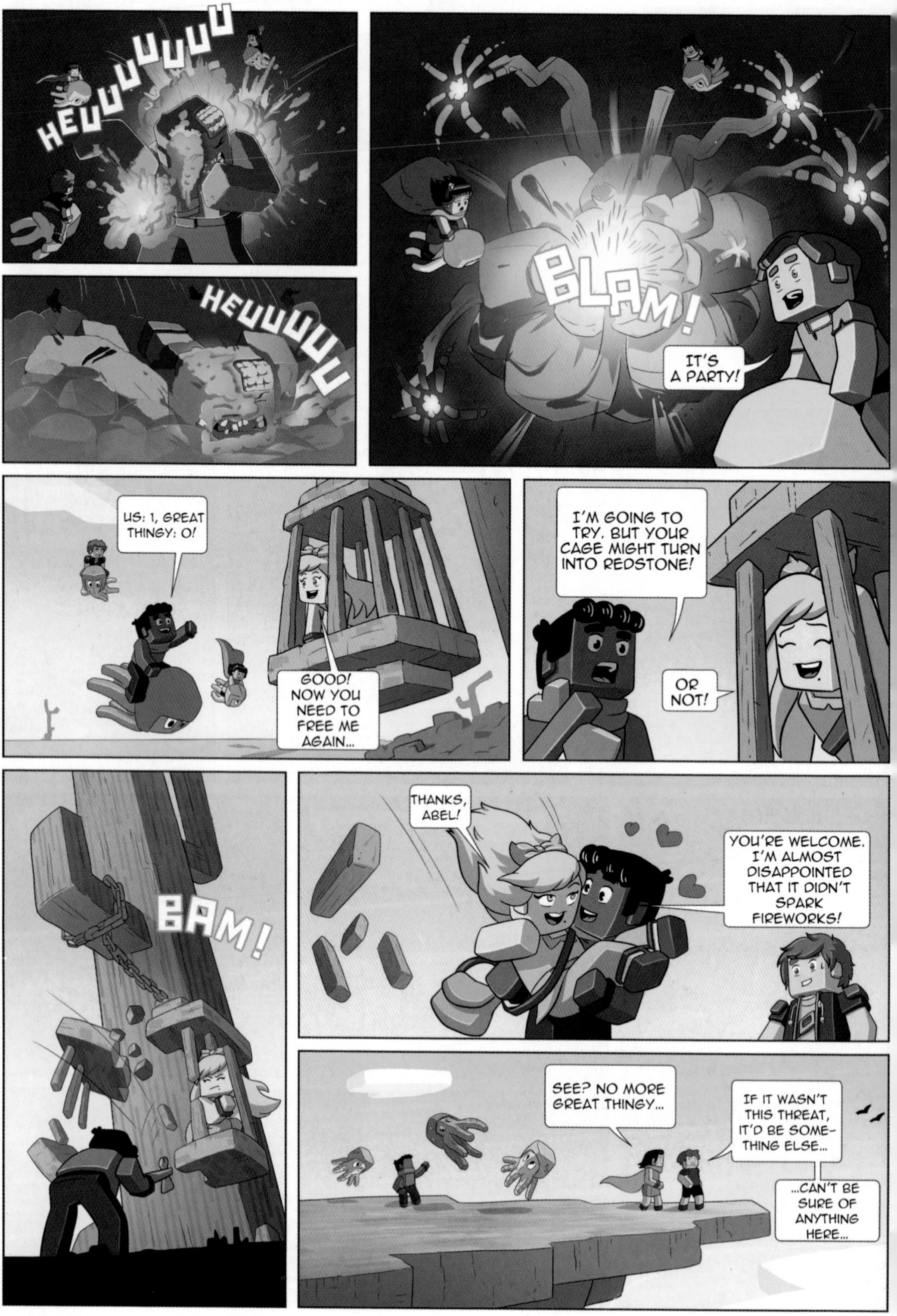
HEUUUUUUU
HEUUUUUU
BLAM!
IT'S A PARTY!
US: 1, GREAT THINGY: 0!
GOOD! NOW YOU NEED TO FREE ME AGAIN...
I'M GOING TO TRY. BUT YOUR CAGE MIGHT TURN INTO REDSTONE!
OR NOT!
BAM!
THANKS, ABEL!
YOU'RE WELCOME. I'M ALMOST DISAPPOINTED THAT IT DIDN'T SPARK FIREWORKS!
SEE? NO MORE GREAT THINGY...
IF IT WASN'T THIS THREAT, IT'D BE SOME-THING ELSE...
...CAN'T BE SURE OF ANYTHING HERE...

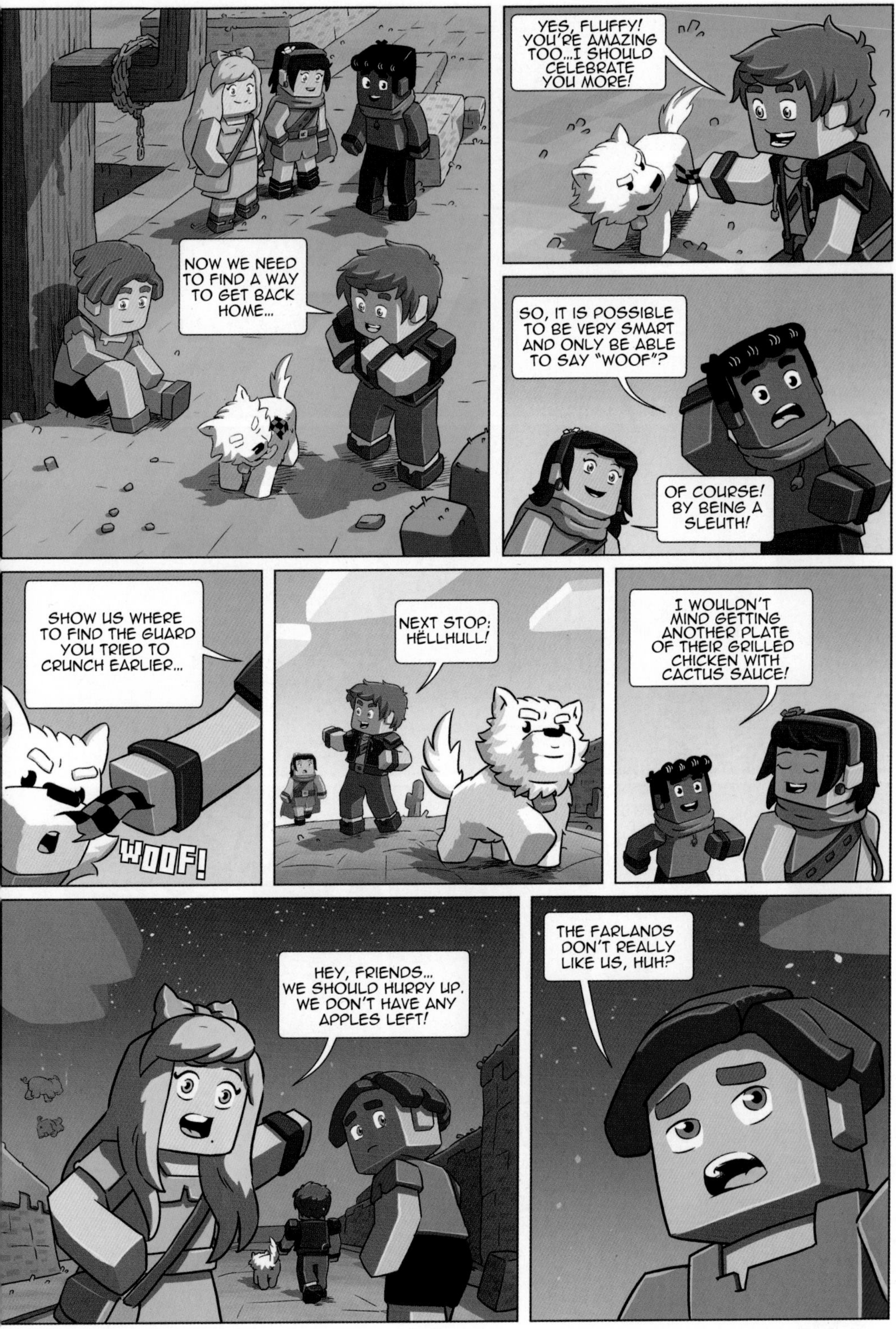
NOW WE NEED TO FIND A WAY TO GET BACK HOME...
YES, FLUFFY! YOU'RE AMAZING TOO...I SHOULD CELEBRATE YOU MORE!
SO, IT IS POSSIBLE TO BE VERY SMART AND ONLY BE ABLE TO SAY "WOOF"?
OF COURSE! BY BEING A SLEUTH!
SHOW US WHERE TO FIND THE GUARD YOU TRIED TO CRUNCH EARLIER...
WOOF!
NEXT STOP: HËLLHULL!
I WOULDN'T MIND GETTING ANOTHER PLATE OF THEIR GRILLED CHICKEN WITH CACTUS SAUCE!
HEY, FRIENDS... WE SHOULD HURRY UP. WE DON'T HAVE ANY APPLES LEFT!
THE FARLANDS DON'T REALLY LIKE US, HUH?

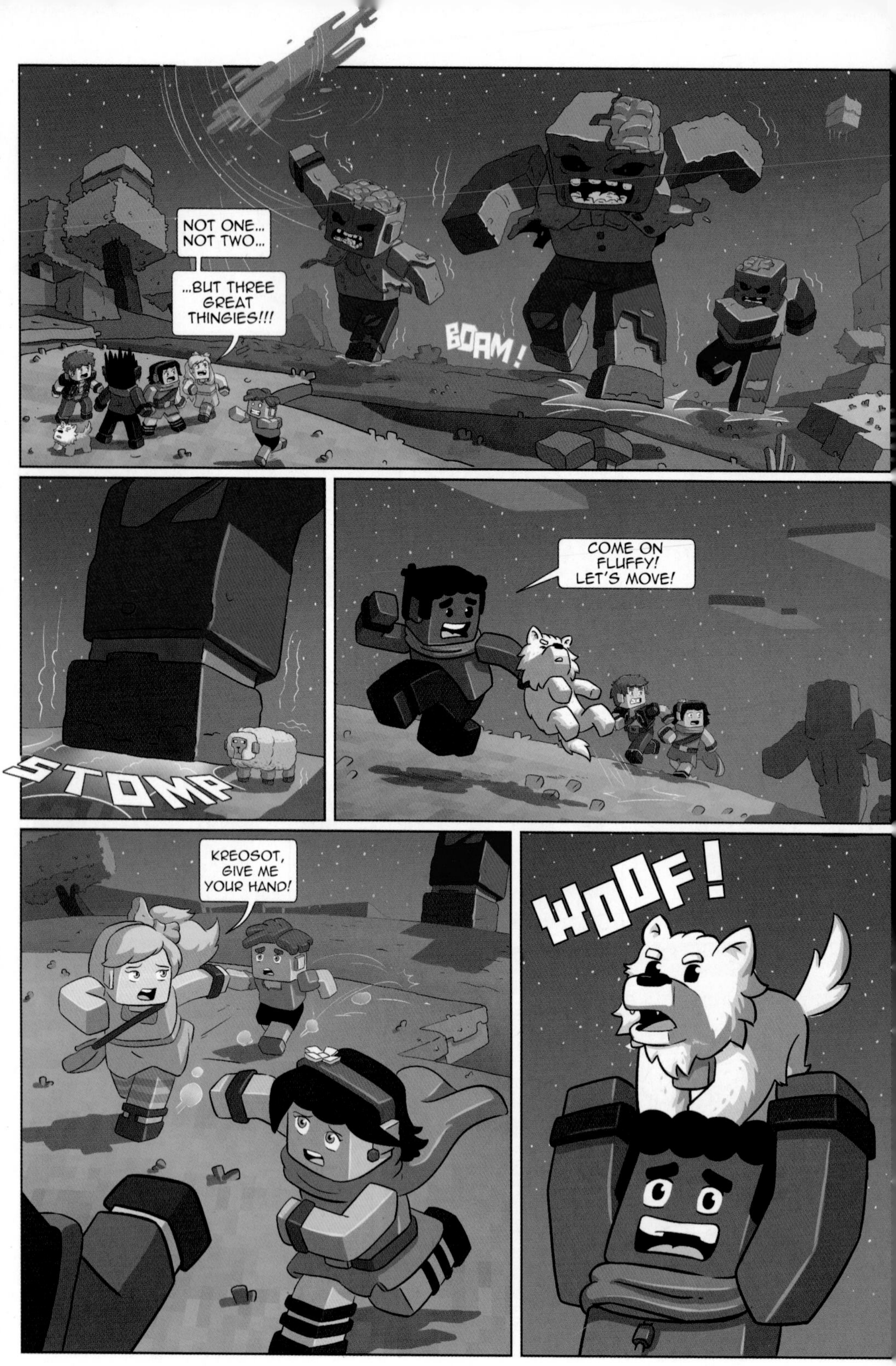
NOT ONE... NOT TWO...
...BUT THREE GREAT THINGIES!!!
BOAM!
STOMP
COME ON FLUFFY! LET'S MOVE!
KREOSOT, GIVE ME YOUR HAND!
WOOF!

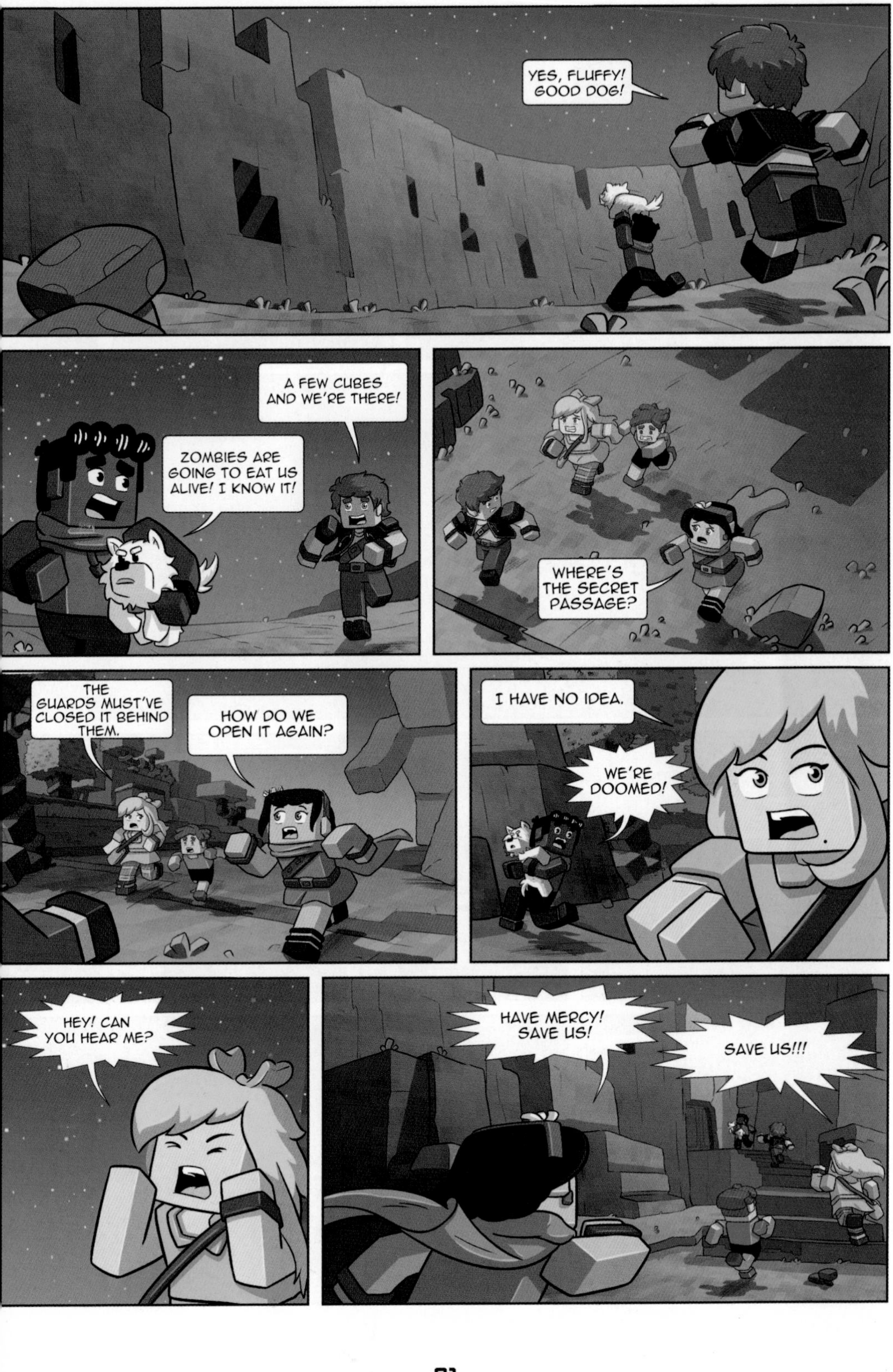
YES, FLUFFY! GOOD DOG!
A FEW CUBES AND WE'RE THERE!
ZOMBIES ARE GOING TO EAT US ALIVE! I KNOW IT!
WHERE'S THE SECRET PASSAGE?
THE GUARDS MUST'VE CLOSED IT BEHIND THEM.
HOW DO WE OPEN IT AGAIN?
I HAVE NO IDEA.
WE'RE DOOMED!
HEY! CAN YOU HEAR ME?
HAVE MERCY! SAVE US!
SAVE US!!!

NOT A SUPER-HEROIC ENDING...KINDA SILLY EVEN!

THIS WALL'S MADE OF BEDROCK, WE CAN'T DO ANYTHING...

GRRR...

WOOF!

WOOF!

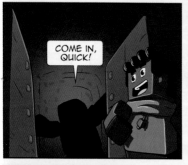

COME IN, QUICK!

GO! GO!

WE'RE ALIVE THANKS TO FLUFFY!

HE WAS VERY COURAGEOUS...

...BUT THE BORDER ACTUALLY SAVED US. THE GIANT ZOMBIES CAN'T LEAVE THE FARLANDS!

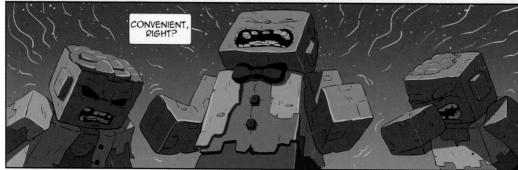

CONVENIENT, RIGHT?

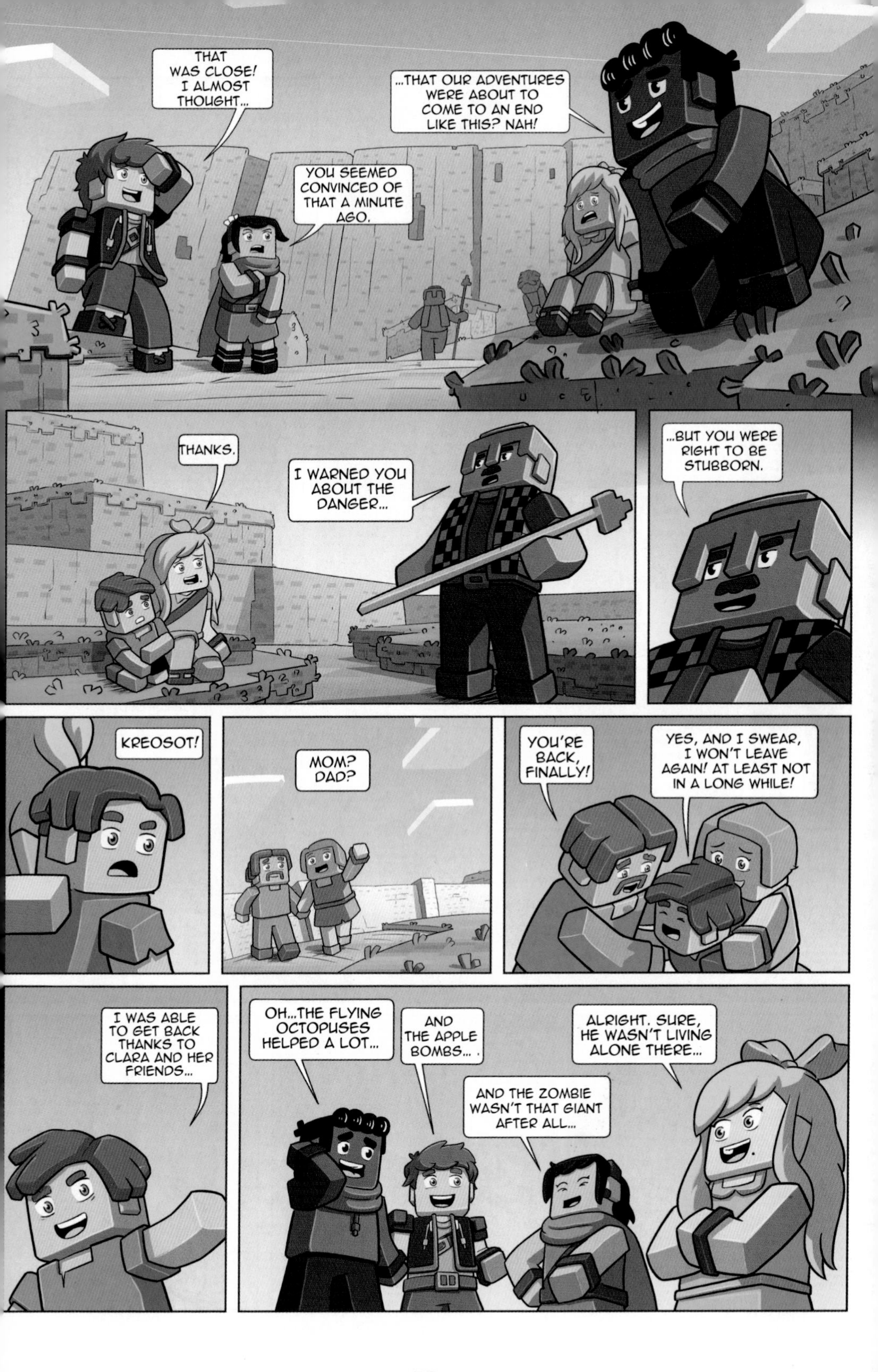
THAT WAS CLOSE! I ALMOST THOUGHT...
YOU SEEMED CONVINCED OF THAT A MINUTE AGO.
...THAT OUR ADVENTURES WERE ABOUT TO COME TO AN END LIKE THIS? NAH!
THANKS.
I WARNED YOU ABOUT THE DANGER...
...BUT YOU WERE RIGHT TO BE STUBBORN.
KREOSOT!
MOM? DAD?
YOU'RE BACK, FINALLY!
YES, AND I SWEAR, I WON'T LEAVE AGAIN! AT LEAST NOT IN A LONG WHILE!
I WAS ABLE TO GET BACK THANKS TO CLARA AND HER FRIENDS...
OH...THE FLYING OCTOPUSES HELPED A LOT...
AND THE APPLE BOMBS... .
AND THE ZOMBIE WASN'T THAT GIANT AFTER ALL...
ALRIGHT. SURE, HE WASN'T LIVING ALONE THERE...

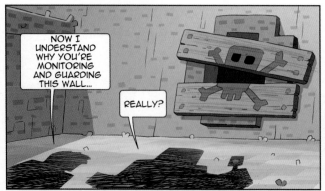

NOW I UNDERSTAND WHY YOU'RE MONITORING AND GUARDING THIS WALL...

REALLY?

I THINK IT'S TIME TO GO BACK HOME, DON'T YOU THINK?

YES. THE SOONER, THE BETTER.

HEY, CLARA, YOU WANT TO COME WITH US? YOU'RE PART OF THE TEAM, NOW.

OH, I DON'T KNOW, I'M NOT A HERO LIKE YOU...

AS YOU WISH...

WE'LL WRITE YOU...

FAREWELL, EVERYONE!

YOU'RE DYING TO GO WITH THEM, SO DO IT!

TAKE CARE, KREOSOT!

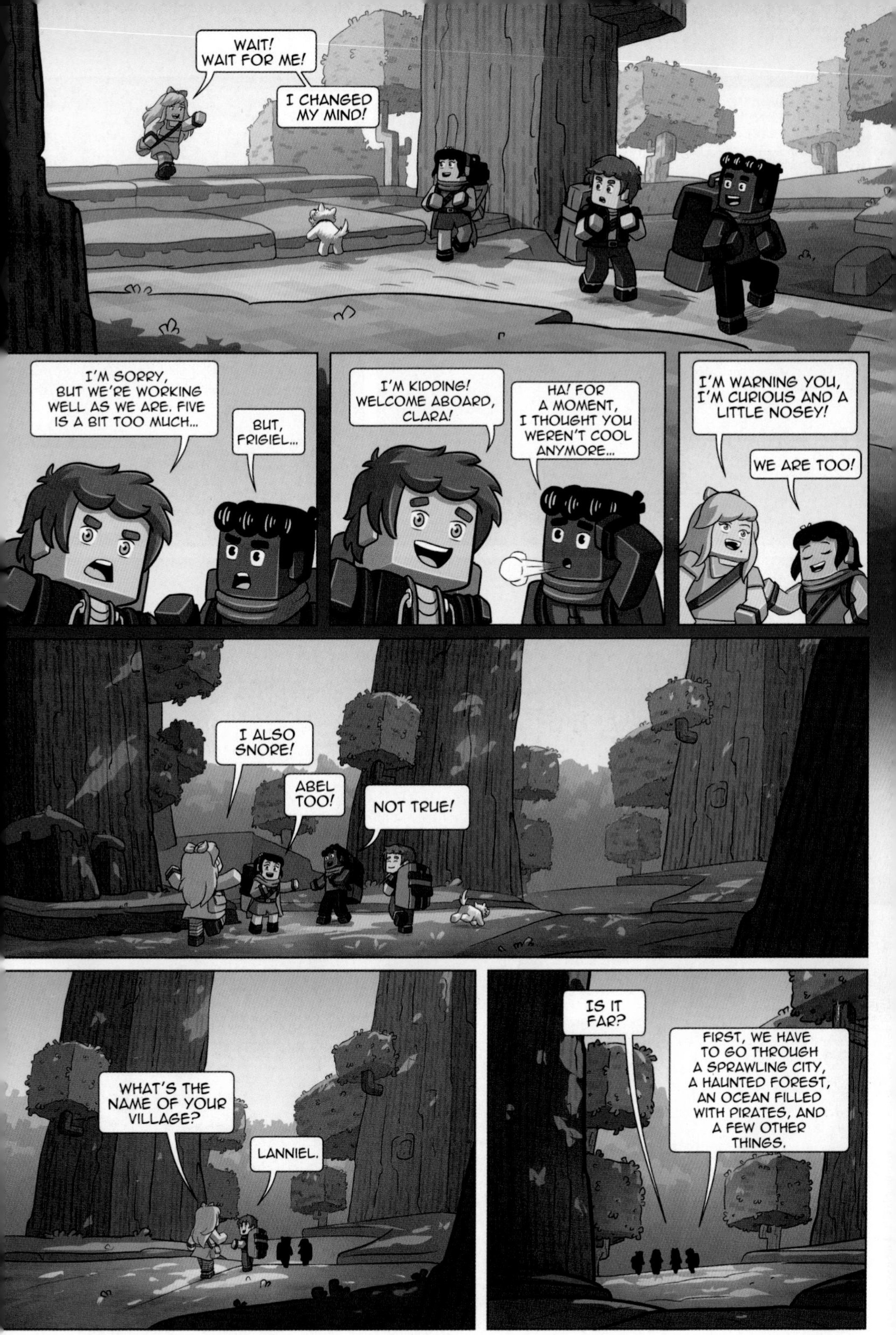
WAIT!
WAIT FOR ME!
I CHANGED MY MIND!
I'M SORRY, BUT WE'RE WORKING WELL AS WE ARE. FIVE IS A BIT TOO MUCH...
BUT, FRIGIEL...
I'M KIDDING! WELCOME ABOARD, CLARA!
HA! FOR A MOMENT, I THOUGHT YOU WEREN'T COOL ANYMORE...
I'M WARNING YOU, I'M CURIOUS AND A LITTLE NOSEY!
WE ARE TOO!
I ALSO SNORE!
ABEL TOO!
NOT TRUE!
WHAT'S THE NAME OF YOUR VILLAGE?
LANNIEL.
IS IT FAR?
FIRST, WE HAVE TO GO THROUGH A SPRAWLING CITY, A HAUNTED FOREST, AN OCEAN FILLED WITH PIRATES, AND A FEW OTHER THINGS.

WHAT'S LANNIEL LIKE?

VERY PRETTY...

AND QUIET?

OH, WE HAD SOME WATERMELON THEFT...

...AND A BLACKMAIL SITUATION. BUT APART FROM THAT, IT'S PEACEFUL.

YOU'LL LOVE IT.

WE CAN ALL REST UP THERE...

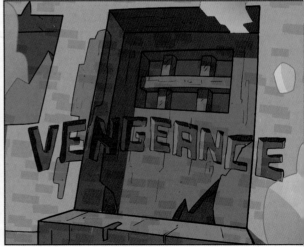

BONUS MATERIAL

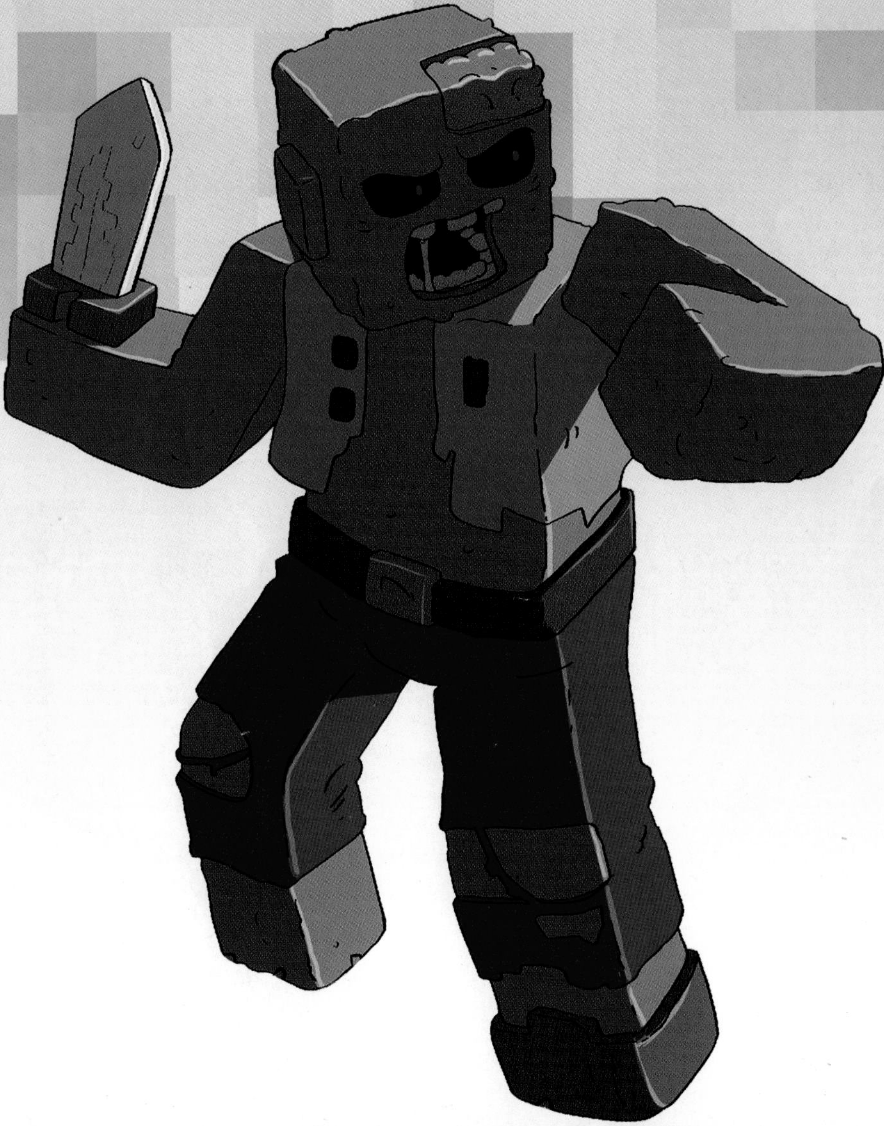

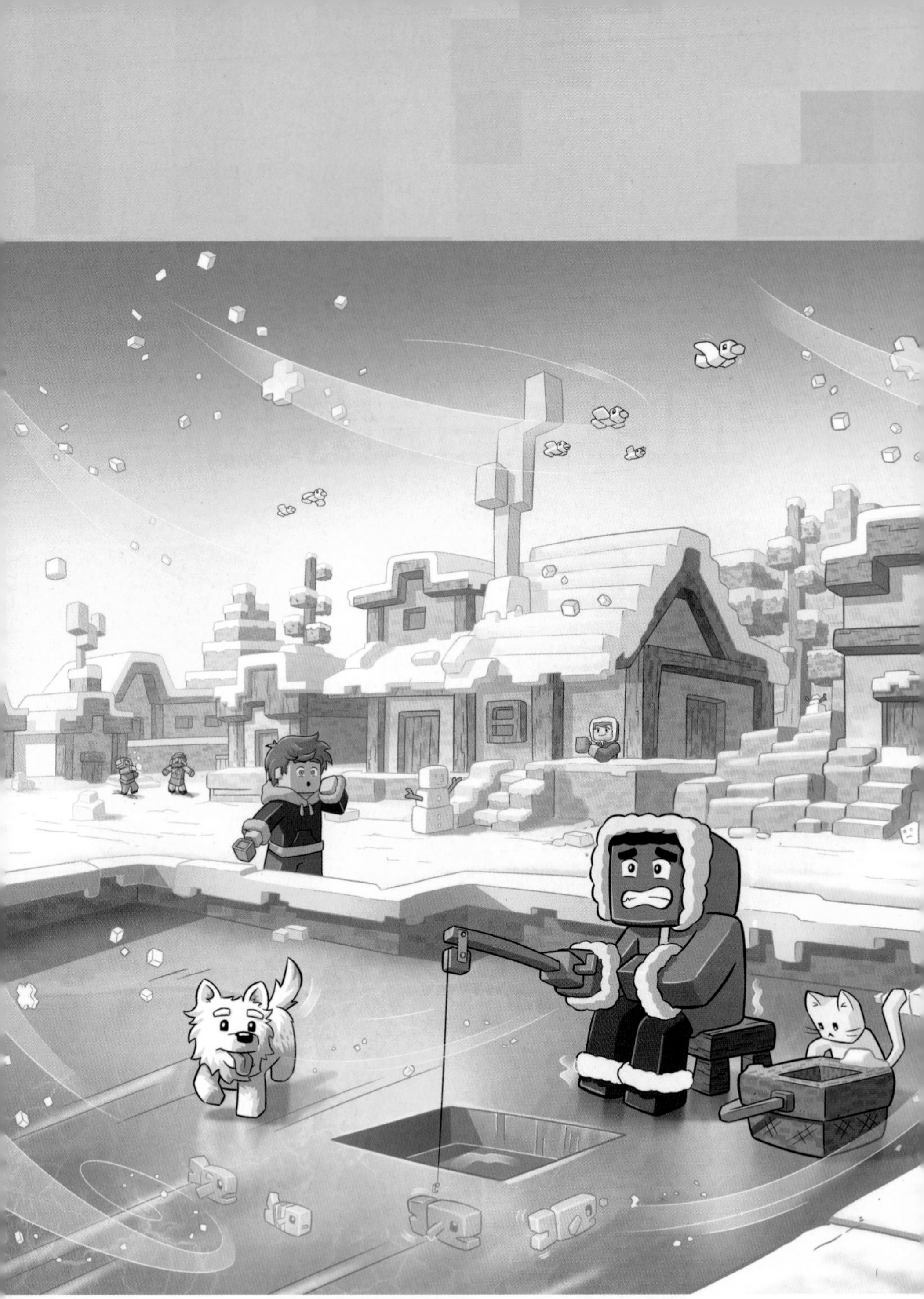

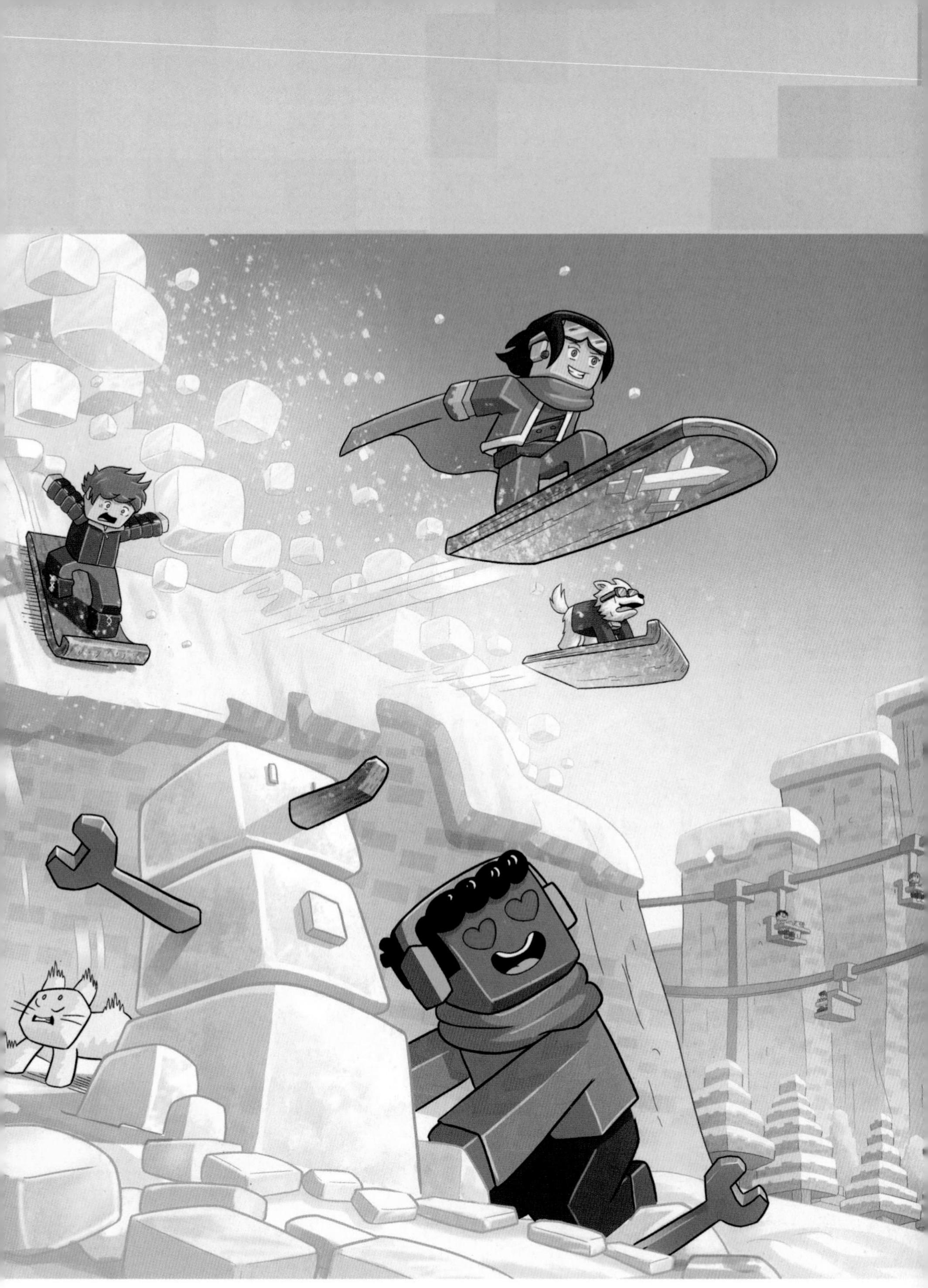

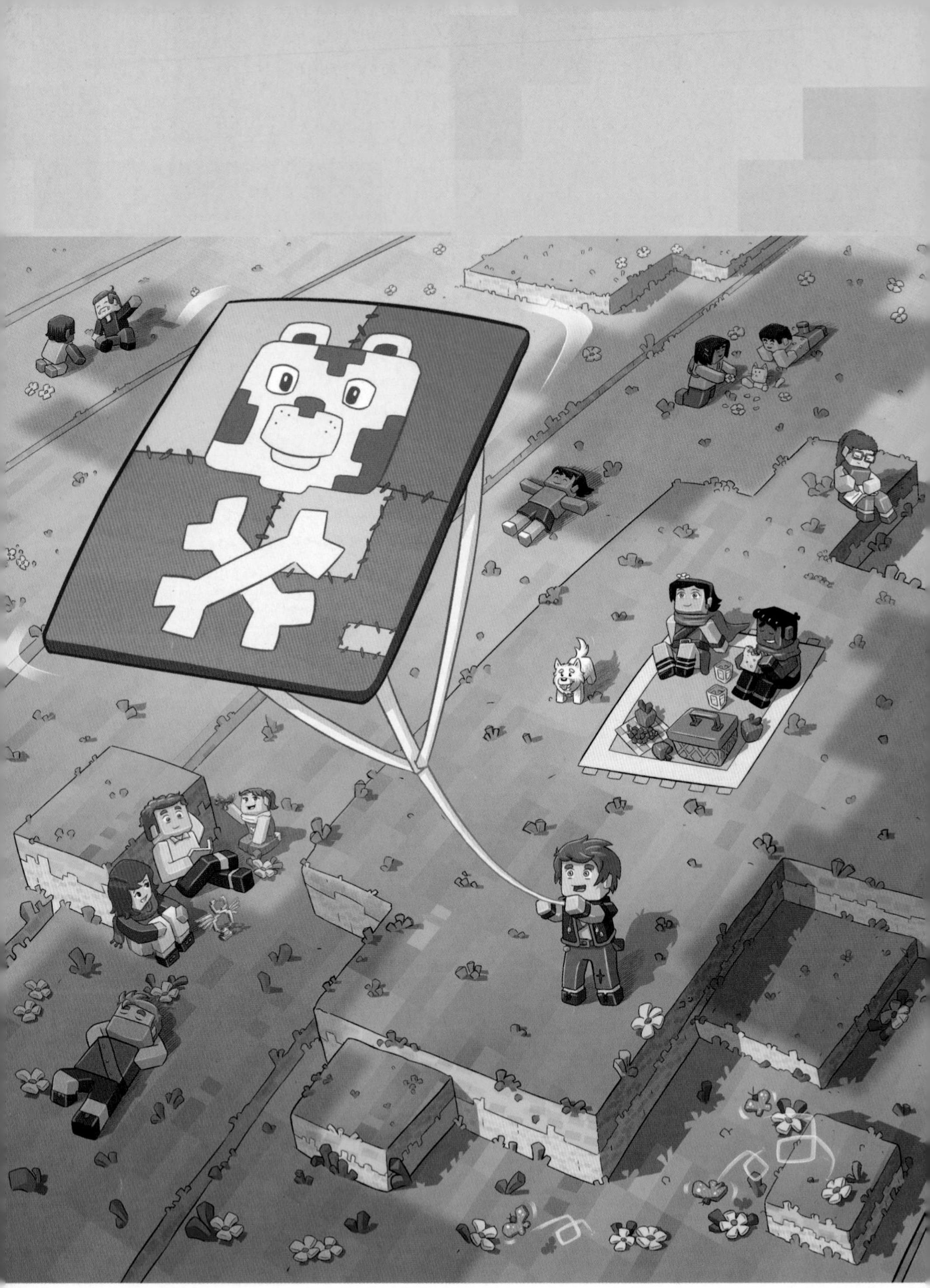

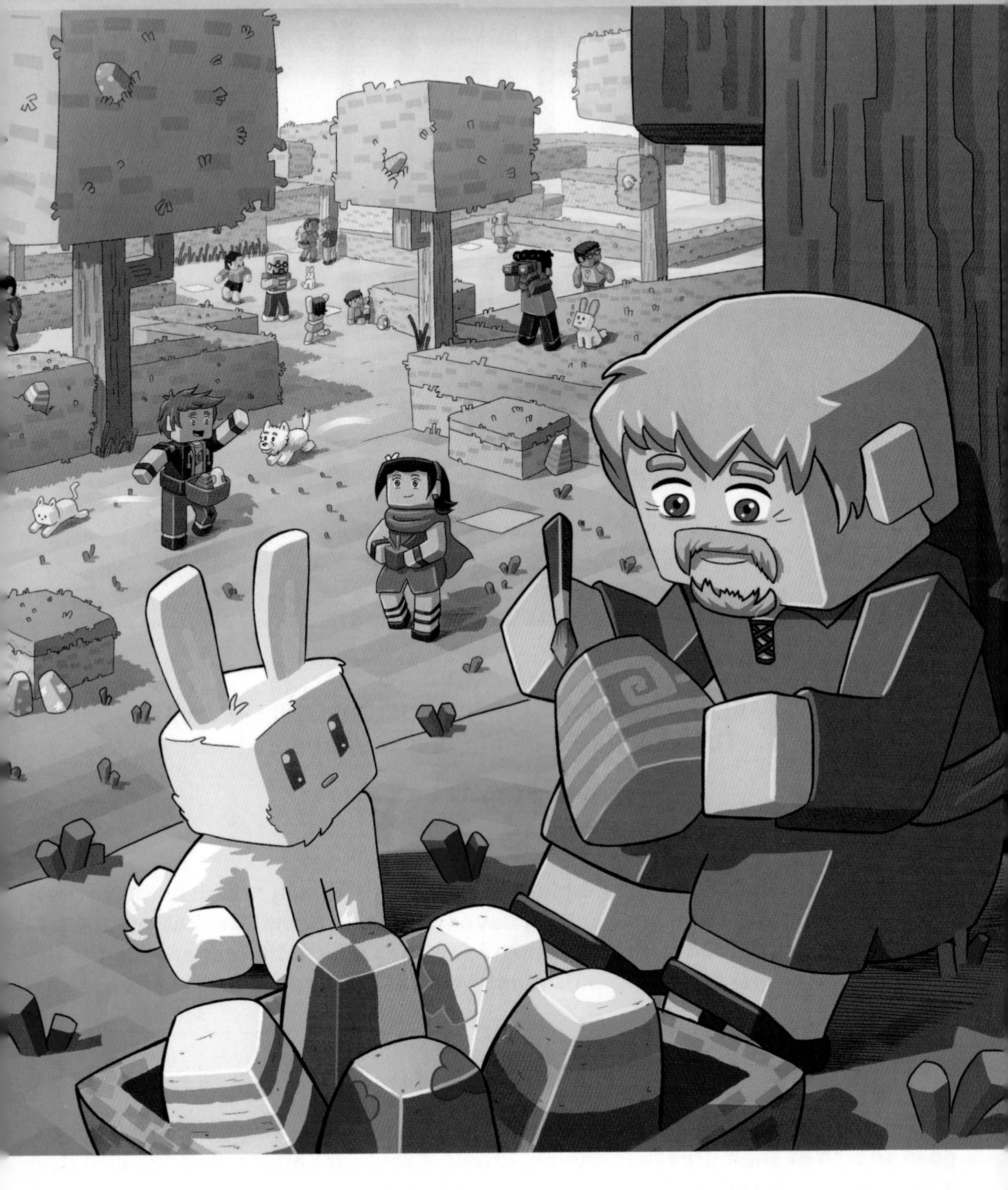

NEXT ON

THE MINECRAFT-INSPIRED MISADVENTURES OF

FRIGIEL AND FLUFFY

**NEW ADVENTURES FULL OF HUMOR AND TWISTS AND
TURNS AWAIT OUR HEROES IN VOLUME 5!**

Featuring two new stories:

SAVING LANNIEL

After exploring the Farlands, Frigiel and his friends finally return home to rest.
But their village, Lanniel, is totally devastated and completely abandoned.
What tragedy unfolded in their absence? Are they indirectly responsible for this
situation? Frigiel and his friends must find the villagers before it's too late!

THE FALLEN GOD

After saving their village from the clutches of brigands, Frigiel and his friends
go in search of their greatest enemy, Ernald's brother Landre. And the situation
is serious: Landre wants to bring a fallen god who could destroy everything in its
path to their dimension! Now, the team must head to the desert and explore a
mysterious pyramid guarded by Endermen...

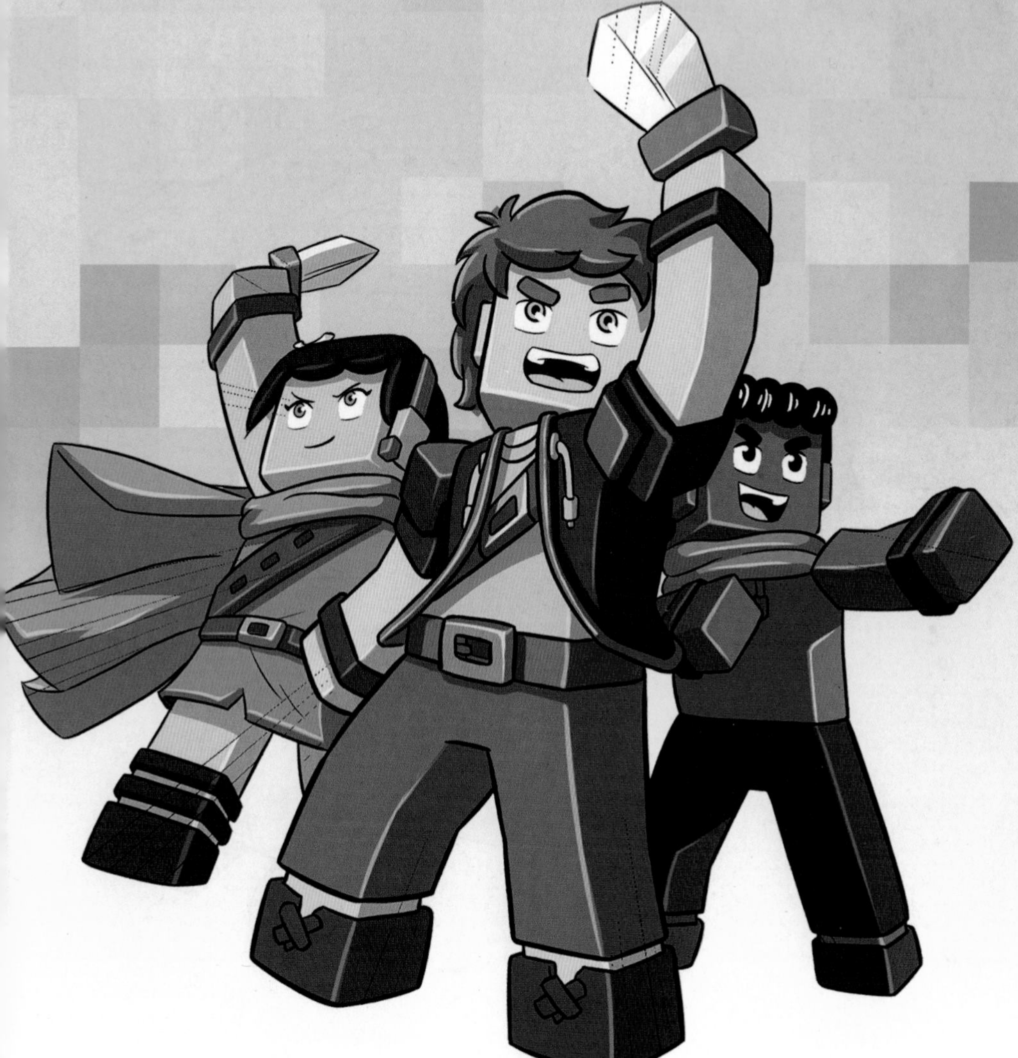

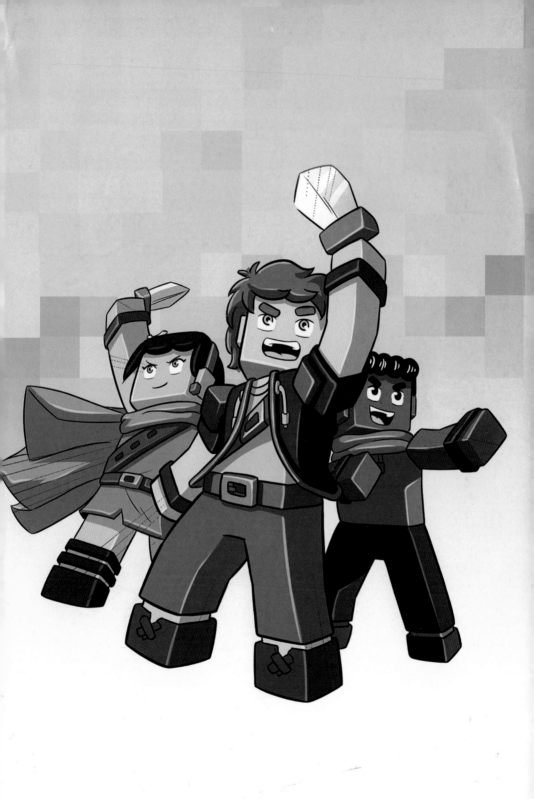

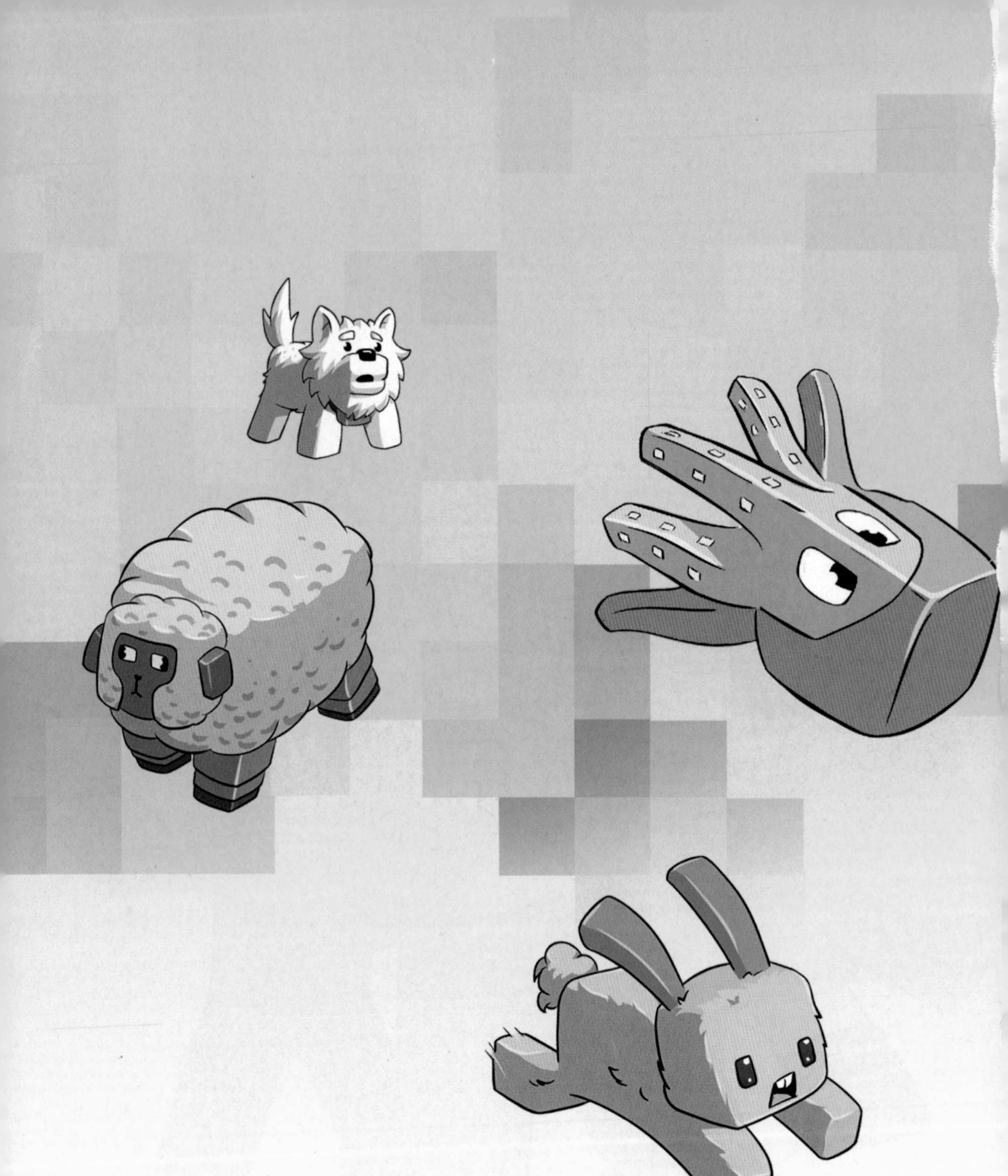